Other books in this series

FLASH: Dogleg Island Mystery Book One
Almost two years ago the sleepy little community of Dogleg Island was the scene of one of the most brutal crimes in Florida history. The only eye witnesses were Flash, a border collie puppy, and a police officer. Now the trial of the century is about to begin. The defendant, accused of slaughtering his parents in their beach home, maintains his innocence. The top witnesses for the prosecution are convinced he is lying. But only Flash knows the truth. And with another murder to solve and a monster storm on the way, the truth may come to late... for all of them.

THE SOUND OF RUNNING HORSES:
Dogleg Island Mystery Book Two
A family picnic takes a gruesome turn when Flash unearths a body buried in a wildlife preserve, and that's only the beginning of the dark secrets that are exposed.

FLASH OF BRILLIANCE

ISBN-10: 0996561048
ISBN-13: 978-0996561044

Published by Blue Merle Publishing
Drawer H
Mountain City Georgia 30562
www.bluemerlepublishing.com

This is a work of fiction. All characters, events, organizations and places in this book are either a product of the author's imagination or used fictitiously and no effort should be made to construe them as real. Any resemblance to any actual people, events or locations is purely coincidental.

Cover art www.bigstock.com

FLASH OF BRILLIANCE

A DOGLEG ISLAND MYSTERY
BOOK THREE

Donna Ball

CHAPTER ONE

If there was one thing Elijah Wiesel—which was actually pronounced with a long *i*, like Wise-el—could say was responsible for his lack of success in life, it was his name. Of course people called him Weasel, which was better than Elijah, and it didn't matter how many fistfights he got into, he never changed anybody's mind. After a while he started thinking of himself as Weasel, and over the years had actually started calling himself that. It suited him. He was small and wiry with sharp yellow teeth, small eyes, pointy chin, and a mangy little tuft of a not-quite goatee. Maybe he'd grown to look like his name; maybe the nickname stuck because of how he looked. All he knew was that he might have had a chance in life if his folks had named him something besides Elijah. Who does that, anyway?

He'd been labeled an "underachiever" in high school and barely squeaked through while reading at a fifth-grade level; he'd joined the army, spent two years playing cards and smoking weed, and was too stupid to know when he had it made. He spent the next year bumming around from place to place, living in his van and picking up odd jobs—construction, landscaping, car wash—until the van blew a gasket in Mississippi and he left it on the side of the road. That was about the time his buddy Bo Tyler—who wasn't really his buddy, just some dude he met in a bar that smelled like piss and served two-dollar hamburgers—turned him on to a job delivering cars. It seemed it was cheaper, when a rich dude moved and had more cars than he could drive, to pay somebody to drive his car to the new place than it was to have it shipped there—and sometimes faster too. Of course, Weasel wasn't entirely stupid. He knew that any operation that conducted business out of a hotel room with cheap veneer furniture was probably delivering more than cars, but they paid him $500 cash up front with $500 more due on delivery, and even gave him a gas card charged up with another $200, all for driving a nondescript Honda Accord with a dented door and a baby seat in back from Mississippi to Florida. Slick.

The man who gave him the cash and the keys wore a fraying blue polyester tie with a white shirt that was stained yellow around the collar and under the arms, and he smoked a cigar that smelled like rolled up turds. He'd typed Weasel's driver's license and Social into a computer—his buddy Bo had warned him they'd check for outstandings—and grunted approval when he came back clear. He'd given him an address and a twenty-four-hour deadline and told him there'd be another job waiting for him on the other end if he was interested. Weasel had asked what the baby seat in the backseat was for, and the guy had replied that cops had a tendency to go easier on a family man, especially one who was on his way to pick up his baby girl for Christmas at Grandma's house. He'd also told him that it would be in everyone's best interest if he did not get stopped by the cops.

That was why, for every one of the last six hundred miles, Weasel had driven like a school teacher. He was making good time in spite of it, though, and had arrived at the east end of Nowhere, Florida, with an hour and a half to spare before his scheduled rendezvous. He hoped that bar where he was supposed to turn over the keys to his contact served food; he hadn't stopped for lunch and he was starved.

Weasel figured there was a hidden compartment somewhere filled with drugs and had even made a halfhearted effort to find it, just so he'd know what he was dealing with. He hadn't found anything, but that only assured him that whoever he was working for was smarter than he was, which wasn't hard. It wasn't until he saw the blue lights flashing in his rearview window that he thought, *Wheel wells*. That's where the drugs were, in the wheel wells. The one place he hadn't checked. He'd been set up to take the fall for a drug smuggling ring and now he was going to prison for the rest of his life for a lousy five hundred bucks.

That was exactly the kind of thing that happened to guys named Weasel.

He pulled over to the curb with the light of a twinkling silver Christmas tree sparkling off a sign that said "Welcome to Dogleg Island, Population 486." The cop car pulled up behind him, blue lights strobing. Weasel rolled down his window, kept his hands on the wheel, and tried not to sweat. He waited while his whole worthless, nondescript life rolled out before him, one bad decision after another, one kick in the ass on top of the last, and not a single break, not once in his whole underachieving life, not a single one.

The cop got out and walked around the car slowly, shining a flashlight in the back—lingering a minute on the baby seat, Weasel was glad to see— then checking out the passenger seat. Weasel frantically tried to remember the story he was supposed to tell about the kid. Going to Disney World? Picking it up from daycare? What?

The cop came to the driver's window and shined the flashlight inside. Weasel tried not to squint. He was sweating like a son of a bitch, he just knew it. He said, "Evening, Officer."

The officer replied, "May I see your driver's license, please, sir?"

"Yes, sir. Absolutely. I have it right here. Sir." Weasel dug into his jeans for his wallet, fumbled it open, took out his license, and passed it through the window.

The officer examined the license with his flashlight. "Is this your car?"

"No, sir," replied Weasel, as he had been instructed to do. "It's a rental." The guy who'd paid him had given him some bogus BS about processing the transaction as a rental car business making it easier for tax purposes, and had given him a set of papers that made it look authentic. Weasel produced them now from the glove compartment and passed them to the officer.

The deputy took the papers and the driver's license, told him to wait there, and went back to his car. He wasn't gone long. By the time he returned, though, Weasel was swimming in sweat.

The deputy returned the rental car papers to him, but kept the license. He said, "Down here visiting for the holidays, are you?"

Weasel swallowed hard. "Yes, sir. My little girl. She lives with my ex-wife. It's my turn for Christmas. Taking her to see Grandma." Grandma, that was it. He'd remembered. And then, realizing suddenly where he was, he added extemporaneously, "At the beach." Which was stupid. He was at the beach, already, with no grandma and no baby. He should have thought of that. He should have left well enough alone. He should have...

The officer peered at him. "Well, Mr. Wiesel..." He pronounced it Wise-el, the way a normal person should have. "Do you know why I stopped you tonight?"

"No, sir," admitted Weasel. He tried not to sound nervous, but knew he wasn't doing a very good job. What was it he had heard about what you were supposed to do when the cops tried to search your car? Would they take you to jail if you said no? *Run*, Weasel decided. When the cop told him to get out of the car, he'd just take off running. He didn't know what else to do. "I wasn't speeding, was I? I was trying to be careful."

"We appreciate that," replied the officer, and passed the driver's license back through the window to him. "On behalf of the Murphy County Sheriff's Office, I'd like to congratulate you on your safe driving habits and wish you a Merry Christmas."

Weasel reached uncertainly for his driver's license, and that was when he realized another piece of paper accompanied it. But it wasn't a ticket. It was a $20 gift certificate to Chik 'N' Waffles, where, according to the caption, they served "the best waffle fries in the world."

Weasel stared at the deputy, and the man smiled back at him. "You and the family enjoy that, you hear? Have a safe holiday, and be careful pulling back out into traffic."

The deputy walked away, and Weasel just sat there, shaking and sweating, staring in disbelief at the gift certificate in his hand. Seriously? Just when he'd been thinking about supper and…seriously?

He poked his head out the window and called, "Umm, Officer?"

The deputy looked back.

Weasel waved the gift certificate at him. "Is there a place around here where I can use this?"

The officer smiled. "Take the next left and go back across the bridge to Ocean City. First stop light, on your right."

"Thank you!"

Weasel sat back in his seat, staring at the gift certificate, grinning in spite of himself. What the hell did you know about that? Finally, a break.

Sadly, it was to be the last one he would ever get.

CHAPTER TWO

Flash had only been in the world a little over three years and he would be the first to admit there were still a few things he didn't know, although he was learning more every day. He didn't know, for example, why there needed to be fizzy water, or why anyone would want to make hot dogs out of soy, or who thought celery was a good idea. What he did know for sure was that whoever had decided to string brightly colored lights across the guardrails of the bridge, both coming and going, was an absolute genius, and that this was, without hesitance or doubt, the best time of the entire year.

Flash was a border collie, which made him a working dog by nature and, in comparison to the general canine population, noticeably more advanced in the area of mental acuity. Most specialists in the field of canine cognition agreed that border collies possess exceptional verbal and problem-solving skills, and Flash was an outstanding example of his breed in this area. His markings were black and white, with a lightning-bolt-shaped blaze on his forehead that Aggie said was a sign of intelligence. He had unusual blue eyes which had the unsettling effect of making people think he knew exactly what they were thinking when he looked at them. Most of the time, they were right.

This would be Flash's fourth winter, so he knew that when the bugs stopped swarming and Grady turned off the air-conditioning at night and Aggie opened up the windows and left the door open so that Flash could sleep on the deck, the holidays couldn't be far behind. The first morning it was cool enough for Aggie to put on her navy Dogleg Island Police Department windbreaker and for Grady to wear his green Murphy County Sheriff's Office shirt with the long sleeves, Flash started to get excited. He knew that in the days that followed there would be even more cool foggy mornings that smelled like fish and salt, and even cooler nights in which the ocean thundered and colored lights twinkled. On the downtown streets of Dogleg Island, light poles would be wrapped in glittering red and white stripes and topped with green wreaths and red bows. Shop doors would be decorated with gold foil and big red bows, evergreen boughs and candy canes, and inside those shops, almost entirely without exception, would be jars of dog treats from which their owners would happily scoop a handful when they saw Flash coming. White lights would twinkle from every window and archway, and the indoor air would smell like cinnamon and chocolate wherever he and Aggie went, which it hardly ever did any other time of the year.

Flash and Aggie would grin with sheer pleasure as they patrolled the streets, taking it all in.

And then there was the bridge.

The bridge was the three-mile-long Cedric B. Grady Memorial Bridge—also known as the causeway—that connected Dogleg Island, where Flash lived, with the rest of the world. Ryan Grady was responsible for keeping the peace on the west side of the bridge, where the Murphy County Sheriff's Office was located, and Aggie and Flash were responsible for keeping the peace on Dogleg Island on the east side of the bridge—although the best part about this time of the year, if anyone were to ask Flash, was that it was almost always peaceful.

This year, for the first time ever, someone by the name of the Murphy County/Dogleg Island Beautification Association had decided to string six miles of red, blue, green and white Christmas lights—along with great big red bows at appropriately spaced intervals—along the guardrails of the bridge. Two twinkling silver Christmas trees, each eight feet tall, punctuated the scene, one on the Dogleg Island side of the bridge, and one on the Ocean City side. It had taken the Beautification Association eighteen months to get all the permits and engineering approvals, but it had been worth it. Already photographers from *Coastal Living* and *Parade* had been down to take pictures, and the holiday-decorated bridge had been featured on six Florida news programs and in the Tallahassee and Tampa/St. Pete newspapers.

Flash had heard Aggie and Grady talking about this and he was sure it was all very important, but for Flash the best thing about the Bridge Project, as Aggie referred to it, was its sheer beauty. The way the lights streaked all together into a single, dazzling, multicolored blur, magnifying and multiplying themselves on the car window and making swirls of dancing color on the dark ocean below as they drove across the bridge; the way the Christmas trees danced and sparkled in the distance no matter which way you were going. The first time Flash had seen it he'd thought all the stars in the sky had somehow fallen down to light up the bridge, and he was awestruck with wonder over how this could have happened without him noticing. Of course, he knew better now, because he had listened to Aggie and Grady talking about it. He learned an awful lot by listening.

"All right," Aggie admitted now from her place in the front seat between Grady and Flash, "it *is* pretty. But Ryan, the electric bill! What's going to happen when that comes due? I certainly hope the Beautification Society saved enough money to take care of that, because the Dogleg Island treasury certainly can't. And what about maintenance? Those bulbs are going to burn out, you know, and who's going to replace them? Not to mention what one strong wind could do to those bows, and you know what kind of winds we get here in December. It might have sounded like a good idea at the time, but nothing in life is free."

The only people who called Ryan Grady by his first name were the women in his life: his mother, his sister, his sister-in-law and his wife, Aggie. Sometimes even Aggie forgot, because they had been colleagues in the Murphy County Sheriff's Office for almost three years before they'd become lovers. Until then, he wasn't entirely sure Aggie had even known his first name, which was why now, every time she said it, he smiled a little on the inside, because it reminded him she was his wife.

"Don't be such a Scrooge," replied Grady, who was driving. "It's the most magical time of the year. Anything is possible. And the Beautification Society has got it covered. Anonymous benefactor, remember?"

"Yeah, well." Aggie sounded skeptical. "That's another thing. I don't trust anybody who won't give his name. Who is this dude, anyway? Santa Claus?"

Grady grinned. "Why not?"

Ryan Grady was thirty-six years old, carelessly good looking, with sun-blond hair and sea-colored eyes. He sported a neatly trimmed blond beard shadow along his jaw despite the fact that his boss, the sheriff of Murphy County, kept threatening to transfer him to the drug task force if he didn't shave. His love of surfing, sailing and running on the beach had helped him to avoid the sagging physique that afflicted most of his colleagues and had earned him the reputation of a pretty boy around the office, although no one called him that to his face.

Aggie Malone had married Ryan Grady in May, after two of the most traumatic and amazing years of her life. Everything about her had changed in those years, from the inside out: the way she looked, the way she thought, even the way she moved. When she'd first met Grady, she had been a cute, raven-haired, twenty-six-year-old with a firm, athletic figure and an acerbic wit; she could out-run him most days and out-shoot him some. If pressed, she might admit to a tiny secret crush on the best-looking guy on the force back in those days, but for the most part she'd thought of him as a big, overgrown playboy, annoying at his worst, amusing at best. And then everything changed.

These days she often couldn't climb a flight of stairs without becoming winded, and she couldn't thread a needle if her life depended on it. She had spent over half of the past four years in physical therapy, occupational therapy, or psychotherapy. She had had to learn to walk and talk and feed herself all over again. Ryan Grady had loved her through it. She had testified before two grand juries, been the subject of national headlines, and had shot a Florida sheriff in self-defense. Grady had never left her side. She had gone from a solitary young deputy whose main pleasure was in her work, to a woman with a family, a dog, a big rambling house, and a police department to run. Ryan Grady was woven into every part of every day that was now her life. Sometimes she teased him that the only reason she'd married him was because he wouldn't stop pestering, but the truth was that she had done so because she had simply reached that inevitable point where it was no longer possible to imagine a life without him.

They'd said their vows in her hospital room while she was still too weak from surgery to stand for longer than the time it took for her to say "I do" and then, breathless and shaky but laughing with nervous delight, she let Ryan help her to a chair where, after several tries, she managed to get the gold band on his finger. She wore a turban printed with orchids over the bandage on her head instead of a veil, courtesy of her new sister-in-law Lorraine, and a white silk kimono over her hospital gown— also courtesy of Lorraine—instead of a wedding dress. She had cried at their wedding kiss. So had Ryan.

She still wasn't fully recovered, and had come to accept the fact that she might never be. Her silky dark hair had been replaced by a pale thin crew cut that almost covered the two scars on her skull: one where the bullet had entered her head and the other where it had been removed. That, and a thirty-pound weight loss, gave her an elfin look that often caused people to underestimate her. It was a mistake they generally only made once. Her husband said he liked her new look. Aggie was getting used to it. She was getting used to a lot of things, like making breakfast for two and picking up someone else's dirty socks off the floor and remembering to buy the kind of coffee he liked. Other things were taking a little longer to get used to, like this whole fascination he had with Christmas.

Aggie had left the office early, changed into her civvies, and picked Grady up from work, so he was still in his uniform while they wandered the big Christmas tree lot in Ocean City. She had been all for taking the first tree they saw, but Grady, as she should have known by now, was not that easy. This one had a bare spot, that one was too skinny, the other one too squat, the next one too dry. While Flash raced around, exulting in the evergreen forest and sniffing out the history of every tree in the lot, Aggie followed Grady from spruce to fir with a tolerant expression on her face, trying not to look at her watch any more than was strictly necessary and reminding him only once, in the most angelic of tones, that the tree would have been decorated by now had they taken the first one they saw.

She kept her hands in the pockets of her jacket because, since the surgery eight months ago, Aggie had been exceptionally sensitive to heat and cold, and her hands had a tendency to tremble, especially first thing in the morning, or when she was tired at night. It was only sixty-two degrees outside, but she was shivering, and she didn't want to spoil Grady's fun by letting him know.

He knew, of course. He always did. And he silently turned up the heat in the truck when they finally made their selection and were on their way home.

The tree that was in the bed of Grady's red pickup as they crossed the bridge toward Dogleg Island was a six-foot white pine—not exactly the first tree they'd looked at, but very close. It was 6:45 and there was, as Aggie recalled, nothing in the refrigerator except half a grapefruit and a package of hot dogs, so she suggested, "Do you want to stop at Pete's Place for chowder?"

Flash's ears perked up at that. Aggie and Grady were both fine cooks, but Pete was the best. He had never had a bad meal at Pete's Place Bar and Grill. Of course, it was rare that Flash had a bad meal anywhere.

Grady glanced at her. "Forget to buy groceries?"

"Nope. You did."

"Oh. Right." He had the grace to look abashed. "My turn. I meant to get to it Tuesday but I got called in on that Randolph case."

"Don't worry about it," she said. "I'm taking tomorrow off. I'll stock up and have everything looking shipshape before your folks get there. They'll never guess we don't live like that all the time."

He grinned. "I should've married you sooner."

She gestured to the flashing blue lights as they exited the bridge onto Dogleg Island. "What's that? Yours or mine?"

"Mine."

Grady kept a police radio in his truck, along with an emergency flasher, for those times that he drove his personal vehicle into work instead of a Sheriff's Office issue. The volume was muted but now he turned it up and picked up the microphone as he slowed in preparation for pulling in behind the unit and the vehicle that was stopped in front of it.

"Three-Six, Captain Grady coming up behind you. What's your status? Do you need an assist?"

Murphy County was a mostly rural, semi-coastal Florida community secured by two small police offices and the Sheriff's Office. Everyone in law enforcement knew everyone else, and it was common courtesy to offer assistance to a fellow officer—even when you weren't officially on duty.

The radio crackled back. "Secure from Three-Six. Just brightening days and spreading cheer, sir."

Grady grinned. The words were a direct quote from Sheriff Bishop when he'd initiated the Santa Cop program, which actually had been Aggie's idea to improve relations between the community and the Sheriff's Office. The gift certificates had been donated by local stores and restaurants, and each man in the department had been given a book of them with the rather gruff command to "Get on out there and brighten some days and spread some cheer" by surprising law-abiding motorists with gift certificates instead of tickets. The program had initially met with resistance. First of all, it added to the workload of road deputies, who now not only had to target real offenders but keep an eye out for those who *weren't* offending as well. Secondly, any traffic stop was risky these days, and most cops had a hard time justifying taking unnecessary chances, even if it was for a good cause.

That was when Chief Deputy Ryan Grady stepped in to lecture the men on what his wife had pointed out only the night before: They were all making this a lot harder than it needed to be. Every man in the department knew who the bad guys were—the sex offenders, the habitual DUIs, the meth-heads and wife beaters. They also knew who the single mothers were, the fathers doing their best to get by on disability and unemployment, the families trying to make it on minimum-wage incomes. Those were the lives they wanted to brighten. Those were the people to whom a twenty-dollar gift certificate could mean the difference between a hot meal and peanut butter crackers. After that it became a matter of pride for the road officers to seek out the beat-up cars with baby seats in back or the mother counting out her change at the Dollar Store, and to make someone's day with a gift certificate. And to everyone's surprise except Aggie's, not only had community relations improved, but so had morale at the sheriff's office.

Grady winked at his wife. "Carry on, Deputy. Grady out."

He dropped his speed to allow the Honda Accord—signaling carefully—to pull out into the street in front of him, then squeezed his wife's knee. "You did good, baby," he said.

Aggie, reading the license plate on the Accord, said, "Mississippi, huh? I wonder what he's doing on Dogleg Island."

"Visiting family for the holidays," suggested Grady, "and spreading cheer throughout the land about what an amazing law enforcement operation we have down here."

After a moment, she shrugged. "I guess it can't hurt to have good relations outside the community too. After all, it's Christmas."

"And end of shift," Grady pointed out. "The guys are supposed to give out three of those a day, and when it gets close to 7:00 they're not all that picky about what county the good will goes to."

Aggie gave a small grunt of wry amusement as Grady made the turn that led to Pete's Place. "Happy Christmas to all, huh?"

Flash, watching the twinkle of colored lights retreat through the back window, thought that sounded just about right.

CHAPTER THREE

Weasel got two chicken sandwiches, a large waffle fries and a large milk shake, and got a voucher for almost ten dollars in return. What a deal. He sat in the car to eat, absently watching the diners going in and out, admiring the Christmas lights on the stores across the highway, and feeling pretty good about the world. It wasn't until he saw a motorist pull into the empty parking lot of a dentist's office across the street and get out to check his back tire that the idea started to form. Of course, it didn't form right away. He watched for a while, munching fries dipped in ketchup and slurping on the shake, while the driver rumbled in the trunk for the tools and started jacking up the vehicle. He was glad he hadn't had any trouble with the tires on the Honda on the way down, but then why should he? The first thing he'd noticed was that the tires, all four of them, were brand new. Brand new tires on a twelve-year-old vehicle with a dent in the door. That started him thinking about the wheel wells again, and why the guys who'd paid him to deliver the car had been particularly careful that he wouldn't have any trouble with the tires.

He sipped the shake and watched the guy across the street straining to loosen the lug nuts. A smart fellow would leave well enough alone. He was within half an hour of getting paid, picking up another car, and hitting the road again. He didn't want to spend that half hour popping wheel covers and searching for drugs. On the other hand, he had a right to know what he was hauling, didn't he, if he was going to pick up another car? Because if it was drugs, he for damn sure wasn't getting paid enough.

He finished up his dinner, stuffed the trash into the empty paper sack, and got out of the car to throw it away. On his way, he opened the trunk and removed the spare tire cover, looking for the tool kit. It would take five minutes to check the wheels, and it was always better to know than not know.

It took him a minute to realize that the spare tire was placed upside down in its compartment. This puzzled him only mildly until he lifted the tire up, still looking for the tool kit, and spotted the black plastic-wrapped bundles stuffed tightly inside the hollow well of the spare tire. He smiled. Bingo.

He darted a quick glance around to make sure no one was looking, then pried one of the bundles out and unwrapped it.

"Holy shit," he whispered.

It wasn't drugs, after all. It was drug money.

The black plastic bag he was holding contained four bound bundles of one-hundred-dollar bills, four bundles of fifties, four bundles of twenties. There were six more bags inside the wheel well of the spare tire. He tried to do the math and couldn't. But it was a lot. A million, maybe. Maybe two. A lot.

He'd driven from Mississippi to Florida for a thousand-dollar paycheck—of which he'd only received half—when all the while he'd been sitting on enough money to set him up for life. "Holy shit," he said again, and broke slowly into a grin. Maybe there was a Santa Claus after all.

He just stood there for a minute, basking in the glow of his good fortune and bathed in daydreams of a future without worry. He started to return the bag to the spare tire, thinking about nothing but fueling up and driving as fast as he could as far as he could. And then he stopped.

The kind of guys who had this much money to transport didn't come by it by accident, and it was a pretty good bet this wasn't the first time they'd done this. They had his driver's license, his picture, the tag number of the car, maybe even one of those tracking devices he was always reading about on the Internet hooked to a fender. There was no way they were going to let him just drive off with a million dollars in cash.

He gave another quick, paranoid look around, his heart pounding in his throat. No. No way. You try to steal some drug kingpin's money and you end up at the bottom of the ocean with no one ever even knowing you were gone, everybody knew that. He was dumb, but not that dumb. No. The thing to do…the thing to do was to take enough so that it wouldn't be missed until he was out of here, long out of here, just enough off the top of each paper-banded bundle that no one looking at it would know anything was missing.

So that's what he did. Sweating, dry-mouthed, he tugged out a few of the hundreds from each bundle, five or six fifties, some twenties. The bands didn't even loosen. He worked quickly, stuffing the money into the takeout bag that held his trash, closing the black plastic wrapping, returning it to the spare tire, taking out another. Before five minutes was up, he had a hundred thousand dollars in the white take-out bag. That was enough. The clock was ticking. He had to be at that bar on the other side of the bridge in half an hour to turn in the car. The last thing he wanted to do was to be late. If he was going to pull this off, the key was to act normal. Normal, that was it. Everything was just fine.

Better than fine. Maybe for the first time in his life, everything was absolutely great.

Angel stood in the shadows of the parking lot outside the bar on Dogleg Island, gazing absently at the Prius parked across the street, thinking about God. That was not something he did very often.

He had picked up the nickname Angel both because of his uncanny propensity for being in the right place at the right time, and for his reputation for generosity when it came to granting favors to those in need—favors that were always expected to be returned, of course, with interest. Most people called him Mr. Angelo, although that wasn't his real name. Not even his closest associates, and those were few and far between, knew his real name. It had been so long since he'd used it, sometimes Angel himself wasn't even sure what it was any more.

He lived a modestly successful life in a simply furnished condo in Savannah, kept a small cabin cruiser docked in the public marina, drove a sensible four-door in a neutral color. He derived a steady income from a few real-estate investments he'd made over the years; nothing too flashy, but comfortable. The majority of his wealth was untraceable, just as he himself was.

He was not one of those people who thought that the point of the game was accumulating the most stuff. The point of the game was, quite simply, winning. He liked the power the money bought him, of course, as well as the protection it afforded him when he needed it. But most of all he liked the game.

He had started out small, a street cop running a dozen or so kids in a podunk town south of Atlanta; he took half their haul, whether it be drugs, cash, or goods, and they got to go back out on the streets with all their limbs intact. If occasionally they screwed up and got themselves thrown in jail, they knew they had somebody on the outside looking out for them. That was the thing about Angel; he looked out for his own, always had and always would. The number one key to building a tight organization was loyalty. Some of those kids were still with him today, although they didn't know it. He'd made certain none of those street thugs—or anyone else, for that matter—would associate the cop he once had been with the man he was today.

He'd stayed on the streets for almost five years, staying low, keeping it simple. He didn't move too fast, he didn't get greedy. He had a plan. There came a time when the police chief started looking at him a little too closely; Angel shot him dead with a long-range rifle as the chief was coming out of a movie theater one night. He had disassembled the rifle and disposed of it in the Flint River, then gone into work that night and started working on the case. He had been one of the honor guard at the police chief's funeral. Three months later, citing a better job offer, he'd left the force, and the case that had torn the town apart was never solved.

Thirty years later, Angel ran his own organization, with enforcement officers, investigators, and undercover operatives on the street. These days, when a cop turned dirty anywhere from Atlanta to New Orleans, the chances were good that he would eventually try to shake down one of Angel's street operatives. At that point he would have a couple of simple choices: join the family, or spend the rest of his short career wondering when the bullet would find him—or his wife, or children. Most men made the sensible choice. As for those who didn't...well, perhaps the second key to building a tight organization was to always keep your word.

Angel took a small percentage off the top for his trouble, but the money, once again, was the least valuable part of the operation. He was building a network, a family, and the role of every member was crucial. His army on the street, whether in uniform or out, was the very foundation of everything he had built. And he took a certain pride in the fact that he had never even attempted to corrupt a law officer who was dedicated to his job, never threatened or bought the loyalty of a good cop. Why should he, when so many of them were willing to sell themselves?

The third key to building a tight organization was that no detail, no matter how small, was beneath his notice. No job was too mundane for him to step in and handle himself. He had personally hauled six thousand pounds of Kobe beef out of dry ice to remove the diamonds that were hidden in the carcasses; he had slit open the guts of monkeys to recover the packages of drugs inside. And though neither one of those things ranked high on his list of experiences to be repeated, he did what was necessary when it was necessary. He had personally inspected each one of the casinos he did business with. He knew the name and background of every single one of his drivers. And he hated what was about to happened here tonight. He really did. But it was for just such a contingency that he had decided to supervise this phase of the operation himself. Well, that and other reasons.

He had set up his business so that, for the most part, it ran itself, and his attitude toward those who worked for him was mostly laissez-faire. They did their jobs, they were well compensated, and he left them alone. That way, when something went wrong, they had no one to blame but themselves. And absolutely no one to point a finger at.

Three and a half years ago, something had gone very wrong in the little Gulf Coast community of Murphy County, Florida. One of his guys—a low-level deputy sheriff looking for an easy way to the good life, like so many of these lazy bastards were—took one chance too many and ended up shooting a fellow officer while trying to cover his own tracks in a double murder that had made the headlines for months. Angel had watched the case closely from afar, but in the end his policy of non-intervention had paid off. Eventually, due to his own incompetence and, Angel had to admit, some unexpectedly impressive investigating by the Murphy County Sheriff's Office, the deputy went down for the murders and was now serving a triple life sentence without parole. Angel had pulled a few strings and arranged for him to serve his sentence in a medium-security facility; he liked his people to know that, no matter how badly they screwed up, they hadn't been forgotten. And, as everyone knew, it was at least as useful to have a cop on the inside as it was to have one on the street.

A week ago, he'd gotten word that his guy was being called to give testimony in another murder, and being temporarily held in a neighboring county jail until his testimony was required. This was somewhat troubling, as one never knew what time in prison, even a medium-security one, could do to a man, nor what kind of deals he would now be willing to make. So Angel sent J.J., one of his top people, to find out.

Only what J.J. had found out was not what Angel had expected. And that was why Angel was here in Murphy County, standing in the dark and thinking about God. About how Fate could stretch its cruel twisty fingers back through time and drag a man forward, about how pieces of a puzzle you didn't even know were missing could suddenly jolt together like magnets finding their poles. About destiny, and patterns, and how, if you took a rock from the Boston Harbor and sliced it down to its tiniest molecular part and examined that part under the most powerful microscope in the world, you would see the shape of the Boston Harbor. Fractal imagery, it was called. Patterns.

Murphy County, Florida, of all places. The ass end of the earth. This is where God had chosen to reveal himself to a man called Angel. And had laughed in his face.

J.J. was one of the smart ones, one of the ones who'd been with him from the old days on the streets, and what he'd found out was, unfortunately, not something that he could be allowed to walk around knowing. He was too smart. He would have put it together eventually. So J.J., as much as Angel hated it, had to be taken care of. And now this poor stupid driver, whose only mistake had been to get too curious, was destined to meet the same fate. But in his operation, there was no room for error. Particularly not in Murphy County, where one unbelievably arrogant crooked cop had let his ambition get out of control and had brought down this mess on all of them. Angel had a feeling a lot would have to be taken care of before he left this place.

Angel had very few vices. A man in his position couldn't afford them. He liked a good wine, a fast car, a woman who didn't ask questions. He could live without all of them. But one of his secret pleasures, and one he never expected to ask himself to live without, was cherry-flavored chewing gum. He always carefully folded the wrapper from each stick, tin foil and all, into neat quarters and placed it in his pocket to be disposed of later. He didn't litter.

He walked across the street and silently opened the door of the Prius, which was unlocked as he knew it would be. He took the gum from his mouth, considered wrapping it in the empty paper in his pocket, and decided against it. He placed the gum in the cup holder of the car and closed the door as silently as he had opened it. Then, hands in pockets, he strolled away.

He hadn't had fingerprints since 1992, and his DNA wasn't in any database in the world. Planting evidence that led nowhere was a technique he'd frequently used to confound the police; just another way of letting his guys know he had their backs. He could have left the gum wrapper, or a cigarette butt, or a meaningless receipt taken from the trash some-where. But this time he'd gone a step further.

There were those who'd say he was tempting fate, and they would be right, to a certain extent. Some might question why, after working so hard to build so much, he would risk it all for something so small. The answer was that he had no intention of risking anything. He was untouchable. He was the game master. And there was no such thing as a small victory.

God, after all, was in the details.

CHAPTER FOUR

The Gradys had been among the first settlers of Dogleg Island back in the seventeen hundreds, when it wasn't even called Dogleg Island and there wasn't much of anything to encourage human habitation except deep pine forests and a couple of shallow fresh-water springs. Those hardy sailor pioneers felled the trees and built a cluster of inland cabins sturdy enough to withstand the fury of the Gulf Coast's frequent storms, and kept body and soul together with salt fish and what little would grow in the thin sandy soil. Early records show that in 1780 the population of Dogleg Island was eight-two. By 1807, after five major storms, a winter in which temperatures dropped below 10 degrees, and a devastating spring outbreak of cholera, the population had declined to twenty-three, fifteen of whom were Gradys. Still, they stayed.

Fortunes began to climb when the War of 1812 produced a surge in demand for pitch, a by-product of the turpentine that was produced from the southern long-leafed pine. As it happened, the Gradys owned almost sixteen thousand acres of pine forests ready to be distilled into turpentine and pitch, and a family fortune was on its way to being made until the great hurricane of 1843 cut the island virtually in half, submerging the central pine forest—which by then was a carefully cultivated and diligently run plantation—beneath a hundred feet of seawater. But the Gradys stayed.

They turned their hands once again to the sea that had always favored them, fishing and shipping and, some maintained, blockade running and privateering during the War Between the States. And though amassing a great fortune didn't appear to be in their destiny, reminders of the mark the Gradys had left on history were still all over the island: Grady Plantation Boulevard that intersected with Long Grady Way which led to the Elmira Grady Botanical Garden which was in itself part of what old-timers still called the Grady Wildlife Refuge, but was actually run by the state park service and leased from the Grady family for a dollar a year. The old Grady shipping warehouse was now the Dogleg Island City Hall and Cultural Museum. There had even, at one time, been a Collin Grady Memorial Clinic on Dogleg Island, but fire had destroyed the building in 1960 and the funds had not materialized to rebuild.

Today the island was home to just under five hundred full-time residents, and only two of them had been born Gradys. Aggie was given to understand that when Ryan's parents decided to retire to Ecuador, they disposed of most of their holdings on the island and gave each of their children an early inheritance. Ryan took the rambling cedar house two blocks from the ocean that his grandfather had built. His sister Lucy, who was married to a CPA and thought island living was for hicks, had taken the cash and built a pretty brick ranch on a fenced, park like acre on the mainland, five miles outside of Ocean City. The oldest brother, Pete, invested in Pete's Place Bar and Grill, which had grown into an institution on the island and eventually afforded Pete and his wife Lorraine a comfortable home on the lagoon with a pool.

Pete and Lorraine had been Aggie's first friends when she moved to Murphy County and took a job with the Sheriff's Office patrolling the streets and beaches of Dogleg Island. Even though Aggie's own family history, if she could even be said to have such a thing, was so different from the Gradys' as to be almost an alien culture, every time she walked into Pete's Place she knew what home felt like. Classic rock pumped from the speakers while ESPN flickered on the four television screens in the bar area. The air was filled with the smell of fried food and the sound of easy chatter. People smiled when they saw her, although if truth be told, most of them were smiling at Flash. A lot of people greeted Flash by name, and almost as many lifted their hands in greeting to Grady and her. Even on a weekend night with as many strange faces as familiar ones filling the tables, it was good to be home.

The wall behind the long, weathered bar was lined with photographs of Grady ancestors and of the early days of Dogleg, and all the other walls were decorated with ship's wheels and anchors, paddle boards and oars and one mounted tiger shark. Tonight Aggie could see Lorraine's touch in the strings of red and white lights that were looped over the bar, their reflections glittering off the glasses that hung from the ceiling, and in the light-studded garland that draped the doorway leading to the dining and patio areas. Pete's aesthetic was represented by the dancing Santa at the end of the bar. It was Friday night and the place was fairly busy—although only a fraction of what it would be on the same night during the summer—and Pete was helping out behind the bar. He grinned when he saw them come in.

"Forget to buy groceries again?" he said when they approached.

Aggie jerked a thumb over her shoulder to her husband, and Grady said, "Can't a guy take his family out to dinner without getting the third degree?"

Flash sailed up onto a barstool and sat politely, causing customers on either side to turn and grin at him. Pete said, "Evening, Flash. How's it going?"

Flash returned a polite bark, and the people around him chuckled. Pete set a bowl of pretzels before Flash and turned to draw a beer for his brother.

"Y'all get your tree yet?" he asked.

"In the truck," Grady said. "She's a beauty, too. You want to come over later and help me untangle lights?"

Pete just laughed and said to Aggie, "What can I get for you, beautiful?"

Aggie said, "That's Chief Beautiful, to you. Do you have any of that cider you were serving the other day?"

"Sure thing. We've been pouring it cold, but I can nuke it for you."

"Sounds good." Aggie returned her hands, which were still chilled from the brief encounter with outdoor temperatures, to her jacket pockets. "Lorraine's not working tonight, is she?"

Pete gave a small grimace and slid a ceramic tumbler of cider into the microwave. "Just try to keep her away from this place during the holidays. I caught her on a ladder yesterday, nailing up Christmas bows."

While they talked, Flash took a pretzel delicately between his teeth and crunched it up, looking around for people he knew. It was something Aggie had taught him—"Always good to know who's in the room, Flash," she'd said—and he noticed Grady did that, too, his eyes roaming casually around, taking the measure of the place. Flash knew just about everyone on Dogleg Island, which included three terriers, six Lab-mixes, two golden retrievers, a one-eyed cocker spaniel and two dozen cats, not including the wild ones that lived in the woods and kept the rat population down. But on weekends at Pete's Place most of the people came from across the bridge where, Flash guessed, they didn't have pretzels, beer or hamburgers. He didn't mind. He liked meeting new people. They always brought interesting smells with them.

For example, the man on the barstool next to Flash smelled like diesel fuel and fast food and cardboard boxes; he drove a delivery truck for a living. He winked at Flash and tossed him a pretzel from his own bowl, which Flash obligingly caught and gobbled up. And the woman at the table in the corner, laughing with her girlfriends, smelled like the vanilla body wash Aggie sometimes used, which made Flash happy. Then there was the dark-skinned man with the steel-wool beard who'd just come in, wearing work boots and a cotton jacket, smelling like Christmas trees and fertilizer and yes, roses. Aggie wasn't wild about roses—she said they reminded her of hospitals—but Flash loved the smell. He wouldn't mind getting to know the man who smelled like roses better, if he had the chance.

Dave, the weekend bartender, went over to the rose man and greeted him like he knew him. The two of them chatted awhile, and Flash lost interest when Pete said to Aggie, "Any leads on our pickpocket?"

Aggie said, "I'm not sure you can call it a pickpocket." She looked unhappy. "After all, only one wallet was stolen. The other things were taken from plain sight."

Grady touched Aggie's shoulder. "There's Lorraine. I'm going to say hi. Meet you on the patio."

Aggie watched briefly as he crossed the room to hug his sister-in-law, then she turned back to Pete. "I hate to say it, Pete, but it's got to be one of the staff.

Mo's running background checks now, but if you'd let us set up a lie detector…"

He was already shaking his head before she finished speaking. "We're not there yet."

Aggie persisted, "A lot of times just the threat of a lie detector will cause the guilty party to show himself."

Pete poured the hot cider from the ceramic tumbler into a footed glass mug, stirred it with a cinnamon stick, and passed it across the bar to Aggie. "It'll scare a lot of my part-time help into quitting, too, and I can't afford to lose staff this close to Christmas." He nodded at the mug and suggested, "That'd be better with a shot of rum."

Aggie sighed. "Don't I know it." Every morning she lined up twelve different pills and capsules on the kitchen counter. Not one of them was labeled *Take with alcohol.*

She wrapped her hands around the mug to warm them and glanced again at Grady and Lorraine, who were huddled together near the entrance to the patio dining area, deep in private conversation. "Those two sure do have a lot of secrets these days," she observed. She looked back at Pete. "What, are they having an affair?"

Pete's eyes twinkled. "Yeah, that's it. It's Christmas, Aggie. Don't be so damn nosey."

"Can't help it. That's kind of my job." She saluted him with the cider and turned to go, then looked back. "Say, Pete," she said. "Do you have any idea what Ryan wants for Christmas?"

He replied without hesitation. "Same thing I do. A happy, healthy wife."

Aggie just smiled and went to join her husband.

When people talk about "low-crime" areas, they're usually referring to crimes against persons, or those involving violence. By that definition, Murphy County, tucked away at the northern curve of the Big Bend area of Florida between Alabama and Georgia, was essentially a low-crime area. Dogleg Island, a mostly undiscovered three-mile-by-twelve-mile stretch of fishing piers and white-sand beaches where every one of the four-hundred-plus residents knew everyone else, was rarely beset by anything more troublesome than teenagers smoking pot on the beach or petty thefts. With rare exception, Aggie and Flash spent their days dealing with administrative details in the office, patrolling lazy streets just to make their presence known, and serving the occasional court order or taking the odd complaint. The kinds of crimes they dealt with were extremely low profile.

There had been, over the past few years, some notable exceptions. Dogleg Island had been catapulted to the headlines by the brutal murders of a dentist and his wife in their beachfront home and by the near-fatal shooting of Deputy Aggie Malone, who intercepted the crime. The entire county had been exposed to a subsequent corruption scandal within the Sheriff's Office, and, more recently, had been the scene of a treasure hunt that had ended in murder. Grady worried that the kind of notoriety their little corner of paradise had been attracting lately would make it even more of a natural target for high-level crime than it already was, but Grady, since he had become a family man, tended to worry about things like that. Aggie was more sanguine.

As for Flash, it was a matter of policy for him to worry about as little as possible. Since he and Aggie had taken over the Dogleg Island Police Department, they'd solved every crime that had crossed their paths, whether it involved a missing cat or a missing person, a stolen lunch or a stolen car. Aggie had told him once that in a place like this, most of the time you knew who the criminal was as soon as you discovered the crime; not always true but usually. Aggie was pretty sure she knew who the thief at Pete's Place was, and so was Flash, although he wouldn't have minded the chance to sniff around to prove it. But Aggie had told him it was impolite to do that kind of thing while diners were present, and besides, he had no doubt Aggie had the situation well in hand. He and Aggie were a team, and they always had each other's back.

They sat on the patio, which Pete had enclosed with sheet plastic to keep out the wind, next to a tall patio heater that gave off a lovely radiant warmth. White lights outlined the star-shaped beams of the ceiling and encircled the roofline, and evergreen wreaths decorated with red bows adorned every post. There was a big Christmas tree decorated with shiny red and silver balls in the corner, and it twinkled with a thousand lights. Lorraine brought Flash an aluminum bowl of water with cubes of ice floating in it—next to the hamburgers, the water was the best thing about Pete's Place—and Flash set about crunching up the ice while Lorraine gossiped with Aggie, and Grady sipped his beer, looking as content as Flash felt.

As soon as Lorraine sat down next to her, Aggie said, "Listen, I don't know what you two are up to, but you need to stop it. I don't like surprises."

Grady looked at her with exaggerated innocence and replied, "I don't know what you're talking about." While at the same time Lorraine said, "You might like this one."

Lorraine gave Grady an exasperated look and added, "Come on, Aggie. Everyone likes surprises at Christmas. Which is not to say," she added quickly, "that we're working on one."

"But if we were," Grady assured her, "you'd like it."

Aggie ignored him and turned a skeptical look on Lorraine. "It has to do with the party, doesn't it?"

She had never met her in-laws, who had retired to Ecuador years before Aggie moved to Murphy County, and in less than a week they were flying in for the holidays to welcome their new daughter-in-law into the family and—more specifically—to celebrate the wedding they had not been able to attend. To that end, they insisted upon giving the newlyweds the gift of an elaborate wedding reception, with cake, champagne, photographs, white tulle bows—all the things that left Aggie feeling baffled and awkward but which, fortunately, her two sisters-in-law enthusiastically embraced. They had taken all the planning and preparation for the party out of Aggie's hands, which was not necessarily turning out to be quite as good an idea as it had originally sounded.

Aggie added, with growing trepidation, "That's it, right? You're planning something crazy, like... like bringing in a snow machine or dropping Santa from a helicopter, aren't you?"

Grady looked at Lorraine, his expression falling. "Crap," he said.

"I didn't tell her, I promise!" Lorraine protested.

Aggie couldn't keep the dismay out of her eyes. "Seriously?"

Lorraine burst into laughter and Grady, grinning, nudged Aggie's ankle under the table with the toe of his boot. "You make it too easy to mess with you, baby."

Lorraine was a tall woman in her early forties who liked to wear colorful caftans with jangling earrings and brightly patterned scarves tied around her head. She also looked great in leather pants and spiked purple hair, but she had shaved her head when she began chemo four months earlier. With a peculiar kind of gallows humor, Aggie and Lorraine had referred to themselves as the Bald Twins throughout the late summer and fall. Although Aggie's hair had begun to grow out after her surgery, she still wore a stocking cap most of the time for warmth. And though Lorraine, who had successfully completed treatment and was now cautiously in remission, had no problem with going bald, she liked the gypsy look of the scarves and continued to wear them. Aggie and she had an ongoing inside joke about which head covering made the most effective fashion statement.

"So," Lorraine said, "we're all set for the folks' arrival."

"Oh yeah?" replied Aggie dryly. "Then why do I have four voice mails from Lucy on my phone since five o'clock?"

Lorraine shrugged. "Because she's Lucy." She stretched her arm across the table to light a mason jar candle centerpiece that was decorated with silk holly and red plaid ribbon. Her engagement ring, a striking marquis-cut sapphire surrounded by diamonds, flashed and sparkled in the candlelight, accompanied by the jangling chorus of a dozen costume-jewelry bangle bracelets. On Lorraine, both the diamonds and the zircons looked perfectly at home.

"Cal and Lucy are picking them up at the airport at one on Thursday," she went on, pocketing the lighter, "which should get everyone to your house by five, unless the flight's delayed." Lucy had volunteered her husband, Cal, for airport duty almost before her parents had decided to make the trip. No one was entirely sure whether or not she had actually informed Cal. "Pete and I will be over as soon as we can with dinner," Lorraine added, "but we probably won't be able to get out of here before six."

Aggie stared at her. "Wait. That means I'll be left with Lucy and the twins for an hour."

Flash looked up in alarm when he heard the word "twins." He liked most people, and children in particular, but he had learned the safest thing to do when the twins were around was to find something under which to hide. He looked cautiously around, but no twins were in sight. Maybe he had misheard. He returned to the ice, but kept his guard up.

Lorraine said, "Well, whatever you do, don't try to argue with Lucy about the agenda. She's still mad that Salty and Lil are staying with you instead of with her and Cal."

"Well, that's just silly," Aggie said. "We're the ones with the guesthouse, not them."

The guesthouse was actually a small 1950s garage that had been converted to a Key West style rental cottage that, while it once had been part of the property now owned by Ryan Grady, was technically owned by both brothers—which meant only that they shared the income whenever they got ambitious enough to rent it out. Aggie had lived there for over a year when she first took the police chief job, and she still thought of it, in many ways, as her house.

"I know that," Lorraine said with a sigh, "but try telling Lucy. No, don't. Anyway, don't worry about cooking while they're here. Pete's making a low country boil the first night, should be enough to last a couple of days. And of course Lucy will have to have them over, and we'll have everybody for dinner Sunday night ..."

"I'm liking the sound of this," Aggie said, sipping her cider.

Grady winked at her. "See, baby, I told you it would be fun."

"Oh, it's going to be the best," Lorraine assured her. Salty and Lil are amazing. You won't believe how ..."

"Wait." Aggie turned to Grady with a mixture of anxiety and accusation in her eyes. "It's not a surprise honeymoon, is it? That's not what you're planning. Because you know I can't take the time off, and there's no way we can afford..."

Lorraine gave a helpless wave of her hands and stood just as the waitress arrived with their order. "You married her," she told Grady, "you deal with her." She started to go, then glanced back. "Stop by the bar on your way out," she told Aggie. "I saw the cutest hat in the catalogue. I tore out the page for you."

The waitress set their orders before them: a mug of creamy clam chowder for Aggie, a basket of fried clams and hushpuppies for Grady, and for Flash, the perfect hamburger—crunchy on the outside, red on the inside, no ketchup, no bun, and a single slice of lettuce. Flash hopped back onto the bench beside Aggie, removed the lettuce to save for later, and took a bite of the hamburger. Nothing better.

Grady said, popping a clam into his mouth, "Guess all you want. I'll never tell."

"No wonder there are more homicides during the holidays than any other time of the year," Aggie muttered.

She picked up her spoon and dipped it into the chowder, but her hand suddenly shook so badly that the spoon clattered against the side of the mug. Grady leaned forward in concern. "You cold, baby? Want my jacket?"

He started to shrug out of his own windbreaker, but she said, "No. No, I'm fine." She forced a quick, tight smile and placed the spoon, very carefully, beside her plate. "Just a little chill for some reason."

She wrapped both hands around the mug with what appeared to be deliberate care, and smiled again at Grady before she lifted it. Grady ate another clam and tried not to look worried. But Flash could tell from the way Aggie smiled that she was not fine, and he thought Grady knew it too.

Chapter Five

Weasel had a plan, or most of one, anyway. The first and most important part of the plan was to act normal. So he pulled up into the sprawling sand and gravel parking lot of Pete's Place Bar and Grill on Dogleg Island right at eight o'clock, just as he had been instructed to do, and parked the car in the back row. He had a backpack in which he'd tossed a change of clothes and a few toilet articles; everything else he owned, precious little as it was, he'd left with a buddy back in Mississippi who'd let him crash on his couch a couple of nights. He started to stuff the Chik 'N' Waffles bag full of cash into the backpack, but decided that didn't look normal. It looked so decidedly un-normal, in fact, as to be stupid, so he dug the money out of the bag and started stuffing it in his pockets, but the cash left noticeable lumps. Starting to panic a little, Weasel began to cram the money inside his tee shirt, which looked even stupider, until he came up with the idea to put on a jacket and zip it up over his shirt. There. That was better. Way better than bringing a backpack into a bar. These days, somebody would probably call the bomb squad. He was freaking himself out. It was going to be fine. All he had to do was act normal.

He wadded up the paper bag, walked casually over to the dumpster, and tossed it inside. Then, double-checking his jacket pocket for the car keys, he went inside the bar, sat down, and ordered a beer. The stereo was playing that Christmas song by Garth Brooks, the one that always made him tear up when he'd had one too many. He made a note to keep his consumption to two.

Weasel hadn't had a bad upbringing. His dad made a pretty good living as a house painter and his mother made sure the kids went to Sunday School. They had a real Christmas tree in Sunday School class and every year the kids decorated it with red and green construction paper chains. Each link in the chain had the name of a missionary written on it in crayon. Weasel always misspelled whatever name he was given, even if it was something as simple as "Brown." What could you expect from a kid named Weasel?

His sister had changed her name at age nineteen by marrying a guy whose family owned a car dealership and, six months later, pumped out a baby boy. She had three kids now, Weasel thought, and worked part time at an insurance agency. Not everybody in his family was dumb.

Funny how he only thought about things like that—family and stuff—at Christmastime.

The plan was this. He was going to sit here and drink his beer until the guy came to collect the keys and give him the rest of his payment for driving the car down here. And then when the guy asked if he wanted to drive the next one to wherever, Weasel would say, Nah, he'd decided as long as he was in Florida he might as well hang out for the winter, see what he could pick up here, but maybe next spring he'd get in touch, what d'ya say? Yeah, that sounded good. Then, as soon as the guy was gone he'd get himself a taxi to the nearest motel—he had cash, he could do that—and first thing in the morning, he'd find a used car for sale in the paper, preferably, or from a dealer if he had to, and then he'd take off for California. He'd never been out west, and by the time the drug boss realized a part of his haul was missing—if he ever did—Weasel would just be a face in the crowd in East LA. Good plan.

The bar was crowded, and warm. Weasel hunched over his beer, and he thought he could feel people glancing at him, wondering why he didn't take off his jacket. He glanced at his watch. Only ten after eight. The guy had said between eight and nine. So he'd wait.

The tune switched to *Jingle Bell Rock*. One of the waitresses, wearing a red felt Santa hat, did a few flirtatious swing steps with the bartender and that made everybody at the bar grin, even Weasel. It was Christmas. Why not be in a good mood?

The door opened and a man came in, looking around for somebody. Weasel tensed. Big guy, tangled red beard, looking tough enough to beat up a Teamster. Weasel hunched down further, the money inside his shirt crackling and scratching at his skin. That was probably him. Who else would they send to pick up a car full of drug money? And when he realized that money had been tampered with...

Weasel cast a furtive sideways glance toward the man at the door just in time to see him lift his hand to somebody at the back of the room and break into a broad, gap-toothed grin. Weasel's shoulders sagged with relief as the big man crossed the room, never once glancing his way.

Weasel put a twenty on the bar and ordered another beer. His heart was still pounding. Act normal. *Act normal.* But that was hard to do with sweat beading on his upper lip and hundred-dollar bills sticking to his skinny chest. He was going to blow this, he just knew it. And when he did, a bomb the size of a truck was going to land on his ass.

The bartender brought his beer and his change, and Weasel managed what he hoped was a normal-looking smile and a nod. His mind was racing with alternatives. The most tempting was to just get up, get in the car that was waiting for him right outside—the one that was stowing close to a million dollars, the one he had the keys to right there in his pocket—and start driving. What had he been thinking, anyway? What kind of plan was that, *act normal?* Maybe the guy who came for the car had no intention of paying Weasel the remaining $500; maybe he'd just shoot him in the head as a thank-you and dump his body off the bridge. Why else would they have arranged to meet in a little podunk place like this with nothing but ocean everywhere you looked? And what did Weasel need with $500 anyway? He had more than enough to get him to California. No, what he needed to do was forget the money, forget the car, forget acting normal and get the hell out of here by whatever means were available.

No. His first plan was the best. Pretend like nothing was wrong, add his $500 to the wad stuffed in his shirt, turn over the keys, shake the man's hand, stroll casually away. That was what he was going to do. It was a good plan. He thought.

What he needed was a sign, just a little hint that fortune was still on his side, that he was not about to be double-crossed and end up at the bottom of the ocean. Just a little something to let him know his luck was changing, like that cop who'd given him a chicken coupon instead of a ticket. Some little sign, was that too much to ask? It was Christmas, after all.

That's exactly what he was thinking when *Jingle Bell Rock* ended and *California Christmas* began. Seriously. *California Christmas.* He heard the door open behind him and two men came in, one with slicked back hair, big shoulders and hard eyes, and the other with a scorpion tattooed on his neck. Two men, of course. One to drive the car and the other to…beat Weasel up and toss him off the bridge? Tie him up and put him in the trunk?

Dry mouthed, Weasel turned his back to the door, hiding his face, trying to think. That was when he saw the cop get up from the table on the patio and start toward him. He did not look like he was there to hand out gift certificates.

Weasel had a hundred thousand dollars of stolen money inside his shirt, with the guys he had stolen it from on one side of him and the law coming at him on the other. He shifted his gaze around, trying not to look frantic. Then he saw the sign.

He got up, leaving his change on the bar, and walked toward it, his heart pounding. The sign said "Men" but Weasel walked right past it and out the rear exit. He walked out of the parking lot, away from the music and the twinkling Christmas lights, head down, shoulders hunched, moving fast, thinking about nothing but putting as much distance as possible between himself and the bar.

He might be stupid, but he knew a sign when he saw one.

The patio was almost full by the time they finished eating and Grady was in a hurry to leave.

"What?" Aggie pretended to protest. "No dessert?"

Flash looked up from licking his paper plate. He wouldn't have minded a dish of ice cream, himself, but Grady was already taking out his wallet. "Come on, honey, aren't you excited about getting the tree up?"

She laughed softly. "You really are a big kid, aren't you?"

"Guilty." He glanced through the bills in his wallet. The official policy at Pete's Place was that family and law officers never paid for meals. That policy did not, as Pete frequently reminded his brother, extend to beer, and Grady never stiffed the waitress. "Do you have any change? All I've got is a fifty and a couple of ones."

"Sorry," Aggie said. "I don't get paid until Monday."

He stood. "I'll get some at the bar. You about ready?"

"Right behind you."

Flash walked out with Aggie, waving his tail at the diners who smiled at him and pausing to let one little boy rub his fur. By the time they reached the bar, which was a lot more crowded than it had been when they came in, Grady was already waiting for his change. Flash looked around, taking inventory of who had departed and who had arrived in his absence. That was part of his job, keeping track. Six people had gone, ten had arrived. The rose man was beginning to smell more like bourbon than roses, and a fellow who lived with a Labrador had taken the place of the man who delivered boxes for a living. There was a man with an interesting looking tattoo on his neck, sitting beside a fellow with mean eyes who smelled like cigarettes. They each slid Grady a glance when he walked up to the bar, then pretended they hadn't. Of course, Flash didn't judge; he'd learned that from Grady, who also noticed the two men but didn't seem particularly interested. A lot of people who came into Pete's looked rough, Flash had heard Grady tell Aggie a long time ago, but most of the time they were just hard-working folks who'd had a bad day. And even if they weren't, it wasn't their job—Grady's and Aggie's and Flash's— to give anyone a hard time unless they broke the law. Live and let live. That was the way they handled things on Dogleg Island.

A woman came in the front door carrying a shopping bag, looking tense and upset, and made her way quickly to the hostess stand. Aggie watched as she began an animated conversation with the hostess, and so did Flash. But just then Dave the bartender brought Grady's change, and Flash lost interest. The money Grady sorted through smelled like chicken sandwiches and waffle fries, two of Flash's favorite things. Sometimes Aggie and he would stop for chicken sandwiches and waffle fries when they had to go across the bridge for business, or to visit Grady at his work. Flash always looked forward to those times. Pete did not serve chicken sandwiches and waffle fries at Pete's Place, which Flash thought was a shame.

Lorraine came up to talk to the woman at the hostess stand, and Aggie turned back to Grady. "I'm going to the ladies' room," she said. "Meet you at the truck."

Grady started to tuck the money into his wallet, then hesitated. "Hey, Malone," he said, "hold on a minute. Look at this."

He held up a twenty-dollar bill and Aggie took it. She turned it over in her hand, glancing at it, and then returned it. "Nice money," she commented.

Grady frowned a little, scraping his thumb nail over the front of the bill. "It doesn't feel thin to you? And look—no ridges."

Aggie lifted an eyebrow and reached for the bill again. "You need to hold it up to the light. It's too dark in here."

Grady leaned an elbow on the bar. "Hey, Dave. Send the big guy over here, will you?"

Aggie held up the bill, trying unsuccessfully to catch a stray beam of light from one of the Christmas lights. "What tipped you off?"

Grady took the rest of the money out of his wallet and examined each bill again. "We had a briefing Wednesday on how to recognize counterfeit. Apparently fifties, twenties and hundreds have been popping up all along the Gulf."

"Yeah, I saw the report. I didn't think it'd reach Dogleg, though."

Grady shrugged. "Merry Christmas."

Aggie returned the bill to Grady just as Pete reached them, propping his hands on the bar with arms akimbo. "What's up?" he said.

Grady slid the twenty-dollar bill across the bar to his brother. "I don't suppose you could tell me how many people paid with twenties tonight, could you?"

Pete laughed. "Only about half the people who've been in. Why?"

Grady glanced at Aggie, but she had just noticed that Lorraine was beckoning her over to the hostess stand, and she looked anxious. Aggie tilted her head apologetically to her husband and said. "Sounds like a problem for the Sheriff's Office. Send me a copy of the report." She edged her way through the crowd toward Lorraine.

Grady turned back to Pete. "Sorry, bro," he said. "It's not good news."

Flash hated to leave Grady, especially with Pete's face turning dark and thundery like it was, but he had no choice. He and Aggie were a team.

The tension that radiated from Lorraine was palpable as they reached her, and to Flash it smelled like metal. But her voice sounded perfectly polite as she introduced Aggie to the woman with the shopping bag.

"Mrs. Carmichael, this is Aggie Malone, our police chief." The look she cast Aggie had an edge of helplessness to it. "Mrs. Carmichael was in earlier and she believes something might have gone missing from her shopping bag while she was dining."

Aggie said, "I'm sorry to hear that." She was, too. She might not have been looking forward to the tree-trimming as much as Grady was, but she really didn't want to spend the rest of her evening taking a report. She rummaged in her purse, found her badge, and clipped it reluctantly onto the pocket of her windbreaker.

"I don't *believe* anything," the woman Lorraine had introduced as Mrs. Carmichael corrected tartly. "I know it for a fact." She was maybe fifty trying to look thirty, with caramel highlights in her bobbed brown hair and makeup creased in the lines around her mouth. The tendons in her neck tightened as she jutted her chin forward, making her look at least three years younger. "When I came in here I had a shopping bag full of Christmas presents, and when

I got home one of them was missing." She looked down sharply at Flash. "Is that a police dog?"

Aggie replied simply, "Yes." She'd found it was easier to give the short answer than to try to explain what Flash's job really was. "What was missing when you got home?"

"A watch from Heller and Sons, in a silver box about this big." She made a rectangle with her hands about six inches long, jostling the shopping bag on her arm as she did so. "I know I had it when I came in because I showed it to my sister while we were waiting for our drinks. It was a gift for my daughter. I only brought the shopping bag in because everybody says not to leave packages in the car this time of year, and I swear it never left my side. It was right beside the table the whole time."

Aggie glanced at Lorraine. "Did you check lost and found?" she asked, knowing already what the answer would be.

"Nothing tonight," replied Lorraine regretfully.

"Did you stop anywhere else after you left here?" Aggie asked Mrs. Carmichael.

"I went straight home," she insisted. "I unpacked my purchases and noticed the watch was missing, then I got right back in the car and came back here. I brought the bag so you could see for yourself." She held the bag up to Aggie triumphantly.

Aggie knew it would be pointless to explain that a shopping bag that might or might not have once contained a missing package was not exactly evidence, so she glanced politely through the items inside: a couple of sweaters, a Christmas CD and a cute pair of shoes from Clara's Boutique on Main that Aggie wouldn't mind having. No watch.

She asked the woman what time she had arrived and when she left, and while she was doing that Flash watched the man with the scorpion tattoo get up from the bar and leave by the front door. Grady and Pete were talking to Dave the bartender. Pete did not look happy.

Aggie asked the woman where she had been sitting, and she pointed to a table on the patio by the Christmas tree. This made perfect sense to Flash, and he started to go check it out. Aggie called him back and he remembered, a little chagrined, that it was impolite to sniff around while people were eating. He went to sit beside Aggie again, but kept an eye on the table by the Christmas tree.

Aggie said to Lorraine, "I'll need to talk to the server and the bus boy for that table. And if it's okay for us to use your office for a minute, I can take down the information I need for my report."

"Yes, of course." Lorraine looked relieved to turn the problem over to someone else, and Mrs. Carmichael looked reassured now that someone was taking charge.

Lorraine lifted an arm to gesture them to the office at the back of the hallway, but Aggie didn't follow. Instead she stood still, staring at her friend's hand. "Lorraine," she said, "Where's your ring?"

CHAPTER SIX

"What is it about the holidays," Grady grumbled to no one in particular, "that brings out the worst in people?"

Aggie suggested, "Christmas tree lights?"

The tree was up in all its naked glory, centered in its stand in front of the bay window in the living room and filling the house with its sweet forest fragrance. Every year Grady told Aggie about the trees of Christmas past that had stood in that very window during his boyhood. None of those stories involved wads of Christmas lights carelessly tossed into plastic boxes to be dealt with next year.

She couldn't resist adding, "You know, Ryan, if you'd just store the lights wrapped around the empty wrapping paper rolls like I told you..."

He shot her a dark look. "Don't start."

Aggie smiled sweetly. "I love you."

Grady sat cross-legged on the floor surrounded by boxes of Christmas decorations, most of which had belonged to his parents. A giant snarl of green-wired tree lights spilled from his lap onto the floor, their multicolor bulbs glinting like dragon's teeth in the lamp light. Aggie sat on the sofa, trying to put ornament hangers on the ornaments, a task that was proving to be at least as frustrating as the lights. Flash helped by carefully removing the delicate glass balls from a big plastic storage box and sorting them into piles for Aggie: red balls to the right of her feet, green balls to the left.

Grady said, "You don't think Lorraine's ring was stolen, do you?"

Aggie shook her head. "In a way it would be easier if it were. At least then we'd have a shot at it turning up in a pawn shop somewhere. It was a family heirloom, wasn't it? God knows how much it's worth." She struggled to get the thin wire hook over the tiny wire loop. It was like threading a needle; she missed every time. "She's lost so much weight, the ring keeps falling off. I know she had it on when she sat down with us, but she could have lost it anywhere in the restaurant after that. Our only hope is that somebody will find it and turn it in. Otherwise, it'll probably end up in a vacuum cleaner bag or thrown out with the trash or stuck in a drain somewhere. Damn it," she said as the ornament loop separated from the glass ball entirely. She tossed it aside and reached for another one.

"Any leads on the thief?" Grady asked.

Aggie frowned over her work. "It's got to be one of the wait staff. All the thefts seem to have happened to people who were eating on the patio, and they only took small things that could be concealed in an apron pocket or under a plate. So we'll be talking to the kids that worked the patio over the past week." Triumphantly, she held up an ornament by its newly installed hanger, admired it for a moment, then put it in the box with the others that were ready to be hung on the tree. "Should I put out a notice to the island merchants about the counterfeit bills?"

"It wouldn't hurt." Studiously, he unwound a final loop in the string of lights, then carefully carried it over to the Christmas tree. "It's probably just a one-time thing—somebody from out of town picked up a bad bill and innocently passed it on. All kinds of people come into Pete's this time of year." He began to carefully tuck the lights into the branches of the tree. "There were a couple of weird-looking cats at the bar when I went up to pay, did you notice? One of them had a scar or something on his face."

Flash looked up with interest, remembering the man with the strange tattoo on his neck, and his friend who'd smelled like cigarettes.

"It wasn't a scar," Aggie said, "it was a tattoo. A scorpion, I think. And it wasn't on his face, it was on his neck."

Grady shot her a curious look. "You saw that? In the dark?"

For a moment Aggie hesitated, wondering exactly how she *had* seen a small tattoo in a dark bar when she could barely get a wire to go through a loop. But since the shooting and the subsequent surgery, there were so many things she didn't understand about herself that she made it a point not to look too closely at any of them.

Flash, on the other hand, didn't know why Grady sounded so surprised. Flash saw lots of things in the dark.

Aggie shrugged. "Women have a better eye for detail than men."

"They do not."

"Sure they do. You take any two eyewitness statements, the woman's is always going to be more detailed than the man's. It's genetic. It's because in prehistoric times women learned to recognize members of their own tribe by focusing on facial features, while men were always scanning the horizon for predators."

Grady considered that for a moment. "Well," he said, "I'm better at untangling lights."

"You can also pee standing up. You're my hero."

He resumed his careful placement of lights along the branches. "Anyway, I think we need to keep our eyes open for a couple of days. Makes me a little nervous that this happened on a Friday night. If somebody cashed a paycheck…"

"The whole county could be seeing those bills by Monday," Aggie supplied, frowning once more over the uncooperative ornament hanger. "The worst part is that the merchants who'll be getting the bad bills are the ones who can least afford it. The bigger stores do most of their business in credit cards."

"I told Pete I'd take care of the Treasury Department report for him," Grady said. "Don't let me forget to print out the form before I go to bed."

Aggie slid him a mildly admonishing look. "Pete knows how to report a counterfeit bill. All he has to do is go to the website."

"Yeah, well, I guess if you have a law officer in the family all you have to do is turn it over to him. Okay, baby, check it out." He plugged in the lights and stood back to admire his work.

Nothing happened.

Aggie looked up sympathetically. "Maybe the next string." She held up another ornament by the hanger, only to have it crash to the floor and shatter, leaving her holding an empty wire. Flash looked up with interest. "*Damn* it," she said.

Grady came over to the sofa, moved the box of ornaments, and sat beside her, drawing her close. "Here's a thought," he said. "Let's do this tomorrow."

She blew out a frustrated breath. "Or never."

"Come on, sweetie." He nuzzled the top of her head with his chin. "You know Santa won't come if we don't get the tree up."

She rolled her eyes at him.

Grady noticed the two piles of Christmas ornaments at Aggie's feet and said, "Hey, look what Flash did. I didn't think dogs could see color."

"Sure they can." Aggie extended a hand to Flash and, grinning, he joined them on the sofa. She tugged affectionately at his ear and he bent his head to her caress. "They just see them differently than we do, that's all." She leaned her head back against Grady's shoulder and looked up at him. "Kind of like the way you and I see Christmas."

Flash rested his head on Aggie's knee and Grady stroked his fur. Aggie laced her fingers through the fingers of Grady's other hand. "It's just that, you know, you and Pete and Lucy had this amazing childhood with reindeer and snowmen and so many presents under the tree you couldn't even see the carpet…"

"Not that many snowmen in Florida," he pointed out.

"I've seen the photos," she reminded him dryly. "Your front lawn looked like a winter carnival."

He chuckled. "It was pretty hokey," he admitted. "Dad would start putting up the lights right after Halloween."

"The point is," she went on, "I never had any of that. That wasn't my life. Those weren't my memories. Christmas just isn't the same for me as it is for you."

Agatha Elaine Malone had been born on her grandmother's bathroom floor to a sixteen-year-old mother who was in and out of Aggie's life until she died of a heroin overdose when Aggie was barely old enough to remember. Her father, whom her grandmother described only as "that no-account lowlife Jimmy Joe Jackson," had been in county detention for some misdemeanor or another when Aggie was born, and shortly thereafter had skipped town, never to be heard from again.

When Aggie first told him about her parents, Grady had the idea to run her father's name through the routine military and law enforcement databases, and Aggie had reluctantly agreed. He knew the chances were good that, if the man had been a juvenile offender in the past he'd continue to show up in the system, but people did change. It was possible. He'd hoped it might make her feel better to know what had become of the man whose DNA she shared, but nothing showed up in the databases. He wasn't sure whether she was relieved or disappointed.

Aggie shrugged uncomfortably and went on, "I mean, it's not that my grandmother didn't try—I mean, she worked two jobs just to keep food on the table, for heaven's sake. She always made sure I had something for Christmas, but we're the ones the church used to bring the charity Christmas basket to, you know? And a tree and lights and all the trimmings, it all just seemed so extravagant, like it belonged in someone else's life, not mine. I know how hard you work to make the holidays special for me, Ryan, but the truth is, they never will be. I just don't have the same feelings about Christmas as you do. I'm sorry."

Grady stopped petting Flash and wrapped both arms around Aggie. Flash didn't mind. He got up, feeling drowsy and content, and curled up on the opposite end of the sofa to have a nap.

"Not just the holidays," Grady said. "I want to make every day special for you because every day that you're here, that you're alive and with me, is special to me. It takes my breath away sometimes, just thinking how lucky I am. So if there's ever a day when you don't feel special, you need to kick my ass for it, because that means I'm not doing my job."

Sometimes Grady's love washed over Aggie like a tsunami, leaving her helpless and baffled and completely overwhelmed by the enormity of it. What did one do with so much love? How could she even hold it all? Other times, like now, being loved by him was like floating in a warm pool, buoyed, surrounded, supported. She had a feeling it could always be that way, if only she would let it.

She turned in his arms, looped her arms around his neck, and tilted her head back to look at him. She said softly, "You are the most ridiculous man."

"But adorable," he countered.

She smiled. "Yeah. That." She kissed him. When she drew back she added softly, running her hand down the length of his chest, "So, here's my idea."

He murmured, "I'm listening."

"Let's go upstairs…"

He kissed her neck. "I like where this is headed."

"Forget about Christmas decorations…"

"I can do that."

"…and concentrate on more important things."

"I am all over that, baby."

His mouth sought hers again and she slipped her hands underneath his sweatshirt, caressing his bare skin. Just then the Christmas tree lights came on. His eyes twinkled as he looked down at her. "Now that," he said, "is what I call electricity."

"That," she returned, giving the muscles of his chest one last lingering stroke, "is what I call a short circuit. Unplug the tree, Ryan."

He kissed her again. "Meet you in the bedroom."

Her phone buzzed as he got up. "You're off duty," he reminded her.

"Couldn't be more off duty," she agreed, and reached for the phone.

The Dogleg Island Police Department was considered a part-time force, with officers on duty from eight to five six days a week, closed on Sundays and Federal holidays. When the office closed, all 911 calls were dispatched to the Murphy County Sheriff's Office, but an automatic text was sent to the Police Department and copied to the chief's phone. Aggie always liked to check. Most of the time the calls were false alarms or routine non-emergencies: a fender-bender in a parking lot, a complaint from a neighbor about someone's party, a drunk and disorderly. But on the rare occasion that there was an emergency after hours—a domestic dispute turned violent, a burglary in progress, or a bad traffic accident, Aggie wanted to be there. These were her people, and as far as she was concerned, no one was better equipped to handle their problems than she was.

Flash sprang to the floor before Aggie finished reading the text, and when Grady looked up from unplugging the tree lights both of them were headed toward the door. "No," he said. "No, no, no…"

She took her jacket from the hall tree and slipped it on, holding the phone out to him. Grady took it and read the text.

"Crap," he said.

He grabbed his own jacket and followed her out the door.

Chapter Seven

A hundred years ago, Flash's ancestors had been in charge of vast ranches over which were scattered thousands of head of sheep. It had been the border collie's job to know where every one of those sheep were at all times, to know which gates were supposed to be open and which were supposed to be closed, to track down lost lambs and herd them back into the fold, and to keep the entire flock safe from predators. Flash's job today was not that much different from those of his predecessors, and his duties were equally diverse, ranging from keeping track of all the residents of Dogleg Island to finding lost and buried things to keeping an eye out for bad guys and making sure they stayed far away from the people for whom he was responsible. For the most part he loved his job. What he liked the least, though, was finding dead things. Fortunately, on Dogleg Island that didn't happen very often.

When they arrived at the intersection of Island Drive and Park Street, an ambulance and a sheriff's cruiser were already there. Grady took the badge that was clipped to a chain in his jacket pocket and draped it around his neck. Aggie did the same. They got out and went to talk to the deputies. Flash went to investigate the dead person on the side of the road.

The EMTs were doing their jobs, but dead was dead. Flash knew it from the feeling—a great sad nothingness, an absence of living—and by the smell: old blood and faint decay, cold flesh, emptiness. There were other smells, too, the smells that told who the person had been when he was alive, what he had done, where he had traveled. Flash set about exploring these from a distance, careful not to disturb the scene. He was in the midst of doing this when Aggie joined him.

Aggie was a lot like Flash in many ways. In the midst of a crisis, she was capable of razor-sharp focus, intense concentration, unflagging attention to detail. She did her job methodically and efficiently; that was what made her a good cop. But inside she was as distressed about finding dead things as Flash was, and that's what made her human. What Flash didn't understand was why she worked so hard to make sure no one knew what she felt inside. That seemed like a waste of energy to him. But of course, sometimes he was wrong.

Aggie stood for a moment looking down at the dead man with her lips pressed tight and her hands closed inside her pockets. She said to the EMTs, "Anything?"

The two men hadn't even unpacked their equipment. One of them shook his head. "No pulse. He's already cold."

"We found some ID," volunteered the other man. "We turned it over to the deputy."

She said, "Definitely a hit and run?"

"Looks like it to me," said the first man.

Aggie told the EMTs to wait for the coroner before moving or covering the body, and they took their equipment back to the ambulance. She squatted down to examine the corpse. His tee shirt was soggy with blood and his right arm and leg were mangled inside a cheap nylon jacket and jeans. His face was relatively unmarred, however, except for a matting of sand on the side where his head had hit the embankment. Small eyes, narrow features, tufted chin. Aggie did not recognize him, and as much as it shamed her to admit it, that was always a relief. Every loss of life should be mourned, she knew, but whenever Aggie got a call like this, she always sent up a little prayer that it was no one she knew.

She stood up and walked a few dozen yards down the road, using her flashlight to search out tire tracks, and Flash walked beside her, pausing to sniff out a couple of indentations in the scrub grass that led away from the tracks, and a cigarette butt floating in a shallow puddle left over from yesterday's rain. Aggie saw them too, but neither told her much. She returned to stand beside the body, looking around thoughtfully.

The night was cool and damp with the sea mist that curled in tendrils across the pavement, tasting faintly of salt and bait fish. It was so quiet that, had it not been for the crackle of emergency radios, Aggie almost might have heard the ocean a quarter of a mile away. In the distance she could see the glow of the colorful lights decorating the bridge, and the twinkle of the star atop the silver Christmas tree next to the "Welcome to Dogleg Island" sign. *All is calm, all is bright,* she thought, and then looked somberly at the body at her feet. *Except for one thing.*

Dogleg Island was home to the only real beaches in Murphy County, as well as some of the best surfing in Florida, so in the summer its roads were busy and its parking lots full. In the winter, however, even during the holidays, shops closed at 5:00 p.m. and the only food and drink establishments worth leaving the mainland for were Pete's Place and The Island Bistro, a semi-fine dining establishment that was only open weekends from 6:00 to 10:00. So at midnight on the island's two main thoroughfares—Ocean Drive and Island Road—traffic was sporadic. Aggie, standing with her hands in her pockets and gazing around at the empty streets lit only by the strobing lights of emergency vehicles, thought it was a miracle the body had been found tonight at all. Which made it likely, in her opinion, that whoever had called 911—and hung up without giving his name—had either witnessed the hit and run, or been the perpetrator.

"His name was Elijah Wiesel," Grady reported, reading from the driver's license one of the first responders had found. "Twenty-eight, Ohio driver's license that's four years old. No emergency contact info in his wallet, but we're running the license now to see what we can come up with."

Aggie nodded. "What's a guy from Ohio doing walking along Island Road this time of night?"

"Maybe his car broke down," Grady suggested. "I'll have one of the guys do a sweep for abandoned vehicles as soon as we're done here."

"Good idea."

"There's something else." He held out a slip of paper to her and Aggie squinted to read it in the strobing lights. "It's a voucher for Chik 'N' Waffles," Grady supplied. "The kind they give out when somebody uses a coupon but doesn't spend the whole amount."

Aggie lifted an eyebrow. "Could be one of the lucky recipients of the Santa Cop program."

"Not so lucky," Grady pointed out.

"Yeah." Aggie once again dropped her gaze solemnly to the body on the ground. "Still, you should check it out. There'd at least be a record of his vehicle if one of your guys made the stop."

"On the other hand, a lot of churches and other community groups are giving these coupons out this time of year, too," Grady said.

Aggie frowned a little, glancing back over her shoulder. "We're how far from Pete's Place? Three, four miles?"

Grady agreed, "More or less."

"Maybe his car is fine," she suggested. "Maybe he was too drunk to drive."

"I hate to tell you, honey, but two years riding the road on the night shift taught me that most people who are too drunk to drive are too drunk to know it. And they hardly ever end up walking."

"They do if they get drunk at Pete's. He's pretty good about taking keys."

Grady looked skeptical. "What makes you think he was even drinking tonight?"

"You're kidding, right? Can't you smell the alcohol?"

Grady bent closer, inhaled cautiously, and shook his head. "Sorry. I don't smell anything."

"It's whiskey," she said. "Maybe bourbon. And something else." She frowned over this. "Something sweet. I can't quite place it."

Flash looked up, interested, waiting for her to reach the obvious conclusion.

Grady called over his shoulder to one of the EMTs, "Hey, Jake, did you smell alcohol on the victim when you got here?"

"Can't say that I did," replied the other man. "I think I would've noticed." He consulted with his partner, who also shook his head.

Aggie said, "Women have a better sense of smell than men. Everyone knows that."

Grady's lips made a small downward turn, and she insisted, "It's true. You ask any gas company employee. If a woman says she smells a gas leak, she's right ninety-nine percent of the time, even when the gas line workers don't smell anything."

It was also true that since the head injury Aggie's sense of smell had become a good deal more acute than it once had been, which her neurosurgeon told her was not unusual. Unfortunately, sometimes the things she smelled were imaginary, otherwise known as olfactory hallucinations, and also not unusual. Grady knew both these things, of course. And of course he wouldn't mention either of them.

She said, "Did anyone search his pockets for car keys?"

"No, just for the ID."

"Maybe someone should," she suggested.

Grady gave a small grimace as he knelt on the ground and patted the dead man's pockets. "Man, I hate this." But he extracted a set of keys from the man's jacket pocket and held them up to her as he stood. "Looks like he did have a car at some point. Now all we have to do is find it."

Flash turned and began to explore the sandy shoulder along Park Street, a residential neighborhood that was even darker and quieter this time of night than Island Road was. There were no houses on the corner, but the sparkle of Christmas lights was barely visible through the branches of pine trees midway down the street. Aggie watched Flash for a moment, remarking, "I'll interview the neighbors tomorrow. Some of them might have seen or heard something."

She turned to watch the approach of another deputy's cruiser, followed by the coroner's van. But her expression was thoughtful. "You saw the tire tracks, right?"

"Yeah. Looks like somebody might've run off the road, maybe swerved to try to miss him. No skid marks, though, which means the driver didn't even brake when he hit the guy."

"Or," she suggested, "the tracks in the sand could mean he pulled over to check on the man he'd just hit, saw he was dead, panicked, and took off."

"Possible," Grady agreed. "They're bringing the big camera; I'll make sure we get some good photographs."

"So," Aggie said, "the driver was headed east, inland. Which means we're looking for a car with damage on the passenger front. Could we borrow a couple of deputies for an hour or two to patrol the streets? The vehicle might still be on the island."

"On it," Grady said. "But don't get your hopes up. My guess is that the perpetrator is the same guy who called it in, and he's not going to leave the damaged vehicle out in plain sight for us to find."

She sighed. "Yeah. That's what I think too. Our best chance is that he'll have an attack of conscience and turn himself in."

Grady gave a small skeptical grunt. "That and other miracles."

"It could happen," she said with a shrug. "After all, it's Christmas."

He gave her arm a light squeeze. "I'm going to log these keys and set up the patrols. Then what do you say we head home? We're not going to be able to do much of anything tonight that these guys can't do better."

"Yeah, okay." Her tone was absent and her gaze was on Flash, who was still investigating the other side of the intersection. "I need to talk to the coroner, then I'll be ready to go."

Grady went back to the cruisers and Aggie walked down the shoulder of the road to join Flash on Park Street, where he waited patiently to show her what he'd found. Aggie took out her flashlight and shone it over the ground near where Flash sat. "Whoa," she said softly, and squatted down for a closer look. A hundred-dollar bill was caught in the spiky dried grass at the edge of the road. "Somebody's going to have some explaining to do when he gets home."

She had gloves and evidence bags in her car, but neither of those items were in high demand during the course of normal duties for a Dogleg Island Police officer, so she didn't usually carry them on her person. She patted her jacket pockets and came up with nothing but a tissue, which she used to lift the bill out of the grass. That was when she noticed a dark stain on one end of the bill. It might have been blood.

She turned and called over her shoulder, "Grady! Evidence bag!"

He lifted his hand in acknowledgment, and Aggie stood, playing her light up and down the shoulder of the road. All she found was another set of tire tracks in the sand, which might have been made at any time during the day or night and could have meant nothing more than someone pulling off the road to make a phone call. Still, it wouldn't hurt to get photos.

Grady finished up with the deputies and started toward her with the evidence bag. Aggie turned off her flashlight and clipped it to the belt loop of her jeans. She stood for a moment surveying the scene: the coroner trudging across the road with his equipment bag, the photographer setting up portable lights near the body, the EMTs packing up to leave. She knelt down and put her arm around Flash, sighing. "Most of the time we do good work in this job, Flash. But this is the part of it that sucks. Somebody's husband or father or son isn't coming home tonight. Somebody else is hiding out somewhere, scared to death, sweating bullets over what he's done. He's going to a jail. One life gone, another ruined. It sucks."

And then she looked at him. "But I was right about the booze, wasn't I? You smelled it too. I was right." She frowned a little. "Wasn't I?"

Flash didn't know why she even had to ask. Aggie was always right. Everyone knew that.

CHAPTER EIGHT

Jerome Bishop was something of a phenomenon, although if anyone had told him that he would have been amused, even embarrassed. He was the first black man ever to be elected sheriff of rural Murphy County, Florida, and he'd held that position, running unopposed in virtually every election, until his retirement thirty years later. His public reason for leaving law enforcement in the middle of his elected term was to take care of his wife, Esther, when she'd been diagnosed with cancer. But there were private reasons too, and those who knew him best guessed them, even though they never spoke about them.

Overnight, his lazy little coastal backwater had been plunged from obscurity into bloody headlines. A mother and father brutally slain, a young deputy sheriff shot in the head, his office shaken to its foundation. He'd seen it through. He'd brought what he thought was justice to the crime, he'd bandaged up the wounded and seen them back on their feet, he'd pieced together the broken parts of his administration and sent it limping on its way. But enough. His wife needed him, his life needed him. He had done his part, but the fight had become too big for him. So, with a silent prayer for forgiveness, he'd walked away.

Two years later his wife was buried and his life a lie. The phenomenon was that he'd been given a second chance. At age sixty-four, he'd waded back into the fray: an office in chaos, its members under investigation, the former sheriff in prison, the county Jerome Bishop had served so faithfully for most of his adult life now shattered and vulnerable. He had two years before the next election, and that was exactly how much time he'd given himself to put back together what he, by turning his back on his responsibility, had broken.

He hadn't expected it to be easy, and it hadn't been. For one thing, he was getting old. For another, there were parts of him that were still raw and wounded, unsure of his ability to do what had to be done should he be called upon to go down that long, mine-blasted road again. But mostly it was because he awoke every day with the nagging certainty, illogical and improvable, that it wasn't over. The worst of it wasn't done. That was why, when the phone call came at 6:30 on that Saturday morning, Bishop was almost relieved.

His work habits had remained virtually unchanged in his thirty years in office. He arrived at 6:00 a.m., departed at 6:00 p.m., and in between did not miss a single thing that went on in Murphy County, for good or for ill. Most people knew that the best time to catch him at his desk was in that quiet hour before the 7:00 a.m. change of shift, but the wise also knew that disturbing the sheriff before he'd finished his first cup of coffee was not a step to be taken lightly. So when his direct line rang, he didn't hesitate or question; he picked it up mid-ring with a single brusque, "Bishop."

"Jerome," replied the voice on the other end. "Glen Derrels here, Jackson County. Sorry to bother you so early."

All of the local sheriffs knew each other, coordinated with each other when necessary, and most of them even liked each other. Some, of course, Bishop liked more than others. Glen Derrels had held the Murphy County Sheriff's Office together during its temporary lapse in administration, and the two men had gotten to know each other fairly well—not well enough, however, for Derrels to be making a social call at 6:30 on a Saturday morning.

Bishop leaned back in his chair and picked up his coffee cup. "Never a bother, Glen," he said. "How's it going over in your neck of the woods?"

The other man sighed. "Well, I'll tell you the truth. I've got a problem, and I'm afraid it's about to become yours."

Bishop sipped his coffee and listened.

"An old friend of yours just got transferred up from Wakulla to my jail," Derrels went on. "He's supposed to give testimony in the Quinlin case next week."

Bishop set his coffee cup down on the desk blotter. "Roy Briggs," he said.

"The same."

And there it was. The other shoe.

Roy Briggs had served under Sheriff Bishop's administration for ten years before Bishop had retired and Briggs took over as sheriff of Murphy County. Later it was discovered that Briggs had been running a protection racket in Murphy County for most of those years that had resulted in at least four murders, but that wasn't the worst thing he had done. That wasn't even the beginning of the betrayal.

Bishop was surprised at how level his voice sounded when he replied, "I thought part of his plea deal was that the out-of-county charges against him would be dropped."

"Right," agreed Derrels. "But we've got a defense attorney over here who thinks he can get his client off with reasonable doubt if he can point the finger at Briggs and get him to testify to the terms of his plea deal. But that's not the problem I'm calling you about." He paused. "Briggs sent a message through one of my deputies. He says he has something for Captain Grady, something he's been looking for. He wants to talk to him."

Briggs had been Grady's partner and friend for five years before the shooting. Now if there was one person in the world Bishop knew to keep away from Briggs, for the safety of everyone concerned, it was Ryan Grady.

Bishop said flatly, "That's not going to happen."

"Yeah, I don't blame you. The SOB is probably lying through his teeth. Who knows what he really wants? But he said to mention a name..." Papers rustled in the background. "Hold on a minute. Here it is." He read from his notes. "Jimmy Joe Jackson. That mean anything to you?"

Bishop drew in a breath and let it out slowly, leaning back in his chair again. "Yeah," he said. "Maybe I'd better take a ride over there."

"Don't waste your time," Derrels replied. "Briggs made it clear he's not talking to anybody but Grady."

Bishop was silent for a minute. "I'm not going to let one of my deputies be manipulated by some sick, twisted..." He broke off, not because he didn't have the words, but because speaking them somehow bestowed upon the object of his contempt a dignity he did not deserve.

Derrels said in a moment, "Right. Best not to play games with these characters."

Bishop said, "Thanks for the heads-up. We're going to have to get our fishing poles out of mothballs one of these days and head up the Appalach."

"We'll do it," agreed Derrels easily. "You take care now."

"Right," replied Bishop absently. He hung up the phone and picked up his coffee cup again, leaning back in his chair with an uneasy frown on his face. He did nothing but gaze at the opposite wall, lost in memories he'd tried hard to forget, until change of shift brought him back to the present again.

And he still didn't know what he was going to do.

Ryan Grady loved being married. He loved using the delicate cycle when it was his turn to do laundry. He loved having someone to call when he was going to be late getting home. He loved setting the table for two. He loved it when his sheets smelled like peaches and his hand soap smelled liked lavender. He loved tripping over someone else's shoes and hanging up someone else's towel, and he loved saying "we." *We'll be over about three. We're just going to stay in and watch the game this weekend. We're having chicken for dinner.* He loved that. He woke up every single day feeling like the luckiest man in the world.

Despite all of that, he was perfectly aware that this amazing creature in whom he had invested all his hopes and dreams was not without flaws—primary among which was that she was not the most understanding person in the world when she was awakened from a sound sleep. It was, therefore, with a certain amount of trepidation that he woke his wife this next morning with a gentle squeeze of her shoulder and the reluctant announcement that the water heater was on the fritz again. She responded by groaning and turning away from him, pulling the sheet up over her head. "Give it another half hour to warm up," he added. "I'll try to get home early to fix it."

The only response was another muffled groan.

"You're taking the day off, right?"

She muttered, "Go to work, Grady."

He said, "I guess this means the honeymoon is over." And he grinned as she made a halfhearted effort to throw a pillow at him which barely made it to the end of the bed. "See you later, baby. I love you."

She replied from beneath the sheet, "Then get out of here, for God's sake." She added, "I love you too." Because they both had looked death in the face once too often not to say that when they had the chance.

Ryan Grady left the house a happy man.

He had joined the Murphy County Sheriff's Office right out of the Coast Guard because it was the first job he was offered. For a guy in his twenties whose ambition didn't go much beyond the next pretty girl or a weekend fishing trip, it sounded like a pretty good gig. Back then the county was small and so was the sheriff's office; the job mostly consisted of handing out tickets and breaking up bar fights, and nobody said anything if, on slow days, he occasionally took a long dinner break and caught some waves. Over the years the county began to change along with the culture; they started to see drugs coming up the coastal highway and along the coastline itself, metal detectors going up in the schools, violence and property crimes rising. The job was not what it used to be. But neither was Grady.

As the senior man in the office and the sheriff's second-in-command, Grady was directly in charge of eight road officers, two investigators, and all ongoing investigations, as well as the training program for new recruits. He was indirectly in charge of all shift supervisors, scheduling and promotions, although he had become very good at delegating most of those responsibilities over the past few years. He was also a member of the emergency services dive team and off-shore rescue, which was called into service for stranded boaters, water accidents and, on more than one occasion, for embarrassed tourists who'd been carried out to sea on their paddle boards or floats. Most of the time, the job was every bit as demanding as it sounded.

But from December through February, time fell away from Murphy County, and it was almost the place it had been fifteen years ago. Shoplifting was the most common crime, family disputes were settled without either party being dragged off in cuffs, and road officers gave out gift cards instead of traffic tickets. Of course, every year there had to be one or two exceptions to their hope for a temporary peace on earth. This year it was Elijah Wiesel.

Grady briefed Sheriff Bishop on the case over coffee and vending machine pastries, but Bishop's attention was only partly on the incident report on his computer screen. Mostly it was on the phone call he'd received from Jackson County, and how much of that he was obliged to share with his chief deputy. His entire office was built on transparency. His relationship with Grady and Aggie was built on trust. But it was Christmas, and he didn't know what to do.

Bishop said, "Island Police are taking the point on this one?"

"Yes, sir. I told the chief we'd offer technical support where needed."

Bishop nodded. Perhaps the only good thing his short-lived predecessor had done for this county was to make sure Aggie Malone was installed as police chief of Dogleg Island. While she would have been perfectly within her rights to turn over major cases to the sheriff's office, she never did, and was as likely to offer assistance as to request it. Bishop had trained her himself, and he knew that if Aggie was on the job, it was being done right. Of course, the fact that she was married to his chief deputy was a stroke of good fortune, and didn't hurt in keeping the lines of communication open.

He said, "I see here we located next of kin, haven't been able to contact them yet. We've given out fifteen gift cards to Chik 'N' Waffles since the program started, most of them to Murphy County folks, a couple out of county, none with Ohio plates. Still, it wouldn't hurt to check the reports."

"Yes, sir, I was about to do that," Grady said. "I'd also like to pull a couple of men to check the garages and body shops. If the car goes in for repair, it'll be on this side of the bridge."

"Good idea," Bishop said. "Let's see if we can get this thing off the books before Christmas." He took off his glasses and gave a single shake of his head. "Poor SOB. What was he doing walking on Island Road in the middle of the night, anyway?"

"Aggie thinks he might've been drunk," Grady said. "I'm going to call the ME's office and see if they can get us a blood alcohol. It won't tell us much, but it's something."

Bishop said, "Keep me in the loop."

"Yes, sir."

They talked for a minute about the Christmas weekend duty roster and the office party, which was always held at a local steak house that gave them a good deal on their surf and turf platter and threw in cake and coffee for free. It was a consistently well-attended event, both because of the food and because of the Christmas bonuses that Bishop took delight in handing out, along with a personalized speech of commendation, to each of his deputies and staff, every year. Bishop had a sterling memory for who had been on duty during the party the previous year and therefore deserved a chance to attend this year; the whole thing gave Grady a headache.

Nonetheless, he dutifully took notes on his iPad, intending to hand the whole thing over to the office administrator as soon as he left here. He'd finished his coffee and was getting ready to take his leave when Bishop leaned back in his chair, folded his hands over his abdomen, and said, "So, am I supposed to bring anything to this reception thing of yours?"

Grady shook his head. "All I know about it is what time to show up. Although I think I did hear Aggie threatening to shoot anybody who brought a gift. She's trying to make it into more of a welcome-home party for Mom and Dad. Mom and Dad want it to be a wedding reception for Aggie and me. But Lucy and Lorraine are in charge. I try to be at the firing range whenever they get together to plan."

Bishop chuckled. "Damn, it'll be good to see old Salty again. What time are they getting in?"

"Thursday afternoon. Lucy and Cal have got airport duty."

"Well, you tell Salty to give me call when he gets unpacked. We're about six years overdue to hoist a few, and it's been so long since I heard one of his tall tales I'm about to go into withdrawal."

Grady grinned and saluted him with his empty coffee cup as he got to his feet. "I'll tell him."

This was the time. If Bishop were going to say anything, this would be the time. The words were in his mouth: *Sit down, Grady, I need to talk to you about something.* But it was Christmas. It could wait.

Bishop put his glasses back on and turned back to the computer screen. "All right, Captain, get out there and start keeping the peace. And by the way…" He glanced up briefly. "Don't take any twenties. Aside from the one you confiscated at Pete's Place last night, we had two more show up on this side of the bridge. If I were you, I'd do my Christmas shopping with a debit card this year."

"Yes, sir," he replied, "I think I will." He gave a single frustrated shake of his head aimed at whoever was making their holiday more difficult with the counterfeit bills, and he left the office.

CHAPTER NINE

A ggie tried to sleep late. They hadn't gotten back to the house after the hit-and-run call until nearly 1:30, and she didn't bounce back from late hours and restless nights the way she once had done. But neither could she still her anxious thoughts, and once she heard the door click behind Grady, they were upon her again. Unsolved thefts. Counterfeit bills. A stranger, dead on the side of the road. She was wide awake, and, after a tepid shower, a futile search for breakfast, and a cup of coffee from the pot Grady had left for her, she was out the door.

The Dogleg Island Police Station looked like a Santa Land Annex when Aggie and Flash arrived at seven thirty. There was an evergreen wreath on one side of the door and a candy cane wreath on the other. Garland lit with twinkling white lights scalloped the walls of the tiny room at ceiling height, and dozens of Christmas cards decorated the walls. There was a sleigh in the corner and herds of reindeer and snowmen on each of the desks. Ceramic carolers in a Dickensian snow village graced the top of the file cabinet, and four Christmas stockings hung over the greenery-framed window, one for each member of the Dogleg Island Police Department, including Flash. A Christmas tree, looped with tinsel garland and lights and crammed full of colorful ornaments, seemed to take up most of the remaining space in the small room. A constant stream of bouncy Christmas music poured from the speakers on the front desk.

All of this was courtesy of Sally Ann Mitchell, the department's twenty-year-old office manager-slash-administrative assistant. For $12.00 an hour, she worked six days a week, managing the day-to-day details of running the office with an efficiency that would be the envy of any major corporation in America while at the same time keeping Aggie up to date on all the town gossip and making sure the staff was provided with an endless supply of home-made cookies, cupcakes and candy. Sally Ann loved holidays, and Aggie was too afraid of losing her to criticize her propensity for overdoing it.

Today Sally Ann wore a green elf hat perched rakishly atop her honey blonde braids, red-and-white striped glasses, and jaunty Santa Claus earrings. She looked up from her computer in surprise when Aggie opened the door. "Hi, Chief," she said. "I thought you were taking a personal day today."

"I am," Aggie assured her, "just as soon as I finish work."

The official winter uniform of the Dogleg Island Police Department was a white long-sleeved sweater emblazoned with the gold DIPD logo on the breast pocket, worn with navy twill pants and a navy billed cap. Because Aggie couldn't decide whether she was officially on duty today, and she *had* to get the shopping done, she had compromised with a Police Department windbreaker and cap over her tee shirt and jeans. Her hope was that she would not be in the office long enough for anyone to notice that she was mostly out of uniform.

She carried an insulated travel cup of coffee and snatched up a couple of cookies from the tray on Sally Ann's desk as she edged past Santa's sleigh to slide behind her own desk only a couple of feet away. Flash went over to the window and sniffed hopefully at the stocking decorated with red and blue felt dog bones. He knew from experience that sooner or later that stocking would be filled with treats. Finding nothing, he turned away, not so much disappointed as informed. Maybe not today. But soon.

Aggie booted up her computer and bit into a cookie. "I'm sending you the report we got from the FBI last week about counterfeit bills. I want you to e-mail a copy to all the merchants and business owners with a link to the US Treasury Department's web page on how to recognize counterfeit bills. Be sure to add a note in bold print that the bills have started to show up here."

"Wow," she said, scribbling a note on her desk pad. "Yes, ma'am."

"Is Mo on patrol?"

Maureen Wilson was Aggie's only other full-time employee, and the only member of the police force besides Aggie who was authorized to carry a gun. She outweighed Aggie by close to a hundred fifty pounds and outranked her by twenty years experience, first as a prison guard and then as a sheriff's deputy. Her dedication to her job was absolute; her devotion to Aggie unquestioned. She had been the only black woman in the Murphy County Sheriff's Office for eight years, and during that time had earned the respect—if not the downright fear—of every man she worked with. When Aggie took the job as police chief with a budget for only one patrol officer, she didn't hesitate over her choice for the job. She had never regretted the decision.

"Yes, ma'am," Sally Ann said. "She left ten minutes ago."

This did not surprise Aggie. Even when it wasn't filled with Christmas decorations and holiday carols, the office was much too claustrophobic for the big woman, and she spent as little time there as possible. "Okay, I'll catch up with her. But in case I miss her, remind her to check the donation boxes for the children's coat drive, okay?"

Most people didn't think it got cold enough for coats in Florida, but on the northern Gulf, snow showers were not unusual at least once a year, and they could look forward to several days of icy rain every January. But because the winter season was so short, coats were the last things a struggling family could afford to spend money on, so every year the Dogleg Island Merchants and Business Association, led by the Dogleg Island Police Department, collected coats to be distributed to the needy children of Murphy County at Christmastime.

"Yes, ma'am, will do," Sally Ann replied. "Did you see last night's log?"

"If you mean the hit and run," Aggie replied, moving her mouse to scroll down a list of files, "I was there."

Sally Ann looked up, her eyes filled with concern behind the peppermint-framed glasses. "It wasn't anybody we know, was it?"

Aggie clicked a file. "He was from out of state. The Sheriff's Office is trying to track down next of kin. Also, we had another theft at Pete's Place. I'm typing up the report now. I told the victim she could pick up a copy after noon today. She needs it for insurance."

"Yes, ma'am, I'll have it ready for her."

Aggie broke the second cookie in two and offered half to Flash, which he accepted gratefully. No one in their house had had breakfast that morning, although he had left kibble in his bowl. Kibble was not his favorite.

Aggie said, "Anything else come in I should know about?"

"A report of suspicious activity at 1808 Old Stillwater Way at 9:00 p.m. It's a seasonal rental, you know. One of Wendy Coker's places." She made a small face as she said it. Sally Ann's father owned Dogleg Island's premier real estate agency—which is to say the *only* real estate agency on the island— and was overtly resentful of Wendy Coker's intrusion on his territory, since she lived and worked across the bridge in Ocean City. "Deputies called the owner—that's Wendy—but she said she was showing the place and not to bother sending anybody out. So they didn't." Sally Ann gave a small grunt of skepticism as she scrolled down the screen. "Showing the place, my foot. Who shows a vacation rental at 9:00 at night? The only kind of showing Wendy Coker was doing did not involve a client, if you know what I mean."

Aggie didn't know whether to be amused, relieved or disappointed. She enjoyed gossip as much as the next person, but when Sally Ann said "suspicious activity" she'd hoped for a moment it might relate to Elijah Wiesel. Old Stillwater Way was a residential street that connected Island Road with Grady Plantation Drive, where a number of businesses—including Pete's Place—were located. She said, "Who made the call?"

Sally Ann scrolled back a line on the computer. "Betsy Everest. You know, old Doc Everest's wife. She's gotten a little spooky since he died," she confided, "and I guess you can't blame her, being married for fifty years and now having to get used to living alone. Mama goes to church with her sister and she says she's been trying to get Betsy to move in with her, but you know how old people are. Plus, Daddy says she'll never get her money out of that house, so she's better off staying where she is. Meantime, she's got nothing better to do than sit at that big bay window of hers on the corner and watch everything that goes on up and down all three streets. How pathetic is that?"

Aggie finished the last half of the cookie. "I hope you never get old, Sally Ann."

"Yes, ma'am," she agreed fervently, "me too. And as long as you're here, Chief, maybe now is a good time to talk to you about the office Christmas party?"

Aggie smothered a groan. "Oh, Sally Ann, I don't know. That's never really worked out. It's such a small department and somebody has to be on duty, and what with all the parades and tree lightings and special events after hours that Mo and I have to show up for, there's really no time…"

"Exactly!" Sally Ann declared, clapping her hands together excitedly. "That's why this year I thought we should sign up for the Christmas Open House. You know, all the businesses have hors d'oeuvres and drinks—non-alcoholic, of course—and the St. Michael's carolers go door to door and everybody just kind of wanders in and out and the public is invited and…"

"Sounds great!" Aggie agreed enthusiastically, mostly just to stop her from talking. She hit send on her report about the watch theft and got to her feet. "Best idea ever! You're completely in charge. Just let me know when to show up. Does this mean no Secret Santa?"

"No, of course not." Sally Ann sounded slightly horrified. "We already drew names!"

"Oh," replied Aggie. "Right." She had given up on trying to point out to Sally Ann the futility of drawing names in a three-woman, one dog office. They all ended up putting something in everyone's stocking anyway, and Flash always came out the big winner. "Okay then," she reiterated, "you're in charge. I've got a couple of interviews to do, then I've got to catch up on errands. Grady's folks will be here next week and we haven't even decorated the tree yet. No calls unless blood is involved, okay?"

"Don't worry, Chief," Sally Ann assured her cheerfully. "I'm on the job."

Flash followed Aggie to the door, watching with interest as she grabbed another couple of cookies. "And Sally Ann," Aggie added, glancing back, "maybe tone down the music a bit? We don't want visitors to think we're soft on crime."

Sally Ann looked doubtful, but Aggie did not linger to hear her objections. She hurried out the door and into the patrol vehicle, Flash bounding at her side.

It was one of those bright blue and white-sand Gulf Coast mornings that made the Christmas tinsel and holiday greenery of the downtown area look ridiculous. Aggie rolled down the windows to the balmy sea breeze and the sound of the ocean, tossing her jacket into the backseat. The SUV's computer told her it was already seventy degrees outside, and barely eight o'clock.

There was a taco stand across from the beach crossover where Heron met Main that was open year round. They served a pretty good breakfast burrito and great coffee, and Aggie knew she would find Mo's patrol car parked in front of it. But before she could reach it, her phone rang. It was Ryan's sister, Lucy.

She debated for a moment whether to answer, but why postpone the inevitable? She punched the button that sent the call to the car's speakers and tried to sound more welcoming than resigned as she answered, "Hi, Lucy."

"Well, it's about time," retorted Lucy. In the background the television blared and children squealed. Aggie had to assume that the twins' school was on Christmas break. Either that, or the twins had been kicked out. It wouldn't be the first time. "I was calling you all night," Lucy went on, miffed. "Don't you ever answer your phone? What if it had been an emergency?"

Aggie started to explain, once again, that her cell phone was also the police chief's phone, and that the only calls that *did* go through after hours were real emergencies, but she was spared the trouble by Lucy's complete lack of interest. Lucy was always fairly single-minded in the pursuit of her own agenda.

"So what is this I hear about you wanting to completely ignore an entire family tradition and, excuse me, *skip* Christmas?" Lucy demanded, barely pausing for breath. "I mean, you *are* kidding, right?"

Aggie blinked, wondering how Lucy had somehow managed to read her darkest thoughts. "I don't think..."

"It's not like my parents are flying halfway around the world just to be here or anything, you know! They haven't seen their grandchildren—their *only* grandchildren—since they were six weeks old!"

She was building up a good head of steam now, growing more outraged with every word, and Aggie still didn't know what she was talking about.

Aggie tried to put in, "I'm not sure..." But her words were drowned out by an ear-piercing scream in the background, which Lucy ignored.

"I just want you to know," Lucy concluded tartly, "that we *will* be having Christmas dinner at my house, just like always, and the boys *will* be having Santa Claus under their own Christmas tree on Christmas morning, and that we *will* be exchanging gifts on Christmas day just like we've always done, and this party of yours doesn't change a thing!"

Aggie made the turn into the sand parking lot of the taco stand, finally coming to understand that this was all somehow related to an offhand comment she had made to Lorraine that it might be easier on everyone, since the party was being held on Christmas Eve, if they didn't try to get together again on Christmas Day. Lorraine had thought it was a great idea. Neither of them thought Lucy would buy it. They were right.

Aggie said, "Oh. Okay."

She waved at Mo, who was sitting at one of the concrete tables beside the small building, her breakfast spread out before her, chatting with Henry, the owner of Paco's Tacos. Henry was a retired high school teacher, a good-looking man as tall as Mo was wide, and a widower. Aggie thought it was entirely possible there was a little flirtation going on there.

On the other end of the phone someone screamed shrilly, "Mommy, Mommy, Mommy, Mommy, Mommy, *Mommy!*" To which Lucy replied, "Here I am, sweetie, Mommy's right here." And to Aggie she added, "Did you get my list of the Play Station games the boys want? Because I'm telling you, if you don't get your order in today, it will *not* get here by Christmas."

Through the speakers came a squeal so high and long that Flash's ears went back and Aggie winced and turned down the volume. "*Mooommmmyyyy!*"

Lucy said, "Indoor voices, sweeties, Mommy loves you." To Aggie she said, "And another thing, will you *please* speak to those awful people you hired to be in charge of the decorations? They want to use white mums in the table arrangements and everyone knows white mums are for funerals. I tried to talk to Lorraine about it but the woman has cancer, for God's sake. Could you take a little responsibility? I can't do everything!"

Aggie said, "What table decorations?"

"Oh for the love of…Aidan! Ethan! I swear to God, if you don't stop that right now, I'll—"

The connection went dead, and Aggie could only hope it did not mean the twins had taken their mother hostage. She looked helplessly at Flash as she turned off the engine. "Ho ho ho," she said.

Flash panted and licked his lips. The sound of all that screaming had made him nervous, even though he had long since learned that sounds on the telephone were generally no threat. Still, with the twins, you could never be sure.

Aggie's phone rang again as they got out of the car. She glanced at the caller ID and answered with, "Bad news. We are never having kids."

"Let me guess," replied Grady. "Lucy called."

"You got it."

Henry called, "Morning, Chief!" and she lifted her hand in return greeting. He hurried across the small lawn to his counter, which, Aggie could see when she reached it, was decorated with a string of red chili pepper lights and a Christmas wreath.

Grady said, "Can you stand a little more bad news?"

"Go ahead. Make my day." She covered the mouth-piece with one hand and said to Henry, "Two breakfast burritos. And can you refill this?" She pushed her coffee cup across the counter to him.

"Yes, ma'am, Chief." Henry turned from the counter to refill her cup from the pot on the shelf behind him, and Aggie returned her attention to the telephone.

"The lab just picked up evidence from the scene, said they'd try to get a report back by Tuesday," Grady said. "Two working days and ten lab techs to tell us what we already know—that it was human blood on the bill you found. Of course, with any luck, they'll be able to match it to the victim, which will tell us exactly nothing. The ME can't do the autopsy on our vic until Monday, but we've got a preliminary time and cause of death."

The county coroner, who had arrived at the scene of the hit and run last night, was an elected official whose primary function was to certify death. Although he could occasionally be persuaded to render an on-scene opinion regarding the time and method of death, he had not felt confident about doing so in this case. Small surprise.

Aggie smiled her thanks to Henry as he returned her refilled cup to her. She leaned her hip against the edge of the counter and took a sip, gazing across the street to the bright glint of sun-diamonds on the water beyond. "Let me ask you something, Grady. How come no one works on weekends anymore except you and me?"

"We're dedicated public servants destined for sainthood, Malone, everybody knows that. Do you want to hear this or not?"

"You have my full attention."

He said, "First surprise, time of death, between nine and nine thirty."

She stood up straighter. "What, really? Is he sure?"

"You heard me say preliminary, right?"

She frowned. "But the 911 call didn't come in until 11:52."

"It's possible some passerby spotted the body on the side of the road two hours after the event."

"Way out in the weeds? In the dark?"

"Possible," he reiterated. "Not necessarily likely. Which brings me to the second surprise. Cause of death: multiple blunt force trauma with crushing injuries. The poor guy wasn't just struck by a car. He was run over."

Aggie had been about to take another sip of coffee, but lowered the cup. "That's weird. I thought it was the force of the blow that knocked him into the weeds. But if he was crushed by tires, how does that happen?"

"Sounds like a question that calls for the unique expertise of one of the top detective minds in the state," he replied. "Unfortunately, my calendar is full, so you're on your own."

"This is how you talk to the woman who's cooking your dinner tonight?" She sipped from the cup. "I'll take another look at the scene. I doubt I'll find anything though. Your guys pretty much scoured it last night."

He said, "I've got a couple of men checking the body shops, and we'll run down the Chik 'N' Waffles coupons before end of shift. We found the next of kin, a sister and a mother in Ohio. We're trying to reach them now."

Aggie sighed. She hated to think of anyone getting news like that at Christmas, and she was grateful to the sheriff's office, which spared her that duty. "Okay, thanks," she said. "Let me know if you find out what he was doing down here. Nothing on his vehicle, I guess?"

"Nope. We logged two abandoned vehicles last night, neither one on the island side, and both the owners identified."

"Yeah, okay. I'm going to check out some possible witnesses and show his photo around, see if we can retrace his steps yesterday. I'll let you know if anything turns up."

"Hey, I just thought of somebody who works on weekends and holidays besides us," Grady said. "The bad guys. Bishop said two more counterfeit bills showed up on this side of the bridge this morning. So far they all seem to be twenties, so keep an eye out."

She stifled a groan. "Terrific. I already sent out an e-mail to the merchants, but I'll be sure to remind them again when I make my rounds."

"I thought you were taking the day off."

"I am, just as soon as I finish work." Henry put a paper plate with two wrapped burritos on it on the counter, and Aggie dug in her pocket for a ten-dollar bill. "Say, Ryan, do you know anything about a list of Play Station games the twins want for Christmas that Lucy was supposed to send?"

"Already taken care of. We got them one about dinosaurs and one about space aliens...or at least I think that's what they are. They're in the hall closet with the other gifts we haven't wrapped yet."

She said sincerely, "You're amazing."

"Baby, you don't know the half of it."

Aggie picked up the plate and said to Henry, "Thanks. Keep the change."

"Thanks, Chief." Henry grinned at her as he put the bill in the register. "You have a good day now."

Flash followed Aggie, his nose lifted to appreciate the good smells coming from the plate, as she crossed the grass to Mo's table. "Did you get any breakfast?" Aggie asked Grady.

"Sure did," he replied. "A whole bowl of granola with yogurt and fruit." And at her reproachful silence he admitted, "Cinnamon buns and Raisinettes from the vending machine. But I know where I'm having lunch."

"Chik 'N' Waffles?"

"Good guess."

She said. "I'll make spaghetti for dinner."

"I'll make the sauce."

"I can do it," she protested.

"Baby, my sauce kicks your sauce's ass."

"Well," she agreed, pretending reluctance, "if you insist."

She could hear the grin in his voice. "Why do I get the feeling I've just been played?"

"Can't imagine. Don't forget about the water heater."

"It's a five-minute fix," he assured her. "I'll stop by the hardware store on my way home. I should be out of here by four."

"Take care of yourself out there today, Ryan Grady."

"You too, baby. Call if you need anything."

Aggie disconnected and sat down across from Mo. Flash jumped up on the bench beside her and waited while she cut his bacon, egg and cheese burrito into small pieces so it would cool faster. While she did that, she filled Mo in on the events of the previous night. Mo listened without breaking stride in her methodical consumption of the remaining two of her three burritos with a side of hash browns.

"So," Aggie said, passing Flash's plate to him, "we're looking for a car with damage on the passenger front. I doubt it's still on the island, but if it is, I want it."

"You want me to go door to door?"

There was nothing Mo liked more than conducting an official investigation, complete with rapid-fire questions, field notes, and an intimidating scowl. Unfortunately, she sometimes forgot that her style could be a little overwhelming for the mostly law-abiding citizens of Dogleg Island. So Aggie said quickly, "No, that won't be necessary. Just keep an eye out."

Aggie unwrapped her burrito and reached for the hot sauce in front of Mo's plate. "Also, we had another theft at Pete's Place last night. An Anne Klein ladies' watch, gold band, crystals where the numbers should be, retails for $179. It came from Heller and Sons, so there's a chance the thief might actually try to return it there for a refund. Criminals aren't always that smart."

Mo grunted her agreement around another bite of her burrito.

"Otherwise," Aggie went on, "watch the pawn shops and flea markets, the usual. Also..." Aggie took a bite of her burrito, wiped her mouth with a paper napkin, and swallowed. "We picked up a counterfeit bill at Pete's last night, and Grady said two more showed up on the other side of the bridge.

All twenties. I sent out an e-mail to all the downtown merchants, but let's make a point to warn the ones who aren't on my list. I'll talk to Henry before I leave. Or…" She tried to disguise her twinkling eyes with an innocent tone. "Maybe you'd rather do that yourself?"

Mo responded with an absolutely blank stare, and began gathering up her trash.

"Okay." Aggie quickly turned her attention back to her breakfast, sprinkling more hot sauce atop her burrito. "Good meeting. And don't forget to check the coat drive boxes before you leave today, okay?"

"Yes, sir, Chief, I am on the job." Mo stood, pulled a Santa hat from her back pocket and plopped it atop her head, which made Aggie grin. Despite her dour demeanor, Mo was as big a fool about Christmas as Sally Ann was and had been doing her patrol in a Santa hat since the first of December. Aggie had also been issued a Santa hat by the intrepid Sally Ann, but it had never left the front seat of her car.

Flash looked up from licking his plate to grin at Mo in the funny hat, but when she dug into her pocket and took out a fold of cash, he grew alert. Mo said, "Anyhow, I thought you were taking the day off. You on duty or not?"

"Mostly not," Aggie assured her. "I've got a couple of things to follow up on and then I'm going home."

Flash's nose twitched as Mo began to thumb through the bills in her hand, remembering how interested Aggie and Grady had been in the last piece of money that had smelled like that. He looked at Aggie. How could she not smell that?

"I don't see how you ever expect to put on any weight if you don't take better care of yourself," Mo grumbled. She was exceptionally comfortable with her own size and proportionately concerned for those less fortunate than she. "And I'll tell you something else—you never mind what you hear on the TV, there's not a man in this world that really likes a skinny woman. A fella likes a little something to hold on to at night, you know what I mean." She sighed and took out a couple of bills from the fold in her hand. "Lord have mercy, a paycheck sure don't go as far as it used to, does it?"

She started to put the rest of the money back into her pocket and Flash, with another quick glance at Aggie, knew it was time to intervene. He sprang down from the bench and ran around to Mo, the better to sniff the tantalizing aroma that was coming from her hand. Mo chuckled, a warm rumbling sound deep in her throat, and rubbed Flash's ears. "Now, what you comin' round here sniffing for? You already had your breakfast, and I didn't save a thing for you. You just hold on and see what Santa Claus brings you."

Flash's ears went forward. He was exceptionally interested in Santa Claus, whose name always seemed to be associated with treats, but at the moment he was even more interested in what was in Mo's hand. To show her, he stood up and put his paws on her knees, thrusting his nose at her hand.

Mo just chuckled and tugged at his ear again, but Aggie watched with narrowing eyes. "Mo," she said, getting slowly to her feet, "that wouldn't happen to be a twenty you've got in your hand, would it?"

CHAPTER TEN

The day, from that point on, did not proceed exactly as Aggie had planned. She put Mo on the task of retracing her steps in an attempt to track down the counterfeit bill, which might have been easier—or at least possible—had Mo lived, shopped and banked on the island. But like the majority of people who worked there, Aggie's patrol officer lived on the other side of the bridge in Ocean City where she had shopped at Wal-Mart, IGA, the Kangaroo gas station and two fast food places since last visiting the ATM. Aggie went back to the office to fill out the paperwork, and before she was finished, Mo called to report that she had notified the store managers at the larger places and had personally gone through the cash receipts of the smaller ones. She was a civil servant who was out twenty dollars, and she was a woman on a mission. Aggie reminded her again, and with regret, that her mission was likely to prove fruitless.

By the time Aggie left the office, the downtown shops were open, and Jason Wendale, one of the owners of the Island Bistro on the corner across from the police station, flagged her down before she could even get into her patrol car. There was no point in ignoring him; her morning was already shot. Besides, Flash had already started across the street toward him. Aggie had had so many meetings with Jason over the past month that Flash was beginning to think that stopping at The Island Bistro was part of their regular morning routine. Aside from being a member of the town council and president of the Downtown Merchants and Businessman's Association—two facts that he seemed to think earned him the right to special treatment when it came to things like overflow parking permits for the numerous private parties his establishment hosted this time of year—Jason and his partner Brett were providing the dessert bar at the infamous reception Aggie spent so much time trying not to be involved in. He was also, presumably, the person Lucy thought Aggie had hired to be in charge of the decorations. She had a feeling the annoyed look on Jason's face as he stood, arms akimbo, in front of his establishment to wait for her, had something to do with the latter.

The exterior of The Bistro was another winter wonderland, albeit a considerably more upscale and slightly more tasteful one than the version Sally Ann had executed at the police station. White garlands wrapped in clear lights and decorated with twinkling snowflake crystals were draped on either side of the short walkway that led from the street to the elaborate grape-vine arbor in front of the entrance, which was also decorated with crystal snowflakes and clear lights. On either side of the arbor were white Christmas trees studded with dozens of red glass ornaments; simple but stunning.

"Hi, Jason," Aggie said, painting on a smile as she reached him. "I'm off duty."

"And don't you look every inch of it." He took her shoulders lightly and kissed the air on either side of her face before stepping back to give her attire a critical once-over. "Love the whole *Les Miz* thing you've got going on," he added, making a circling gesture to include her baggy jeans, stretched-out gray tee shirt and billed cap. "Very retro-chic." In a single swift motion, he lifted the cap from her head, turned it backward, and replaced it on her head. "Perfect," he declared.

"Don't flirt with me, Jason." Aggie removed the cap and put it on again with the bill facing forward. "I told you, I'm not looking for a gay best friend."

He looked pained. "Darling, I can be your gay best friend, or I can flirt with you, but I simply cannot do both."

Flash liked Jason okay, even though Jason pretended not to like dogs and always made a fuss whenever Flash got too close to the threshold of his restaurant. However, Flash *really* liked Jason's partner, Chef Brett, who saved soup bones for Flash and often sent take-out bags to them for lunch when he and Aggie stopped by close to the midday hour. His ears and nose told him the hour was too early for take-out bags today, though, so while Aggie talked to Jason, Flash felt free to pursue another avenue of investigation.

One thing he had learned from listening to Aggie and Grady talk about their work—particularly the part of their work that involved figuring things out—was the importance of putting things together. It was like putting the red balls with the red balls and the green balls with the green balls, until pretty soon all the balls were where they belonged and things made sense. It was the same with figuring things out. If you just kept putting things together, one would lead to another until pretty soon you had a trail. And almost always, that trail led to something interesting. The things he was putting together now were smells—or, more accurately, the memory of a smell with the remnant of a smell. He wasn't entirely sure why, but he had learned these things often didn't make sense at first. The important thing was to keep letting one thing lead to another until they did.

Aggie watched as Flash, nose to the ground and paws busy, followed the sidewalk to the corner, paused to wait for traffic, then bounded across the short expanse of street to the lawn of St. Michael's Episcopal Church, where Father Dave, in shorts and a "Jesus is the Reason" tee shirt, was setting up a plastic nativity scene. The priest paused in his work to rub Flash's ears, looked around until he saw Aggie, and raised his arm in greeting. Aggie waved back and returned her attention to Jason.

Aggie said, "What can I do for you? Did you get my e-mail about the counterfeit bills?"

"Oh, please." He waved a dismissing hand. "We are a fine-dining establishment. We rarely deal in cash."

"Your wait staff might," she reminded him. "Put the word out. And a little in-service training on how to recognize counterfeit wouldn't hurt. The more of these bills that go into circulation here on the island, the more everyone suffers."

He gave that due consideration for a moment. "I suppose so," he agreed, and punctuated that with a sigh. "People can just be beasts this time of year, can't they?"

Before Aggie could think of a reply to that—if in fact there was one—he saved her the bother. "So," he said, businesslike now, "here's the thing. You know I have nothing but the greatest admiration for you and your team, I truly do, and I completely sympathize with how overworked you must be. But seriously, you have *got* to get control of that sister-in-law of yours."

Aggie felt obliged to ask, even though she knew the answer, "Which one?"

He gave a slight heavenward shift of his eyes. "The mean one, of course. Honestly, I only volunteered to be in charge of the decorations because of my contacts, and she certainly was quick enough to take me up on my professional discount, and of course since we're doing the dessert table it's absolutely essential that the rest of the decor matches. But I cannot, simply cannot, be road blocked at every turn. The plans for the wedding cake were approved months ago..."

"Wedding cake?" Aggie looked at him in dismay. "I thought we were doing a cupcake tower."

This time he made no attempt to disguise the roll of his eyes. "Oh, please. That's *so* five years ago. Believe me, the best thing—and by that I mean the *only* good thing—about this event is that I do *not* have to accept the input of an ill-formed temperamental bride." He smiled sweetly. "No offense, of course." He added briskly, "Three-tiered white cake with raspberry filling, white chocolate frosting, decorated with white mums and raspberries, what could be simpler?"

Aggie wondered if Ryan even liked raspberries. It seemed like something a wife should know.

"Angel cookies, lady fingers, a white chocolate fountain with red and green fruit—red and *green,* can you believe that?—and red and green sugared almonds in the guest bags, if we could get more cliché. But did I object? The soul of cooperation, I assure you, the absolute soul. But this, my dear Chief Malone-Grady…"

At this Aggie winced and felt compelled to interrupt. "It's just Malone. Chief Malone."

"My dear Mrs. Grady," he corrected himself with a meaningful look, "this is just too much. Your budget allows for a decor built around white mums and holly, elegant, simple, holiday appropriate and, if I may say so, ultimately affordable. Suddenly I'm given to understand mums are out? What, I pray you, am I supposed to do about that? Do you have any idea what lilies cost this time of year?"

"Lilies?" she parroted. "Did Lucy say lilies?"

"My words exactly," he replied with a satisfied nod. "Now, all I want to know is, am I in charge of the decorations or not? And if I am, could you *please* authorize the floral? I mean, your mother-in-law, the original Mrs. Grady, sounds perfectly lovely on the phone, but she couldn't make a decision if her life depended on it, not to mention the cell phone reception in those third-world countries can be more than a little iffy. All she ever says is 'Whatever Aggie wants.' So I'm asking you: What do you want?"

Aggie sighed. "What I want," she said, "is for this thing to be over." She added with a scowl, "Anyway, I don't know what you're complaining about. You're the one who wanted this job so badly. Grady and I would've been happy with catfish nuggets and a soft-serve ice cream machine."

He made an awful grimace. "That," he replied darkly, "does not even merit a reply. And if you repeat it to anyone I'll swear you were under the influence. Now, focus. Flowers."

Aggie watched Flash playing with Father Dave on the church lawn, and said distractedly, "Roses. What's wrong with roses?"

His pale eyebrows almost touched the top of his spiky blond hair. "Aside from the fact that you hate them and specifically said to me 'no roses'—not to mention that they cost the earth—not a thing. I'm a huge fan. In fact, I have a source who might be able to get them for—"

She came back to herself with a shake of her head. "No, not roses. I hate roses. What are those little pink things you see everywhere?"

He stared at her blankly.

"Carnations," she remembered abruptly. "They come in all colors and they're cheap. Get carnations. And the next time Lucy calls, don't answer. I know I won't."

He screwed up his face. "Carnations," he muttered. "I hate carnations."

"Brief your staff on the counterfeit bills," Aggie said, turning to cross the street. "I'll see you later."

Flash saw her coming and trotted to the door of the sanctuary, waiting to be let in. Father Dave laughed. "Looks like our young friend there is in need of sanctification," he observed, nodding at Flash. "Never a bad idea this time of year. Merry Christmas, Chief."

"Merry Christmas, Father."

Aggie had been raised Southern Baptist at the strict insistence of her grandmother, who had been known to bop a child over the head with her Bible for fidgeting in church. However, perhaps not surprisingly, Aggie had not attended services regularly since she left home, and was never entirely comfortable around the clergy. Perhaps it was a remnant of the good old-fashioned Southern Baptist guilt her grandmother had worked so hard to instill in her; perhaps it was because most of her encounters with men of God had been under extremely unpleasant circumstances. Even now, approaching the young priest on this bright sunshine-filled island day, all she could think of was that sick-sweet smell that seemed to cling to hospital walls, which was ridiculous because Father Dave hadn't even been in Murphy County when she had been hospitalized.

The truth was, she liked Father Dave, who, according to the islanders, had brought a welcome breath of fresh air to the parish. In addition to expanding the youth program and adding guitar music to the early morning service, he had applied with her office for a permit to hold "beach church" shortly after he arrived at St. Michael's. The service had proven surprisingly popular with surfers and fishermen from May through October, and she, Grady and Flash had even attended once or twice before their schedules and the need for sleep got in the way. Aggie worked with Father Dave on several community outreach programs, including the children's coat drive, but she never stopped feeling as though she should apologize for her lack of church attendance every time they met.

She glanced at the plastic Mary, Joseph, wise men and baby Jesus who were scattered about the lawn on their sides amidst bales of pine straw. The camels, donkeys and sheep were already in place beneath the plywood stable roof and secured by guy wires against the wind. "Are you going to be able to do this by yourself? Don't you have any help?"

"One of the parishioners is coming by this afternoon to put up the lighting," he assured her. "I feel a little bad that we're the last building on Main to get our decorations up, but you should see what the Hospitality Committee did with the sanctuary, and the florist is setting up the Christmas tree in the Parish Hall now. Everything was donated, and it's really something." He gestured companion- ably toward the door where Flash was still waiting patiently. "Come on in, I'll show you."

Aggie said, "Actually, I have to be going. I'm kind of on a case."

His face clouded as she told him, as briefly as possible, about last night's hit and run. After all, the more people on the lookout for a car with front-end damage, the better, and Father Dave saw a lot of people in the course of his day.

He shook his head sadly when she finished. "I'll pray for the family," he said, "and for whoever is responsible. He'll never know a moment's peace until he comes forward."

Aggie thought privately that the perpetrator's life would likely not be all that peaceful after he came forward, either, but said only, "Thanks, Father." She glanced around at the sound of a car pulling into the parking lot near the church office, grateful for the opportunity to make a graceful escape. The car parked next to the white florist's van, and Aggie said, "Maybe that's some of your volunteer help, now."

Father Dave lifted his hand in a friendly fashion to the driver of the car, a dusty ten-year-old Ford with rust-eaten bumpers and a taillight covered in a red plastic. Aggie thought about saying something to the driver about the taillight, but changed her mind when the woman behind the wheel got out. It was Linda Ayers, who struggled every month to make her health insurance premium for her little girl, who had cerebral palsy. Her husband worked construction, which always slowed down this time of year, and her eighteen-year-old, Jenny, was a waitress at Pete's Place, which made her, in essence, the only full-time wage earner in the family.

Linda, a thin, weathered woman in jeans and a faded tee shirt, smiled shyly when she saw Aggie, and said, "Morning, Father. I talked with your girl, Miz Baker, and she said it would be okay if I come by this morning to pray with you for a spell. I hope it's okay."

He replied warmly, "I'm so glad you did, Linda. Go on inside and have Helen pour you a cup of coffee. I'll be right in."

The woman smiled again, fleetingly, at Aggie before she went inside, and Aggie smiled back. Father Dave said sadly, "I guess you heard Bill fell off a ladder last month. He'll be okay, but it'll be a while before he can swing a hammer again. The church is doing what it can, but it's a hard time for them right now."

Aggie thought about her own childhood, and the Christmas baskets the church people brought by every year. She said, "It's not much, but I have some gift certificates from the Santa Cop program the Sheriff's Office is doing this year, and the Ayers sound like just the kind of family we want to help. I could have Mo bring them by this afternoon when she drops off the coats from the coat drive."

He smiled. "Santa Cop? Now that sounds like something I want to hear more about. Thanks, Chief." He touched her arm lightly and started to turn away, then looked back. "I'll see you and the family tomorrow night, I hope. You're coming to our Christmas program, right? We're having a blessing of the animals on the lawn here before the program starts, and the church Christmas party afterwards. Everyone on the island will be here."

"Oh." She forced a quick smile. "Of course. Wouldn't miss it."

She raised her hand to Flash who, after a quick confused look back at the closed door of the sanctuary, came down the steps to her side. Aggie started back to her car, wondering how she could have possibly overlooked the Christmas program—not to mention the blessing of the animals—and hoping Grady didn't have plans.

Flash, for his part, wondered why Aggie had not cared to investigate the smell of bourbon and roses, and hoped he hadn't made a mistake in putting things together.

CHAPTER ELEVEN

G iven his choice, Grady would rather be in a patrol car than behind a desk any day. On days like today, when flu season and the holidays had put them two men down, he didn't hesitate to take a call or team up with a road officer when necessary. Before ten that morning he had sent an investigator to the scene of a break-in that had occurred the night before—the third in the same neighborhood this week—taken a report of a cell phone stolen from an unlocked car, dispatched two deputies to pick up a suspected shoplifter from Wal-Mart, and had himself responded to a B&E, auto, and a theft by taking of sixteen oxycodone pills from a residence on Hill Street. Additionally, he had two men searching the county's garages, body shops and gas stations for a vehicle with right front side damage, and put all road deputies on alert for the same. Regarding the B&E and the oxycodone theft—both of which were reported by the same seventy-three-year-old victim—the suspect, who also happened to be the victim's grandson, was fairly easy to find. He was apprehended on the soccer field of the local high school, attempting to sell the oxycodone—still in its original prescription bottle—to a fellow classmate. It was his second offense for virtually the same crime, and after a few halfhearted and completely unconvincing arguments, he allowed himself to be cuffed and escorted to jail.

Grady left the teenager at booking and returned to his office to write up the report—his least favorite part of the job—in time to catch a call from the Panama City lab that handled their forensics. He answered with, "Well, this is a first. A lab report that's actually earlier than promised."

He should have known better. There was a hesitance on the other end, followed by a female voice. "Captain Grady, this is Stella Anderson, and I'm the log-in clerk at ACW Analysis. I have you as the contact person on item 107-348692 date stamped 12:43 this morning? A counterfeit one-hundred-dollar bill stained with an unknown substance?"

He stared at the telephone. "*What* did you say?"

She repeated patiently, "Item number 107-348..."

"No," he interrupted, "I mean, what did you say about the bill? It's counterfeit?"

"Yes, sir, according to the initial visual. But the examining technician kicked it back for clarification on the paperwork. Did you want a fingerprint match as well as a substance analysis? Because the box for fingerprints isn't checked."

He said, "Counterfeit? You're sure?"

"Sir, all I have to go by is the technician's notes, and that's what they say. Also, that there is a partial fingerprint visible in the stain on the corner, which is why…"

"Yeah, yeah, sure," Grady said. "Fingerprints, too. How much longer will that take?"

She said she didn't know but could request an estimate from the proper department as soon as the evidence was received. However, she could tell him that with holiday staffing issues most departments were running three to four days behind. And yes, she assured him when he asked again, the lab tech definitely described the item as a one-hundred-dollar bill, counterfeit.

Grady thanked her and hung up the phone thoughtfully. Bogus twenties were one thing, but hundreds? That kind of phony cash could do an awful lot of damage in a short amount of time. And what had it been doing at the scene of a hit and run?

This case had just gotten a whole lot more interesting.

Aggie knocked on doors up and down Park Street in the vicinity of the accident for over an hour, hoping someone might have heard or seen something helpful. No one had, although one person reported seeing a vehicle parked on the southbound side of Park Street when he returned from a family dinner on the other side of the bridge about nine thirty. It might have been white or beige, and it might have been a minivan. He thought there was writing on the door. Was it writing or a picture? He wasn't really paying attention. No, he hadn't gotten a look at the driver, but he had the impression he'd pulled over to make a phone call. No, he couldn't *really* say the driver was male, but might have been. And no, he hadn't gotten a look at the passenger side of the vehicle at all, so he couldn't say whether it was damaged.

Aggie went back to the corner, but the tire tracks from the night before had already been muted by sea mist and crisscrossed with the tracks of other vehicles that had cut the corner too short, or pulled over on the narrow lane to let another car pass. She brought up on her phone the pictures taken at the scene the night before, and compared the two sets of tracks— the one on Island and the other on Park—side by side. To her inexpert eye, the two appeared to be the same. So had the perpetrator hit Wiesel, pulled off the side of the road on Island to check the damage, then turned the corner onto Park and pulled over to call 911? The problem with that was that, according to the ME, death had occurred around 9:30, and the 911 call hadn't come in until 11:52. So it seemed unlikely that whoever had pulled over on Park at 9:30 was calling in the hit and run. It was, however, more than a little possible he had seen something helpful, if not the actual incident itself. And only an expert would be able to tell whether the tire tracks on Park were even related to the tracks on Island.

She was returning to her vehicle when she got the text from the Sheriff's Office about the counterfeit hundred-dollar bill. "Terrific," she muttered. She was embarrassed that neither she nor Grady—nor in fact any of the officers who'd been present at the scene last night—had thought to check the bill before bagging it, and she guessed Grady was too, especially since he was the one who'd spotted the first phony twenty.

The picture was pretty clear. Either the victim or the perpetrator had somehow gotten hold of a significant amount of counterfeit. "On the other hand," she told Flash as she opened the driver's side door, "the first thing they teach you in police school is never to accept the obvious."

Flash jumped in and went to the passenger side window, where he took in the smells from the night and early morning. He loved listening to Aggie figure things out. She was almost always better at it than he was, and he never failed to learn something new. For example, that thing about not accepting the obvious. He'd be sure to keep that in mind from now on. He wondered if that was why she'd lost interest in the smell of bourbon and roses.

"After all," she went on, climbing behind the wheel, "Mo ended up with counterfeit, and so did Pete, and neither one of them were involved in the hit and run. It could be totally unrelated. Maybe this is the one case where you *don't* follow the money." She chewed on her lower lip, her eyes thoughtful and determined. "But I don't think so."

She blew out a breath and took off her cap, which had already started to grow damp around the brim, tossing it in back with her jacket. She started the engine. "I'll tell you another thing, Flash," she said.

"Nine times out of ten when we receive an anony-mous report about a hit and run, it's the perpetrator calling. He wants to do the right thing and get help, then panics and hangs up. But this call came two hours later. If it was an innocent citizen, why didn't he stay with the victim, or at least give his name? It doesn't make sense."

With a brief, frustrated shake of her head, she checked for traffic and made a U-turn on Park, heading back onto Island Road. Flash settled back in the front seat and was glad when they made the turn that led to Pete's Place. Sometimes, when things didn't make sense despite your best efforts to put them together, the smartest thing to do was just to start over.

At least, that had been his experience.

During the autumn, which coincided with the worst of Lorraine's chemo treatments, Pete's Place had modi-fied its hours, from 11:00 a.m. to midnight Monday through Saturday, to 3:00 p.m. to midnight Monday through Friday, opening for lunch on Saturdays at 11:30. Even though Lorraine was back on a part-time schedule now, the latest bout with cancer had reminded them both about priorities, and Pete and Lorraine had decided to keep those hours through the winter. Sometimes Pete didn't even come in on Saturdays until it was time to set up for the dinner crowd, so Aggie was glad to see his car in the lot when she pulled in a little after 10:30 that morning.

Flash, of course, preferred to visit Pete's Place during lunch, but Pete's was always a happy place, with good smells promising even better things to come, and plenty of people to scratch his ears and ruffle his fur. So he walked in with tail waving beside Aggie when one of the lunch hostesses unlocked the door for them, and paused to let the girl make a fuss over him while Aggie went over to the bar where Pete was setting up.

"Hey, kiddo," he greeted her, setting a bin of clean glassware on the bar. "Did you bring my twenty dollars back?"

"Sorry, I'm afraid you're going to have to take that one as a tax write-off. Any luck finding the ring?"

Pete was only six years older than his brother, with the same easygoing manner and healthy good looks. The past few months had taken their toll on him, though, and there were traces of white in his close-cropped blond hair that were not due to the sun. Today he looked even wearier than usual, with shadows beneath his eyes and worn lines of worry around his mouth. He gave a sad shake of his head and turned to start putting away the glassware. "We tore this place apart last night. Didn't get home until almost two. Nada."

Aggie tried to sound convincing as she said, "It still might show up. It could've rolled behind something or gotten wedged somewhere. This is a lot of territory to cover."

He gave her a look over his shoulder that told her he appreciated the effort, however futile they both knew it was. "She's pretty upset. Didn't come in today. Maybe you could stop by the house?"

"As soon as I leave here," she assured him.

Aggie took out her phone and leaned on the bar, scrolling for the picture. Flash went over to Miguel, who was sweeping beneath one of the tables, and made sure he noticed a peanut someone had dropped on the floor. "Pete," she said, "take a look at this."

He turned around, took the phone from her, and winced. "Jesus, is this guy dead?"

"Sorry," she said, retrieving the phone. "I forgot you're not in the business." She paged down and brought up another picture, returning the phone to Pete. "Here's his DMV photo."

"Baby, whatever kind of business you're talking about, I'm glad I'm not in it." He took the phone reluctantly and looked at the new photo. "What happened to him?"

"Hit and run on Island Road last night," she said. "I thought he might have been walking because he was too drunk to drive. So what about it? Do you recognize him?"

He studied the picture. "Recognize might be a little strong," he allowed after a moment. "Familiar, maybe. He might've been in here."

"Last night?" she prompted.

"Could be," he admitted. "But I didn't serve him." He turned and called, "Hey, Dave. Come up here for a minute, will you?"

Dave appeared from the storeroom carrying a case filled with bottles. The writing on the case said "Four Roses."

"Yo, boss," Dave said, "we're going to need another case of JB next time you order. Morning, Chief. How ya doin', Flash?"

Flash replied by scrambling up onto a barstool and putting his paws on the bar, which sometimes earned him a pretzel. This time it didn't, but Dave's scratch under the chin was almost as good.

Aggie watched as Dave set the case of bourbon on the bar. "Roses," she said softly. "*That*'s what I smelled."

Pete said, "What's that, hon?"

Aggie frowned a little and gave a dismissing shake of her head. "Nothing. Just...nothing."

But Flash just smiled at her. He knew she'd figure it out.

Pete showed Dave the picture on the phone. "Did you serve this guy last night?"

Dave set the case of whiskey on the bar and looked at the phone. It barely took him a moment to reply, "Yeah, sure, I remember him. Never been in before, the kind of face you don't forget."

Aggie said, "Was he alone? Did he talk to anyone?"

"Nah, he just came in, ordered, sat there for a while. Looked nervous every time somebody came in, like he was waiting for somebody. I figured him for a blind date. He wore a jacket zipped up to his chin, like he was trying to look dressed up."

"Was he drinking bourbon?"

Dave shook his head. "Beer. He ordered two, but only drank one. Left early, maybe eight thirty or so. I thought he'd just gone to the john, kept waiting for him to come back, but he never did. Left change from a twenty on the bar. Hell of a tip for two beers. You remember a thing like that." He returned her phone to her. "Is he in some kind of trouble? Because I swear he was sober when he left here."

She shook her head, not wanting to go into an explanation now. "Just trying to figure out why he was walking down Island Road last night."

Dave shrugged. "Like I said, I'd never seen him before."

"Okay, thanks, Dave."

She pocketed her phone and Flash, remembering unfinished business from the night before, sprang down from the barstool and made his way to the patio.

Aggie said to Pete, "Is Jenny Ayers working today?"

"I think so." He was busy with the glassware again. "She usually comes in at three on Saturdays."

"She was working the patio last night, right? I wanted to talk to her but couldn't find her before I left."

"Could be. I'd have to check with Lorraine. She keeps the schedule." He turned around then and gave her a suspicious look. "Why?"

Pete was very protective of his staff, and, like his brother, found it impossible to believe evil of anyone he cared about. So Aggie just said, "I saw her mother in town, that's all. I heard her dad is out of work."

Pete said levelly, "Look, Aggie, these kids handle thousands of dollars a night. If they were going to steal, don't you think they'd be a little smarter about it? Run the credit card twice, forget to report the cash receipts, forge a tip…there are a dozen ways to skim off the top that would take days, if not weeks, for me to notice, and all of them a lot easier than lifting merchandise from customers. A town as small as this, where would they even fence it?" He gave a dismissive shake of his head. "Sorry, babe, but you're way off track on this one."

Aggie hated to admit it, but he had a point. There *were* easier ways to make an illegal living these days, and anyone with access to the Internet knew most of them. On the other hand, when desperate times called for desperate measures, it was important not to overestimate the sophistication level of the average crook.

Pete glanced at his watch and said, "I've got to get to work in the kitchen. Hey, Dave, finish up here for me, will you?"

"You got it, boss."

Aggie said, "See you later, Pete." She looked around for Flash.

Pete said, "Say, honey, I just thought of something."

Aggie replied, "That's Chief Honey to you."

He grinned. "You want to investigate something, you might want to run the tag on that overnighter in the back parking lot." An overnighter was what Pete and Lorraine called cars that were left overnight in their parking lot, usually because the drivers had found alternate transportation. It happened fairly regularly. "A gray Honda Accord, backed in against the fence so I didn't see the plate," he said. "We usually give them forty-eight hours, but given the fact that your guy was here last night..." He shrugged. "It might not hurt to check it out."

She said, "Hey, thanks, Pete. I will."

Aggie looked around again for Flash, and only spotted him because of the swaying of the Christmas tree on the patio. "Flash, be careful!"

Flash backed out from under the tree, dislodging a couple of ornaments with his tail as he did so. Pete chuckled and re-hung the ornaments on his way to the kitchen. "Guess he was looking Santa Claus."

Aggie gave Flash a mildly reproving look when he joined her at the door. "No time for games now, Flash. We're working."

Flash thought that was an odd thing for her to say since working was exactly what he had been doing when she called him away. But he understood when Aggie started across the parking lot toward the back, where a single car was parked against the fence. A car that smelled like chicken and waffle fries.

All you had to do was put things together.

Flash raced ahead of her and was sniffing the tires when Aggie reached the Accord. She used the hem of her tee shirt to wrap her hand and checked the doors; they were locked. She walked around to the back, checked out the tag and smiled. "Bingo," she said softly, and dialed her husband's cell phone.

"Do you know what I like?" he said by way of answering. "The way your picture comes up on my phone every time you call. Hang up and call me again."

She said, "Slow day at work, huh?"

"Not even. I've already taken more offenders off the streets today than you will in a week. What's up?"

"I take it you haven't finished going through the reports on all the Chik 'N' Waffles coupons your guys gave out last week."

"What makes you say that?"

"Because if you had, you'd've found a match for a Santa Cop stop made yesterday about, oh, six thirty or so just across the bridge on Dogleg. Mississippi license plate Seven Niner Tango Eight Two Charlie Three. I'll bet you lunch it comes back to Elijah Wiesel."

He said, "Mississippi, huh? His driver's license said Ohio."

"People move, hotshot."

"That must be why they pay you the big money, Chief. I'll check it out and call you back."

"Better yet, meet me at the beach in an hour. Bring the car keys you took off Wiesel last night. And lunch."

"Chicken sandwiches?"

"I'll bring the blanket."

"You just earned yourself some waffle fries."

She disconnected, smiling, and Flash joined her with tail waving as they walked back around the building to their vehicle. His hearing was excellent, even over the telephone, and he was looking forward to those waffle fries.

CHAPTER TWELVE

When Aggie and Flash entered Lorraine's normally well-kept house, it looked like a bomb had gone off. Sofa cushions were tossed on the floor, books swept from the shelves, potted plants overturned on the tile floor. The only thing that appeared untouched by whatever tornado had roared through the room was the Christmas tree that stood before the patio sliders. Even the hearth in front of the fireplace was scattered with ash, and the entire place smelled like burned cookies. Aggie looked around cautiously and Flash paused on the threshold, muscles tensing, ready for whatever unpleasant force had wreaked such havoc. And then Lorraine appeared from the kitchen in flour-smeared paisley silk pajamas that were too big for her, no makeup, no scarf, her eyes red from crying and her arms crossed defiantly over her chest. Seeing her, Aggie relaxed.

"I hope you got a description of the guy who broke in," she said. She returned a cushion to its place on the sofa and restored a fichus tree to its upright position. Flash came inside, carefully avoiding the spilled potting soil as he crossed the room, and Aggie closed the front door. She looked at Lorraine sympathetically. "You're not going to find the ring here, you know," she said. "You were wearing it last night at dinner when you sat down at the table with us, and it was gone when we got ready to leave. Unless you came back here in between, the ring is at the restaurant."

Lorraine scowled at her. "This," she said with a curt gesture around the room, "wasn't a search. It was a temper tantrum."

Aggie nodded her understanding. She had had more than one of those herself.

Lorraine said, still scowling, "Do you want a cookie? I'm baking a batch to take to the hospital. Yeah, that's right. I've got cancer, I feel like shit, I spend half the life I've got left arguing with the insurance company over medical bills that are bigger than the national debt and now somebody's stolen the only thing I've ever owned that I really cared about, but it's Christmas and I'm baking cookies for the less fortunate because I guess somewhere in this world there *are* people less fortunate than me and because bad things always happen to good people, am I right?"

"So I hear." Aggie returned the last cushion to the sofa and sat down. Flash jumped up beside her and rested his chin on her knee, watching Lorraine with quiet eyes.

After a moment Lorraine sat down hard beside Aggie and slouched back, resting her head on the back of the sofa. She was silent for a time, staring at the ceiling. Then she said, "Five-minute rule?"

They had an agreement between them that had begun years ago, when Aggie first started physical therapy after the shooting: for five minutes a day they each could cry and bitch and rage and complain and throw things if they needed to. They could express their darkest thoughts and deepest fears, things they would never admit to their husbands, and know that those words would go no further. For every other minute of every day they were brave, confident, optimistic. But for five minutes they could tell the truth.

Aggie slid down in her seat, rested her head against the back of the sofa, and fixed her gaze on the ceiling. "Go," she said.

Lorraine said, without looking at her, "That ring was Pete's great-great-grandmother's, back during the turpentine boom. She wore it until the day she died, and then it passed to her son, who gave it to his wife, who wore it until the day she died, and willed it to her daughter, who willed it to her oldest grandson, Pete, after she died. It never left her finger until she went into the hospital for the last time. I'm going to die. Lil and Salty say they're coming home for you and Ryan, and to see the grandkids, but they know it. They're coming to say good-bye to me. They're coming home and the ring is gone and…" She took a slow, shaky breath. "I don't know what Pete's going to do without me. He doesn't know where the household accounts are kept or how to do payroll or who to call when the gutters have to be cleaned. I mean, the man's a genius in the kitchen and a sharp businessman, but he can't do everything by himself.

And he lets those kids at work run all over him. If it weren't for me we'd be paying them to play soccer half the time. His heart's just too big, you know? And when I die, that great big heart is just going to crack in two and there's not going to be anybody there to put it back together again. That's the hardest part, knowing what it's going to do to Pete. I think if it weren't for him I would've died a long time ago, but God, it's just so unfair to have to worry about hurting the person you love because of something you can't even control. Damn it, dying is not my fault!"

She sniffed wetly and flung an arm across her eyes. "You don't survive cancer twice," she said thickly. "I don't care what the doctor says. It'll come back. It'll be in my liver, or my pancreas, because that's what I am, a freaking cancer machine, and nobody gets out alive from that. But oh, the fun part is I get to know what's coming, I have to live with it every day, and just to make sure I never forget, there're the monthly checkups and the concerned family and friends always asking how you're doing and damn it, I hate being bald. I hate that none of my clothes fit, I hate being ugly, I hate being sick and I hate Christmas!"

She was crying now, tears rolling down her cheeks beneath the paisley sleeve of her pajama top, and Aggie let her. She reached across and held Lorraine's hand; the other hand she rested in Flash's fur until the tears slowed, and stopped.

Aggie called time quietly. "Five minutes."

They sat in silence for a while, holding hands. Aggie stroked Flash's head.

Lorraine's voice was tired as she said, "I'm never getting my ring back, am I?"

Aggie admitted, because she owed her friend the truth, "Probably not."

Lorraine said, "Shit."

Aggie agreed sadly, "Yeah."

Aggie glanced at Lorraine and said, "Do you think you're going to die today?"

Lorraine sighed and replied, without removing her arm from her eyes, "Probably not."

"Good. Because I'm supposed to meet Ryan for lunch in less than an hour."

Lorraine said, "Take him some cookies. I've got plenty."

Lorraine removed her arm from her eyes. Aggie smiled at her. Lorraine smiled back, tiredly.

There was another silence, more comfortable this time. Then Lorraine said, "Do you believe in God?"

Aggie was surprised. She had to think for a minute. "I don't know. I used to. Then when I got shot...for a long time I didn't. I know it was stupid. After all, I was the miracle woman, the amazing girl with the bullet in her head, the one who should have died but didn't...but it just seemed to me the real miracle would've been if I hadn't gotten shot at all. That if there was a God, the bad guys wouldn't have won."

Flash turned his ears forward with interest. Bad guys were something he was still trying to learn about, so he paid particular interest when they were mentioned.

Aggie went on, "But then...one day I realized that if I hadn't walked into that house where the bullet found me, if I hadn't opened that door... then I never would have met Flash, or loved Ryan, or become the woman I am today, and as messed up and complicated and hard as it all was, if I had to do it all over again, I'd walk through the door. I'd take the bullet. So I guess, in a way, if that's what God is, somebody who sees the big picture, who puts it all together even when you can't...then yeah. I'm okay with that."

Flash listened alertly. Someone who could put things together even better than Aggie could? Better than he could? Sounded like somebody that would be worth knowing. He decided to pay particularly close attention in the future, in case such a person should cross his path.

Lorraine held her hand, still gazing at the ceiling, and she said, "I think God brought you here. For me. For Ryan too, but for me. Because nobody could have gotten me through this except someone who's been through it, only worse. So it's like, I hate it for you, that you got shot in the head...but I'm glad too. Sorry about that."

Aggie's throat felt full. She didn't know what to say.

Lorraine squeezed her hand and sat up straight, brushing away the last of the tears. "Come on, I'll pack up some cookies."

Aggie stood as Lorraine did, and glanced around. "Do you need some help putting this place back together?"

Lorraine started toward the kitchen. "No, the cleaning service will be here this afternoon. Hell of a thing, when you have to plan your temper tantrums around the maid's schedule."

"High-class problems," Aggie pointed out, and Lorraine smiled.

Aggie watched as Lorraine filled a plastic storage bag with snickerdoodles and thumbprint cookies filled with bright red jam. Flash watched even more intently. Lorraine handed her the bag and the two women hugged each other for a long time, not saying anything. Then Aggie stepped away.

"Tell Pete where the household accounts are," she said. "Show him how to do payroll."

Lorraine dropped her eyes, giving a quick shake of her head. "I can't. It'll make him think I've...you know, given up."

"Then write it in a letter," Aggie suggested. "Put it with your important papers. He'll probably never even need it, but it'll keep you from waking up in a cold sweat at night, worrying about it."

A slow smile touched the corners of Lorraine's lips as she looked up at Aggie. "That's a good idea," she said. She hugged Aggie again, and when she stepped back her smile was easier, more relaxed. "See?" she said. "Sent by God."

Aggie said, "I'll call you later."

Flash left the house thinking that this God thing was something he definitely needed to keep on his radar.

CHAPTER THIRTEEN

Sometimes the sound of the ocean was so big and so powerful that Flash could feel it rumbling in his bones, tilting the earth up and sloshing it down again like a giant teacup in a crazy saucer. Today was not one of those days. Today the ocean lay shimmering and quiet, lapping at the shore with sleepy puppy tongues. Flash, replete with chicken and waffle fries, drowsed in the sun beside the bench where he, Aggie and Grady had had their picnic, eyes half open to the blue water, listening to Aggie and Grady talk.

"Cold front's moving in," Grady observed. He sat atop the concrete picnic table with his feet resting on the bench, eyes squinted at the sea, munching on a waffle fry. "Bet it doesn't get above fifty Monday."

Aggie cast him a look that was half-amused, half-annoyed. He was never wrong about these things. "How can you tell?"

He gestured with his fry. "The water always gets flat before a change. Also…"

"The Weather Channel, I know," she supplied, and he bumped her shoulder affectionately with his own.

There were a dozen or so people on the beach, taking advantage of the weather while it lasted, and Aggie and Grady watched them in easy silence for a while, finishing their sandwiches and sharing the last of the fries. They'd chosen to eat in the grassy picnic area adjacent to the beach parking lot because neither of them wanted to get sand in their food, and because Grady, who hadn't checked out for a dinner break, couldn't get out of radio range.

Among the beachgoers that day was a certain Mr. Angelo, lately of Savannah, Georgia, visiting Murphy County on business and accepting the Chamber of Commerce's invitation to "enjoy the sugar-white beaches of Dogleg Island." He parked his rental car in the parking lot next to a dusty jeep with a kayak carrier on top and walked down to the dune crossover on the west side of the park, where he took a seat on one of the wooden benches built into the wide deck there, stretched out an arm across the rail, and tilted his face to the sun. He wore flip-flops, a straw hat, sunglasses and a logo tee shirt he'd bought at a souvenir shop. There was a camera around his neck, and now and then he lifted it, tracked the flight of a gull across the sky, and snapped a picture. That the camera also occasionally captured the faces of the young couple having lunch with their dog at a nearby picnic table was not coincidental.

Angel didn't need the pictures; there were plenty to be found of both Aggie Malone and Ryan Grady on the Internet. He just wanted them. The camera was also a foil for a small sound-enhancing microphone, and he found listening to their conversation mildly entertaining, if not exactly enlightening. He had people whose only job was to know what law enforcement officers like Aggie and Ryan Grady—and more importantly, their bosses—were talking about, and he was here only to observe. Another one of the top five most important keys to running a successful organization was knowing when to delegate.

On the other hand, when the young couple's conversation turned to matters concerning their work—and his—Angel was very glad he had not delegated this particular trip. It would turn out later that knowing what they were thinking and where they intended to go after their meal would be crucial to the smooth continuation of his own operation. Being a hands-on boss definitely had its rewards.

Aggie and Grady caught each other up on the details of their morning, but Aggie couldn't stop thinking about poor Elijah Wiesel as she ate.

"Dave said he kept his jacket zipped up while he was in the bar," she remembered, for no reason at all. "But when we found him it was open, wasn't it?"

Grady dipped his waffle fry into a paper cup of ketchup. "Yeah, I think so. I'd have to look at the photos to be sure."

She said, "Huh." She nudged his hand aside to swirl her own fry in the ketchup. "And nobody at the Chik 'N' Waffles remembered him?"

"He probably went through the drive-through," Grady pointed out. "Not that easy to get a good look at a face at night. But they did have a record of cashing the coupon, and it was the only one they got yesterday. So he was there. Adams remembers making the stop, of course, but nothing unusual about it except us happening to come by at the same time. So far none of this is taking us anywhere. Too bad he didn't give out the coupon to the perpetrator, instead of the victim. That'd make him a lot easier to track."

Aggie sighed. "Yeah."

"Anyway, I've got the keys we found in his pocket. If they open the Honda in Pete's parking lot, maybe we'll find something inside that'll help us out."

"They'll open it," Aggie assured him. Then she said, "Hey, Ryan, do you like raspberries?"

His eyes were easy on the water, one elbow resting on his upraised knee as he sipped his soda. "Nah, I'm allergic." And at the alarm that crossed her face he winked and nudged her shoulder playfully. "Just kidding. Lucy told me about the cake. Honey, I told you not to make yourself crazy over this."

She frowned. "I'm not. I just wish it were over, that's all."

"It's going to be fun. The Gradys give knock down, blow out parties. Always have, always will."

She didn't point out the obvious—that she was not born a Grady. "I just don't want your folks to be disappointed. It's so generous of them to pay for everything and they don't even get a real say in what it's going to be like."

Grady said, "As long as there's booze, music and food—pretty much in that order—they're going to love it. You about finished?"

She glanced down at the remnants of sandwich bun in the paper wrapper on the table beside her. "Should I give this to the gulls? It's got ketchup on it."

"Better not." He gathered up their trash and stuffed it back into the paper sack. "Finished with your drink?"

She shook down the ice, slurped the last drops of soda from the straw, and handed him the cup. "Rinse this out and fill it with water for Flash, will you?"

Grady took the bag to the trashcan and filled the cup from the water fountain. A woman carrying a Pekinese with sandy paws came up the stairs of the dune crossover, and a man with a camera who'd been sitting there got up, stretched, and waited for her to pass before he went down to the beach. Grady returned to Aggie.

"I'll follow you over to the bar," he said when he set the cup in front of Flash. "Now that the twenties are showing up all over the county, I need to get Pete to sign a statement. Mo, too, when you get a chance."

"No problem." She opened the bag of cookies Lorraine had sent and offered it to Grady. He took two. Aggie rested her elbows on her knees and gazed out over the ocean, her expression relaxing into one of quiet contentment. "Gosh, it's peaceful here, isn't it?" She slid her gaze toward her husband, smiling. "Do you ever think about how lucky we are?"

"All the time." He draped his arm around her shoulders, and for a time they remained that way, eating cookies, watching the ocean and the beach-goers on the sand before them, listening to Flash lap up his water. Then Aggie said, "Lorraine is really upset about her ring. She's got this superstitious thing in her head about losing it, like it means she's going to die."

Grady frowned. "Damn."

"I know."

Aggie said, "I feel so bad for her. I wish there was something I could do."

He cupped her neck lightly with his hand. "Yeah, I feel bad too. Maybe we could all go out on the boat tomorrow. Get out in the sun on the water, better than sitting at home thinking about it, right?"

Aggie gave him one of those smiles that women give the men in their lives who are doing their best, but who really don't get it. He acknowledged it with a wry shrug. "A dollar short, right?"

"Just about," she admitted. "Besides, I kind of promised Father Dave we'd go to the service tomor-row night, and you know how tired you are after a day on the water. They're having a blessing of the animals, and I thought we could take Flash."

It was, in fact, she who was always exhausted after a day of boating, and they both knew it. So Grady agreed amenably, "Cool. Everybody should go to church at Christmas, right? And that'll give us the whole day Sunday to get the tree done. Good plan, Malone."

She said, "Glad you approve. But I've still got shopping to do, so let's get back to work." She used his shoulder to brace herself as she stepped down from the table. "Flash, finish up. Let's go."

Flash took a last few hurried slurps of water and raced to the car, fueled and ready to get back to work. Aggie followed more slowly, her arm around Grady's waist, smiling as she talked to him. Watching them made Flash smile a little inside too, and he wagged his tail in the sand as he waited for them, thinking what a good day this was, and how good it was to be here with the people he loved.

Later Flash would feel bad that he hadn't noticed the bad guy watching them. Aggie hadn't noticed either, but that didn't make him feel any better. Noticing was his job.

He wouldn't make that mistake again.

There was a big colorful building across from Pete's Place Bar and Grill called Beachfront Supplies that specialized in renting sporting equipment by the day or week: kayaks, bicycles, paddle boards, camping gear, even pop-up camping trailers. Upstairs there was a real estate office and a swim shop, so the parking lot was always busy. It wasn't unusual for cars to remain parked there while their owners were camping on one of the nearby primitive islands, so that's where Carson and Sting had set up, parking inconspicuously near the waterfront in between a stack of kayaks and a display of bright orange inflatable rafts. From there they had an unimpeded view of the back parking lot of the bar, and in particular of the dusty gray Accord that had been abandoned there since 8:00 p.m. yesterday.

It had been a long night.

They didn't have a key to the car, but either one of them could have popped the trunk, accessed what was inside, and been out of there inside of two minutes. That wasn't the problem. The problem was the car shouldn't have been abandoned in the first place. Sting—whose real name was Stan Lindon but who'd earned the name Sting because of the scorpion tattooed on his neck—had assured Carson that the owners of the car were not going to just let it sit there, and that by now whoever was supposed to pick up the keys had already reported the no-show. Somebody would be here. All they had to do was wait.

So that's what they did.

"Jesus," complained Sting, hanging his head out the window as Carson lit another cigarette. "Can I get lung cancer from this? I've been breathing your damn smoke for forty-eight damn hours, I can get lung cancer. If I do, I'll sue your ass, I swear to God."

Carson exhaled into the windshield, unconcerned. "You do that."

The bar had opened an hour ago and the smell of fried food had been making their mouths water ever since. Sting had been all for going over and ordering something, or at least getting a burger to go, but Carson thought it was a bad idea to show up again in the same place so soon. So they waited. He smoked; Sting finished off a bag of stale peanuts and fidgeted.

"This is a bad idea," he said, not for the first time. "What if they spot us when they come for the car? They know me, man. We need to get the hell out of here and try again next time. Or..." He slid a quick greasy glance toward Carson, who was behind the wheel. "We do what I said. We pop the trunk, we take the loot, we head for Mexico. It's sitting right there, man, ours for the taking..."

"Shut up," said Carson, and sat suddenly forward. He ground the cigarette out absently in the car's overflowing ashtray and watched the crew-cut figure in jeans and tee shirt approach the car with an easy confidence. A black and white dog followed close behind.

"Jesus," said Sting, watching alertly. "That's the same kid that was nosing around this morning. What's he doing back? He can't be more than twelve years old! This ain't right, man, something's off."

"It's not a kid," said Carson. The first time he had noticed the duo he'd suspected he was about to witness a break-in, but he'd been wrong. They'd left. Now they were back and this time it was different. He watched with narrowed eyes as the figure took out a key and inserted it into the driver's side door. "I think it's a woman."

Sting looked at him skeptically. "Come on, are you kidding me?"

But Carson wasted no more time. "I'll check it out," he said, opening the car door. "Stay here."

He tucked his berretta into the back of his jeans, made sure his tee shirt covered it before he got out of the car, and started across the parking lot toward the Accord.

Flash recognized him immediately, and so, once Flash got her attention, did Aggie. It was the guy from the bar last night; the one with the big shoulders and hard eyes who had sat next to scorpion-tattoo man. Flash could tell by the way he moved—stride a little too casual, eyes a little too watchful—that his intentions were not friendly. By the time the man was ten feet away, Flash could smell the gun that was hidden in the waistband of his jeans. This was not particularly troublesome, because Grady often carried his gun like that, and Aggie sometimes put her gun in her purse or her jacket pocket, where no one but Flash would know it was there. But she had not done so today.

So it wasn't the hidden gun that made Flash uneasy; he had dealt with guns before. It was the way Aggie's face went all still and tense when she looked up and saw the man approaching; the way her muscles hardened and her pores opened. Aggie had almost as good an instinct for danger as Flash did, and together they were never wrong. He moved closer to her.

Aggie was leaning into the driver's seat of the car when she saw the man coming toward her with purpose in his gaze, and the first thing she thought was, *Oh crap.* She was out of uniform, breaking into a stranger's car, and she did not want to get into an awkward confrontation. The second thing she thought—in fact, it was almost simultaneous—was that she was unarmed. She was not armed and she would have bet everything she'd learned in her ten years as a law officer that the man who was coming toward her was.

Aggie straightened up, keeping the open door of the vehicle between them while glancing around for the man with the scorpion tattoo. She didn't see him immediately, but neither did she see anyone else. Except for a few employee vehicles, the back parking lot was empty and would likely remain that way until 7:00 or 8:00 tonight. Grady had gone inside to talk to Pete. She and Flash were on their own.

The man, only a couple of strides away now, grinned at her in a way that wasn't at all reassuring and said, "Hey there, sweetheart, whatcha doing with my car?"

Aggie was on the verge of identifying herself as a police officer, but with those words she hesitated. The registration had come back to a Mississippi rental car company; the paperwork had been issued to Elijah Wiesel. If this man was connected to either one of them, she needed to know about it. She said, "Your car? Do you have some ID?"

He chuckled and managed to make the sound menacing. "I'm not the one breaking into a parked car. I don't need ID."

She held up the key. "And I'm not breaking in. Who are you?"

His gaze moved from the key that dangled between her fingers to her face. His eyes narrowed. He took a step toward her. Flash, who was mostly concealed behind the car door, started to growl, but Aggie made a small shushing motion with her hand and pulled the door a little closer to her chest, holding the man's gaze.

He said in a low, smooth tone, "Okay, sweet thing, this is how it's going to go down. You're going to hand over those keys and then you and me are gonna have ourselves a little talk. Maybe I'll take you inside, buy you a beer. You good with that?"

Aggie edged the car door a fraction closer. "What if I'm not?"

"Then maybe you end up in the trunk of this car. Hot day like this, right in the sun…" He cast a brief, squinting glance skyward. "I give you an hour. So how about you play nice? We're just gonna talk."

He took another step, grabbing for her, and Aggie shoved the door open with all her might. It slammed into his torso and knocked him back just as Flash launched himself out of concealment, barking furiously. He weighed forty-five pounds after a good meal, but speed and muscle gave him the impact of a one-hundred-eighty-pound man. He threw himself at the assailant's chest and knocked him off his feet. It was at that point that Flash saw, out of the corner of his eye, the man with the scorpion on his neck running toward them. Flash leapt over the man on the ground and charged toward the new bad guy, teeth bared in a roar of barking that would have done justice to a dog twice his size.

Aggie saw the man on the ground twist around and reach behind him for what she assumed was a gun. She drew back and kicked him hard in the shoulder. The gun went flying, but the force of the kick—and the fact that she was wearing sneakers, not boots—overbalanced her and she fell hard onto the gravel beside him. The shock of the fall reverberated through every bone in her body. Her heart slammed in her ears and her vision strobed in rhythm—*bam! bam! bam!* She felt his hand on the back of her neck and suddenly it wasn't. She scrambled away and her peripheral vision caught the green uniform of a Florida deputy sheriff slamming her assailant back to the ground. She heard Flash barking, saw him running. The gun was on the ground a few feet away. She flung herself toward it.

Aggie grabbed for the gun. Her fingers wouldn't close. The man twisted away from Grady, and Grady hit the ground hard. Finally, her fingers closed on the grip of the gun. The weapon slipped out of her stiff and shaking fingers before she could lift it. Grady had the advantage now, slamming the man face down on the gravel and twisting his arms behind his back. He jumped up, gun drawn, and shouted, "Police officer! On the ground, asshole! Let me see your hands!"

Aggie got to her feet, her hands wrapped firmly around the assailant's gun now. She steadied the weapon, and shouted, "Grady, I've got him! Get the other one!"

It was only later that she realized the entire episode had taken less than ten seconds. As she stood there, holding the gun in a death-grip with both hands, desperately hoping her body wouldn't betray her and trying to keep her focus on the man who was trying to pull himself up from the ground, she caught the glimpse of blood on Grady's face, saw him swing his weapon toward the squeal of tires, saw Flash running back across the parking lot toward them. Ten seconds. That was all it took.

The man with the scorpion tattoo was gone. Grady followed his flight with the barrel of his gun for a moment but did not shoot. Flash, who had chased the bad guy back into his car, raced back to Aggie's side, tongue lolling and adrenaline soaring, ready to do the next thing that needed to be done. Grady grabbed the man on the ground by the collar and jerked him to a kneeling position, his weapon aimed at his head. "Hands!" he shouted.

Aggie's hands, gripping the suspect's gun with all her might, began to tremble.

The man, bracing himself on his knees, laced his hands behind his head. He winced as he did so, and Aggie liked to think the pain it caused him was due to her kick in the shoulder. Then he said, sounding tired and resigned and frustrated and angry, "At ease, Deputy. I'm a federal agent."

CHAPTER FOURTEEN

Aggie pressed a plastic bag filled with ice gingerly against the scrape on Grady's cheek, her eyes dark with worry. "Are you sure you don't want to go the ER?" she insisted, not for the first time. "You might need stitches."

Grady took the bag of ice from her and replied levelly, "Aggie, honey, I love you with all my heart, but if you say that one more time, I'm going to leave you. Swear to God."

Aggie sucked in a sharp breath to speak, changed her mind, and sat down in the plastic office chair opposite him, her hands clasped between her knees. From across the room they glared at each other, although Grady broke eye contact first, gingerly pressing the ice bag against his face and pretending it hurt more than it did. Flash, who knew they weren't really mad at each other and who wasn't nearly as worried about Grady as Aggie was, took the opportunity for a brief nap beneath Aggie's chair.

They were in Sheriff Bishop's office, where they had been sternly ordered to wait more than an hour ago. They had not strictly obeyed, going back and forth to the vending machine, the communications room, and the investigators' desks until finally accepting there really was nothing for them to do but wait. Aggie was just about to lurch to her feet again when the door burst open and Bishop strode through, followed by the man who, only a short time earlier, Grady had arrested for assaulting a police officer. Bishop looked angry and impatient. The prisoner, who was not wearing cuffs and who—except for a few scratches where his face had hit the gravel—appeared to be perfectly unharmed, simply looked annoyed.

Bishop slapped a folder on his desk and said brusquely, "This is Special Agent Mike Carson of the United States Secret Service. Agent Carson, Captain Ryan Grady and Police Chief Aggie Malone, Dogleg Island." He went behind his desk, jerked out his tall-backed, faded leather desk chair and sat down. He scowled at the man he'd introduced as Carson and commanded, "Sit down. Let's get this straightened out."

Aggie took the folder from Bishop's desk, opened it, and examined the faxed photo, Secret Service ID, and partial assignment record—much of it blacked out as classified—of Agent Mike Carson. She passed the folder to Grady, who did the same before returning it to her.

Carson sprawled out in the only remaining guest chair and glowered at Aggie. "Police chief, huh? You should have identified yourself."

Aggie bristled. Her foot still throbbed from having kicked him and she thought her big toe was starting to swell inside the sneaker. "So should you." She replaced the folder on Bishop's desk.

He returned, "I'm undercover."

Grady put aside the bag of ice and looked the other man over with an expression that was barely on the safe side of furious. "You mind filling me in on what they teach you in federal law enforcement school about the procedure when you're apprehended by an officer of the law? Because you almost got your undercover ass shot."

Carson regarded him coolly. "That would have been unfortunate," he said, and added deliberately, "For you."

Flash's ears tilted forward alertly and he watched the stranger from beneath the chair, but he didn't get up. He had learned from Aggie's trick with the car door what an advantage surprise could be. He was going to remember that one.

Aggie's eyes flashed. "I hope you're aware that you have no authority whatsoever over a deputy sheriff in this county, and as far as I'm concerned you're still guilty of assault."

Carson rubbed his shoulder and glared at her meaningfully. "So are you."

Grady tensed. "You really are a first-class—"

"All right, ladies and gentlemen," interrupted Bishop mildly, "let's settle down and see if we can get to the bottom of this, shall we?" He turned his gaze on Carson. "Special Agent Carson, you have the floor. Make it good."

Carson shifted his weight in the chair, appearing to think it over. He patted his pockets for cigarettes, found them empty, and looked even more annoyed. He settled back in the chair, pretending to relax. He deliberately did not look at Grady.

He said, "For the past six months we've been tracking the movement of large amounts of counterfeit along the Gulf Coast. The primary method of distribution is via a string of so-called vehicle transportation shops that sometimes disguise themselves as private rental car agencies. The counterfeit is stowed inside the vehicle, some poor schmuck is hired to drive it from Point A to Point B, where he turns in the car to an intermediary, picks up another car, and starts the process all over again. As far as we can tell, the drivers aren't part of the scam. They're just doing a job and getting paid. That car you broke into was carrying over a million in bad bills."

Bishop nodded grim confirmation. "We found it under the spare tire while the boys at impound were doing a routine search."

Aggie said, "That explains the bad twenty at Pete's Place." She addressed herself to Bishop. "Wiesel was in there last night, and the bartender said he paid with a twenty."

Carson frowned. "That doesn't make any sense. They never pay these guys with bad money. It's too risky."

Bishop said, "Then it looks like somebody screwed up. We've had over a hundred dollars in bogus twenties show up here in the past forty-eight hours."

"Not to mention the hundred we found at the scene of the hit and run last night," Aggie reminded him.

Carson frowned. "Yeah, the sheriff said the driver was killed last night."

"Do you think it might not have been an accident?" Once again Aggie directed herself to the sheriff. "Now that we know about the counterfeit, that is."

Bishop looked to Carson for the answer, but the other man just shrugged.

Aggie said, "What about your friend? The one with the tattoo. Is he supposed to be a federal agent too? Why did he run?"

Carson scowled. "His name is Stan Lindon, they call him Sting on the street. He's a CI that helped me set this whole thing up." He smiled politely at Aggie. "That stands for criminal informant, in case you're wondering."

Grady glared at Carson, but Aggie just returned his smile. "We call them plain old snitches around here."

"He worked for the operation as a go-between," Carson went on, unfazed, "delivering cars to the drivers, picking them up and transferring the money, until we busted him last October. Since then he's been feeding us information and helping set up this bust. As for why he ran—what would you do if you were an ex-con trapped between a deputy with a gun and a crazy dog that was coming at you like a freight train?"

Flash looked hard at Carson from his place beneath the chair. He wasn't entirely sure what the big man meant by "crazy," but he suspected it wasn't a compliment. And anyone with even basic observation skills should have been able to tell that the only thing Flash had done today was his job. Just like everyone else.

Carson said to Bishop, "Your boys better find him, and quick. I don't like the way this is shaping up, and without him, I've got nothing."

Bishop replied without expression, "We've got a BOLO out on him."

Grady said impatiently, "So why don't you get to the part where you interfered with an officer of the law in the performance of her duty and then threatened to lock her in the trunk of a car? And while you're at it, maybe you can explain why anybody would want to transport a million in counterfeit to Dogleg Island."

Carson ignored the first question and answered the second. "That's the MO. They use small towns like this as drop-off points because they're less likely to attract the attention of understaffed police agencies, and also because of their proximity to the final distribution point. A guy walks into a bar, has a drink, trades out a set of keys, walks out and gets into a different car with no one the wiser. Easiest thing in the world. I'd be surprised if your little berg isn't a regular stop on the underground express."

"What do you mean," demanded Grady with a frown, "final distribution point?"

Carson seemed to debate for a moment whether to answer. Then he said, "We think the bad cash gets into circulation through casinos, where it's paid out in winnings a little at a time. Those winnings go out all over the country, where they start showing up in such small amounts, generally speaking, they're almost impossible to trace. There are three big casinos within two and a half hours of here."

Aggie said, "Wait a minute. Casino cashiers are the sharpest people in the world at spotting bad bills. Wouldn't they notice?"

A brief spark of what might have been respect flickered across the other man's eyes, and was gone. "Right," he said. "So this isn't a small-time operation. Casino managers, bank managers, cashiers— some if not all of them are accomplices along the way, and you'd better believe they're being well compensated for their cooperation. So we're not talking about a penny ante operation." He hesitated, again seeming to debate how much more to reveal. "The focus of the Secret Service operation was to find out how deep the counterfeit ring goes. We're not interested in the drivers, the car shops, the mules that get the money from one place to the next. We want to know who it goes to and who sends it."

Aggie said, "So is that what you were doing at the bar last night? Trying to intercept the guy Wiesel was turning the car over to?"

Once again Carson absently patted his pockets in the manner of a habitual smoker, possibly not even aware he was doing it. "This was the last stop before the money was distributed to the casinos. Our information is they don't send mid-level operatives for that. This would've been somebody close to the top. It took over a year to set us up as the bodyguards who were going to make sure the money got where it was going. If he had showed up, we could've caught him in the act of transferring the counterfeit, which would have given the federal government one big-ass bargaining chip toward bringing down the big guys. But when the driver bailed, all we could do was stake out the car and see who claimed it. It was a good bet they weren't going to let a million in counterfeit get towed for a parking violation." He looked at Aggie. "When you showed up with the key, I figured you for the target. You should have identified yourself."

Aggie said nothing, because he was right. She should have.

Carson turned impatiently backed to Bishop. "Are we about done here, Sheriff? I have to report in."

Bishop looked at the other man long and hard. "I hope you include in that report how you managed to mistake a deputy sheriff in full uniform for an assailant, not to mention why you tried to pull a gun on one of my officers."

Carson's lips tightened, and he glanced reluctantly at Grady. "I'm sorry, Captain," he said stiffly. "That shouldn't have happened. I was worried about losing my suspect and you came at me from behind. It was my fault."

Bishop nodded his approval, and almost smiled. "That's better. Let's try to remember we're on the same team here." But the pleasant expression faded as he passed a piece of paper across the desk to Carson. "Here's the receipt for you weapon. You can pick it up on your way out—and I hope you know I mean out of my county. Your behavior was reckless and unprofessional, it endangered the lives of my officers and the public, and that's what I'm going to put in *my* report." He added, hard-eyed, "But the next time you boys are in town, be sure to stop by and introduce yourselves. You're bound to get a lot more cooperation. Now get out of here."

Bishop waited until Carson, without saying another word, left the room and closed the door behind him. Then he turned to Grady and Aggie. "As for you two..."

His phone rang.

He snatched it off the hook, scowling. He said, "Yeah...Yeah..." and "Okay." He punched another button on the phone without looking up at the two people in his office, and he spoke abruptly into the receiver. "Is Special Agent Carson still in the building?" A pause. "Send him back here."

Aggie and Grady glanced at each other. Flash, who hadn't understood the significance of the words he'd heard on the phone but knew from the way Bishop's voice changed that this was no time for a nap, came to sit between Aggie and Grady, ready for whatever was next. Bishop hung up the phone and folded his hands atop his desk. He looked at them with somber eyes.

"The state patrol responded to a report of a vehicle over the embankment on Highway 98, description and tag matching our BOLO. The car missed going into the Gulf by a dozen feet, but a man matching the description of our Mr. Lindon was behind the wheel. He's dead. Shot through the head."

Chapter Fifteen

Aggie and Grady were mostly silent on the ride home. Grady drove her car, Aggie sat in the passenger seat, and Flash stretched out on the bench seat behind them, listening to the tension in the car. He had learned a long time ago that sometimes the best thing to do was just be quiet and listen.

Grady tried to start a conversation once or twice, but received only monosyllabic replies. Finally he said in exasperation, "What the hell's the matter with you, Malone?"

She was silent for a moment, hands twisted in her lap. Then she said, "I screwed up."

"Well, gee, that must be tough, seeing as how you're the first person in history ever to do that."

She said tightly, "Don't forget to stop at the grocery store."

He stifled a groan. "Baby, I'm done for the day. Why don't we just grab a pizza…"

"No!" Her voice contained enough force to cause Flash to raise his head from the backseat. "I'm making dinner. I said I would and I am. I'm making the damn spaghetti and you're making the damn sauce and we're having a salad! I want eggs for breakfast and milk in my coffee so just stop at the damn grocery store, will you?"

Grady's jaw went tight. He checked the traffic, signaled a left turn, and swung into the parking lot of the IGA, then into the nearest parking space. He slammed on the brakes with enough force to make Aggie's seat belt lock, then turned off the engine. He sat there, hands on the wheel, waiting.

It wasn't quite twilight, and the sky was streaked with fading stripes of pink and orange. Red and white "Merry Christmas" banners flapped from the light poles in the parking lot, and the store windows were outlined in twinkling lights. There was a big display of poinsettias by the entrance, and two plastic snowmen swayed in the breeze on either side of the door. Aggie fixed her gaze on them for a long moment.

Then she said quietly, steadily, "I'm supposed to keep you safe. I stop the bad guys on Dogleg Island, so they don't cross the bridge to you. You're supposed to keep me safe. You stop the bad guys from getting to Dogleg Island. That's the deal. I didn't do my job. I screwed up and you got hurt."

Grady was silent. Sometimes, like Flash, he knew when that was the best thing to be. It often took him a little longer to catch on, that was all.

Aggie said, "I shouldn't have tried to engage him. I had time to call you."

"I was already on my way. Couldn't have gotten there any faster."

"But next time...I should teach Flash to go get you when there's an emergency. I shouldn't have tried to take him on my own."

Flash looked up, puzzled, and Grady said with only a touch of impatience, "Flash doesn't need to be taught anything. He did exactly what he was supposed to."

Flash started to relax, but Aggie said, "Flash shouldn't have chased that guy, that Sting. What if he'd had a gun? And anyway, he might be alive now if Flash hadn't gone after him, and now the operation is blown..."

Flash was confused, and more than a little hurt. Had he done something wrong? His job was to keep the bad guys away. Hadn't he done that? Then why was Aggie disappointed in him? He rested his head on his paws, feeling not so happy as he had been a moment ago.

Grady said, "You about done?"

Aggie drew in a breath. "I dropped the gun, Grady," she said, almost in a whisper. "I saw it and I couldn't pick it up, I couldn't make my hands work, and then I picked it up and I dropped it."

He reached across the seat and covered her clasped hands with his. For a moment he just sat there, holding her hands. Then he asked, "What does the doctor say about the tremors?"

She gave one swift fierce shake of her head. "I can't take another pill, I can't go through another battery of tests, I can't..." She didn't finish, but he understood. Every day both of them lived with the possibility of what the truth might eventually be, and were grateful for every day that they didn't know it. "Not yet. Not now," she said.

She took another breath. "I was conducting police business out of uniform. I should have identified myself but I thought I was going to be the big shot, get a leg up on solving this thing...I just screwed up. If Carson had been a real criminal, lives might have been in danger. You might have...Jesus, that guy Sting was *right there* and he ended up with a bullet in his head. Maybe if I hadn't been such an idiot..."

"Okay, that's stretching it," Grady said firmly. "Carson was responsible for his snitch, not you, not me, not Flash."

She leaned her head back against the seat. "You're right. You and Flash did your jobs."

Finally, Flash relaxed a little.

Grady said, "So did you." His fingers tightened briefly on her hands, and he gave her a moment to let that sink in. Then he addressed the one thing she had not. "The Dogleg Island Police Department doesn't require its police chief to wear a uniform. Or carry a gun."

She glanced at him with a mixture of gratitude and despair. "Ryan, I'm one of two law enforcement officers on the whole island. I need to keep people safe. I'm afraid that...in an emergency...I can't."

Grady pried her hands apart and lifted the fingers of her left hand to his lips. He kissed them and gently returned her hand to her knee. "This is what we're going to do," he said. "Next week, we'll go to the shooting range. I've got Wednesday off. I'll take you through qualifying, compare it to your last score, see how you stand. You might be steadier than you think. At least we'll have some stats to take to the neurologist. We'll get this fixed, baby. Compared to what we've been through, piece of cake. Just relax. I've got your back."

Aggie slowly unfastened her seat belt, stretched across the console, and kissed him. Grady gathered her close and kissed her back. Aggie's elbow hit the horn, startling them apart, and they smiled.

In the backseat, Flash smiled too.

It was full dark and the lights on the bridge were streaking their psychedelic display by the time they started home. The cargo area was filled with groceries, including, Flash couldn't help noticing, salted caramel ice cream, which was his favorite. He sat up to watch the lights while they crossed the bridge, panting in sheer delight, and then stretched out on the backseat again once they reached Island Road.

Aggie said thoughtfully, "I know Sting's murder is out of our jurisdiction, and so is this counterfeit scheme, but I still think Wiesel is the key. I mean, why did he run? If Carson is right, and the drivers weren't in on it, he was minutes from picking up his pay when he bolted. So what spooked him enough to make him set out on foot in a strange place? Do you think he could have found out what he was carrying?"

Bright green and red lights from a row of LED Christmas trees that lined the curb flashed across Grady's face as he shook his head. "No way. He had less than two hundred dollars in his wallet, all of it genuine, by the way. Why would he walk away from a car full of cash, even if it was counterfeit and even if he did know it? He could have gotten a long way on what was in that trunk, and he wouldn't have been walking, either."

"Then where did the counterfeit hundred come from? His killer?"

"Maybe." Grady's voice was thoughtful. "I've got investigators on it, but we don't have a whole lot to go on. And, not sure if you noticed, but the Secret Service wasn't exactly tripping over themselves to help us out here."

At the end of the day, in response to Sheriff Bishop's question, Special Agent Carson had replied briefly that his assignment ended with the death of Sting. That investigation was in the hands of the Florida Department of Law Enforcement and, potentially, the FBI. He was headed back to Miami headquarters, and he had no information about how the investigation into the counterfeit ring would proceed from here. All of this was, of course, a not particularly polite way of saying that they should mind their own business and stay out of the federal government's way.

In the flickering lights of a passing yard display, Grady slid a grin at her. "I wish you could've seen yourself, kicking that SOB when he was down."

She returned his look uneasily. "You saw that?"

"I've never been prouder."

Aggie struggled to hide her own smile—after all, she deserved a little self-congratulations—and replied instead, "I think I broke my toe."

He inquired, straight-faced, "Do you want to go to the ER?"

She punched him in the arm.

Grady said in a moment, "I hate to say it—I mean, the guy is dead and all—but I'm glad they found that Sting character before end of shift. A manhunt cancels all days off, and I'm really looking forward to a quiet Sunday."

Aggie gave him a look that was part derisive, part exasperated and part—although she liked to think it was a very small part—understanding. The job of a law officer was often filled by heroes, but it was, nonetheless, a job. He got tired. So did she.

Aggie said, "Don't get too comfortable. It might still come back to bite us."

"You're talking about Wiesel?"

She said, "Wiesel walks away from a car full of counterfeit cash and is killed—maybe by accident, maybe not—an hour later. Sting runs away from a stakeout after I try to confiscate that same car full of counterfeit, and is killed—what? Two hours later? Those dots are definitely connected, my friend. We just have to put them together."

Flash's ears rotated forward. Putting things together was something he knew a little about. Before they knew it, there would be a trail to follow, just like the one that led to the church. Although Flash wasn't entirely sure how important that particular trail was anymore.

Passing headlight beams caught the faint shadow of Grady's frown. "You think the killer followed both of them from Pete's Place?"

That made Flash lift his head in mild alarm. A killer at Pete's Place? And he hadn't noticed? How had that happened?

Aggie said, "I think it's pretty likely whoever shot Lindon was either watching him or in contact with him somehow today. He caught up with him too fast."

"Yeah," agreed Grady thoughtfully. "The murder might be out of our jurisdiction, but there's a good chance it started here."

He made the turn onto Seahorse Lane, whose name had been changed from Grady Loop Road after Ryan Grady petitioned the Roads and Mapping Authority to do so when he took ownership of the house. It was little more than a sandy cul-de-sac, with only two other houses besides their own, that connected with Dolphin Drive on one side and Grady Plantation Way on the other. The Fitzsimmons house was dark and empty, its occupants having routinely departed after Thanksgiving to return in March. The house on the Dolphin Drive end of the street was happily decorated with artificial palm trees outlined with green Christmas lights. In the center sat the Grady house. The minute they saw it, they said in unison, "What the...?"

Grady put his foot on the brake instinctively. Flash sat up from the backseat and grinned at what he saw. Aggie stared at Grady. "Ryan, did you...?"

He stared back at her. "Did you?"

She said simply, "No."

He pulled into the driveway and they just sat there for a moment, gazing at the spectacle before them. There were Christmas lights on the balconies, wrapped around the railing of the deck, dripping from the eaves over the front porch. Lighted candy canes marched across the front yard and a fully decorated Christmas tree was visible from the eastern-facing bay window. There was even a tinsel wreath on the front door.

As they watched, dumbfounded, that door opened, and Grady began to grin. "Dad?" he said uncertainly. He flung open the car door and jumped out. "Dad!" he cried. "Mom!"

CHAPTER SIXTEEN

Some people might have been amazed by how quickly a day could turn from dark to light, from angry to happy, from chasing down bad guys to having a party, but not Flash. He had been around too long. One minute you're eating waffle fries and the next a big man with a hidden gun is coming toward you. One minute Aggie and Grady are yelling at each other, and the next they're buying salted caramel ice cream. Life was like that. That was why it was important to pay attention.

Grady ran toward the house and two people ran down the steps toward him, arms open. They met in the middle, laughing and embracing. Flash bounded after him, excited by all the happiness and knowing there would be petting involved. Aggie followed a little more slowly. There was, in fact, petting, and as soon as Aggie arrived, more hugging and half-finished exclamations of, "How did you…?" "When did you…?" "Look at you!" "Wanted to surprise…" "Why didn't you…?"

Aggie heard Grady's mother exclaim in her sweet southern drawl, "Ryan! *Darling*! What happened to your *face?*"—managing to give every word at least two syllables for emphasis, which from another person might have been annoying. But from Lil Grady it was simply charming.

Grady replied dismissively, "Work-related injury." He was grinning from ear to ear as he stretched out his arm to draw Aggie forward.

But almost before he had finished speaking, Lil turned to Aggie, placed her hands on either side of Aggie's face and beamed, "Look at you! Look at her, Salty! Those eyes, those cheekbones! Oh, you're even prettier in person!" to which Salty replied boisterously, "The Grady men always get the prettiest ones!" He slapped his son on the shoulder, scooped Aggie away from Lil, and kissed her hard on the forehead. "Daughter," he said, smiling at her, "welcome to the family." Then he hugged her so hard that Aggie thought her ribs might snap.

Aggie had talked with her parents-in-law over the phone, and Skyped with them once or twice, so she knew to expect larger than life. Still, she wasn't entirely prepared for the reality, or how to react to it. Sean Grady—or Salty as he had been called for over forty years—was a broad-shouldered man with thick wavy white hair and a neat white sea captain's beard. He had a strong baritone voice and booming laugh and—as Ryan had warned her—the gift of the Irish for storytelling. His wife Lil was a smaller, plumper version of her husband in bright yellow capris and a lime green tee shirt with a beaded toucan embroidered on it. She had a platinum bob and a bubbling smile and Ryan's eyes. It was impossible not to love them on sight, even though they were, individually and as a couple, a little overwhelming.

"I hope we didn't overstep," Lil said anxiously, slipping her arm through Aggie's as they went back toward the house. Flash led the way, and the men, carrying the groceries, followed. "A friend of ours has a charter business—"

"Amazing fellow," interrupted Salty. "Two bronze stars, flies medical personnel into the jungle in his spare time—"

"And it happened he was flying a couple to Tampa this weekend," Lil went on.

"Split the fare, ended up costing less than a regular flight," Salty added with satisfaction. "Took half the time and no fighting the holiday crowds. Who says no to that?"

"Of course, we should have called," Lil added. "But it came up at the last minute and then we got into Tampa so late last night—"

"Stayed at the Treasure Island Resort," Salty put in. "Now there's a place you need to see if you get a chance. Best breakfast I ever had, right there by the waterfall with parrots flying overhead."

"So we said," Lil went on, "why not just rent a car and drive up to surprise the kids? But I hope we didn't overstep. I told Salty we were overstepping. You don't just walk into someone's house and start putting up Christmas decorations—"

"A few lights!" objected her husband, close behind. "They were already out of the box!"

"But we saw the Christmas tree," Lil went on, "and thought it might save you some time if we got started. Of course, we left plenty of ornaments for you," she assured Aggie quickly. "I know how much I always enjoy taking out each ornament and seeing it again for the first time every year."

"Oh," Aggie said quickly, "no, it's fine, thank you, it's just—I wanted to put fresh sheets on the bed in the guesthouse and..."

Lil laughed and squeezed her arm. "Oh, honey, don't worry about it! Already done."

"Oh," Aggie said, a little dazed.

Lil opened the door and Flash bounced inside, then stopped still, nose lifted appreciatively to sniff the air. Grady came in behind them and stopped as well, a smile of delight breaking over his face. "Mom?" he said. "Is that pot roast?"

Aggie said at the same time, "Dinner? You made dinner?"

Lil looked at her in dismay. "We overstepped," she said. "Salty, I *told* you we were overstepping. You don't just—"

Grady laughed and hugged his mother with his free arm and Aggie just looked at them both, dumbfounded.

"It's too much," Lil declared with an emphatic shake of her head. "I *knew* it was too much. You don't just go into another woman's kitchen and make dinner. And I so wanted to get off on the right foot with you!"

Aggie, aware now that everyone was looking at her, released a breath and an uncertain smile. "Wow," she said. "What do I have to do to convince you to move in?"

It was one of the happiest times Flash could remember. They sat around the big table in the dining room, which Aggie and Grady never used except sometimes to clean their guns, and ate roast beef with gravy and little potatoes with carrots and peas. Flash thought Grady's mom might even be a better cook than Pete, although he didn't want to be disloyal. Aggie made a big salad and dinner rolls from the grocery store, and afterwards there was salted caramel ice cream. The Christmas tree sparkled with lights and filled the house with a fresh green scent that smelled almost as good as the pot roast. Beneath it were dozens of colorfully wrapped presents decorated with curly ribbon and tinsel bows. Flash sniffed every single one.

After dinner Lil and Salty called Lucy and put her on speaker so everyone could hear her squeal with excitement and then complain because she had just put the boys to bed and why hadn't they called her earlier and how dare they sneak into town like criminals? In the end Lil and Salty promised to come over tomorrow after church and spend the entire day, and ended the call with lots of noisy kisses sent over the phone to their sleeping grandchildren. By that time Pete and Lorraine had arrived and there were more hugs and kisses and exclamations of joy. Pete brought two bottles of wine and a case of Guinness, and Lorraine brought a big tin canister filled with cookies. She hugged Aggie as she handed her the cookies and whispered, "Not a word to Lil about the ring. I'll tell her when I'm ready."

Aggie said, "Feeling better?"

Lorraine's answer was a rather sheepish smile.

Grady built a fire in the fire pit and everyone moved outside to the patio, which, to Flash's amazement, now had tiny white lights strung across the wooden pergola, so that it looked like a thousand little stars dancing right above their heads. Flash decided that Grady's dad might be the only person in the world who appreciated Christmas lights as much as he did, which was only one of the reasons Flash liked him. He also gave great ear rubs and told the most amazing stories. Flash fell asleep in the glow of the dancing fire listening to a story about a big fish while Pete and Grady drank beer and hooted with laughter and the women talked and giggled among themselves with voices that sounded like music.

"Aggie, me darlin'," declared Salty, who could slip in and out of an Irish brogue as naturally as another man might change his shirt. He stretched out a hand to his newest daughter-in-law. "Come sit beside me while I tell you the story of your children's great-great-great-grandmother, the first police chief of Dogleg Island, Peg O'Brien Grady, and how I knew it was you me boy was destined to marry long before he knew it himself."

Aggie was intrigued, both because of his reference to children yet unborn, and because of the way Ryan wrinkled up his face in a pretense of parental indulgence.

"Now, Dad, don't go bending Aggie's ear with more of your blarney," he said. "Besides, you couldn't possibly have known I was going to marry her before I did because I knew the minute I met her."

"That's the truth," chimed in Lil, her smile benevolent. "He called me that very Sunday, the week after you started at the Sheriff's Office, and he said, 'Mom, I've found the girl I'm going to marry.'"

Grady, who had told Aggie that story multiple times during their courtship, lifted his bottle to her with a twinkle in his eye and an "I told you so" nod. Aggie was a little uncomfortable being the focus of attention, so she said, "Tell me about the police chief."

She left the women's side of the fire pit and went to sit on the arm of Grady's chair. He rested his hand on her hip and offered Aggie a sip of his beer. It would have been un-Irish of her to refuse, so she took one, medication be damned, while Salty regaled them all with the tale of his ancestress, a "wee slip of a lass" with a "passel of young ones clinging to her skirts" who had organized the women of the settlement of Dogleg Island to fight off a band of marauding pirates one brutal winter while the menfolk of the township were off on a hunting expedition. Upon defeating the "dastardly Spaniards" to a man, the people of Dogleg Island raided the invaders' ships for enough supplies to set them up for several winters and rewarded Peg Grady both with a chest of jewels taken from the pirates and the title magistrate for life over Dogleg Island.

Though she doubted a word of it was true, Aggie thought that was one of the best stories she had ever heard, even when Pete pointed out, "The way I heard it, it was a band of Tuskegee Indians she fought off."

Lorraine added, amused, "And the last time you told it, wasn't she six feet tall? Fierce, I believe, is the word you used."

Salty waved a dismissing hand. "Tall, small, Indians, pirates, the details nary matter. The point is that when I heard my boy was keeping time with a woman with the fine Irish name of Aggie Malone, and a lady of the law to boot, I knew it was a match destined to produce another grand line of Grady heroes."

"Hear, hear," declared Pete, and everyone chimed in, lifting their glasses to her. Aggie ducked her head in embarrassment.

"So what happened to the jewels?" Aggie asked when the clamor died down.

Lil replied easily, "Oh, they're still around..." She made a vague gesture with her hand. "Somewhere."

Everybody laughed, and Salty added, "Sure and Begorrah, that's how the grand Grady fortune you see around you today got its start."

Grady got up, grinning, and gave his father a one-armed hug. "I love you, Dad. Another round, everybody?"

Aggie followed him inside, looking in the back of the cabinet for a container big enough to pass for an ice bucket while he took beers from the refrigerator. Except for the ache in her toe and the scrape on her husband's cheek, she could hardly remember the fight in the parking lot, and the picture of the man with the scorpion tattoo shot dead in his car had faded into practical obscurity.

She found a big silver vase that looked as though it might have been a trophy of some sort in its former life, and Grady dumped handfuls of ice into it. He said, "What's that goofy smile for?"

"It's not goofy. I was just thinking what an idiot I was for not marrying you the first time you asked. And what pretty babies we're going to have."

"You're right about that." He brushed a kiss across her lips. "But it is a goofy smile, and you're swaying on your feet." He took the improvised ice bucket from her and stuffed the beers inside. "Why don't you go on up? It's been a long day."

"What, and miss all this?" Aggie gestured through the open back door to the group around the fire pit, who were listening to Salty describe the colorful details of their life in South America. Apparently they grew avocados the size of melons on a tree in their backyard, and picked pineapples, oranges, bananas and lemons year around. Chickens cost a dollar a piece—not a pound, but a piece—although Lil was quick to point out you had to pluck them yourself, which sent everyone into gales of laughter. Except, perhaps, for the story about the family of monkeys who had invaded their pool or the one about the three-foot-long iguana that had somehow found its way to their kitchen countertop, it sounded like paradise.

"Besides," she added, "tomorrow's Sunday, I can sleep in." And then something occurred to her. "Except we should probably make breakfast. Do you think it has to be early?"

Grady cupped her neck affectionately. "Nope. Dad and I make waffles on Sunday. It's a tradition."

"Wow." Aggie leaned against him. "I really do want your folks to stay forever. Maybe if we hired them a maid and a gardener and planted some avocado trees…"

He grinned. "Go to bed. You're getting punchy."

Aggie said, "You all make it seem so easy."

"What's that?"

She shrugged. "The whole family thing. I mean, I love it, and it's great and all, but…" She was momentarily at a loss for words. "It's all a little overwhelming, isn't it?"

He chuckled. "Says the woman who just six hours ago kicked a Secret Service agent's ass."

She looked at him in alarm. "Don't you dare tell your mother that."

"Don't worry." He rubbed his nose wryly, careful to avoid the scrape on his cheek. "Then I'd have to tell her how he kicked mine."

Flash, who had been dozing beside Salty's chair, got up suddenly and trotted inside, staring up at them. A second later Grady's phone rang. Grady said, looking at Flash, "How does he do that?"

"Well," explained Aggie, "cell phones give off a high-pitched signal just before they ring that only dogs can hear..."

"Seriously?"

"Totally made that up," replied Aggie, noticing the way Grady frowned over the caller ID.

"Work," he said, just as she knew he would, and he turned away. "Yeah. Grady," he said and walked a couple of steps away.

Aggie rummaged under the sink for a tray and had just finished putting the ice bucket and an open bottle of wine on it when Grady came back, staring at the phone in his hand with an expression on his face that she had never seen before. Flash waited expectantly for him to speak.

Grady said, "You know how you were just saying family is a little overwhelming for you?" She nodded and he added, "Well, you're going to love this. Your brother-in-law is about to be arrested."

Automatically her eyes swung to Pete, who was clinking his bottle of beer against his father's and laughing at something that had just been said. Before she could even draw in a horrified breath, Grady said, grimly, "Billings' Body Shop called in a report of a car with right-side damage that was dropped off right before closing tonight. There was blood on the fender, human, same type as our victim, Wiesel. The car is registered to Cal Bertram. Lucy's husband."

CHAPTER SEVENTEEN

Flash understood how quickly order could turn to chaos and joy could turn to tears. That was why, of them all, he was the only one who was prepared for the disruption and disorder of the next few hours—although he had to admit that, next to himself, Salty was the most level-headed. While Grady and Aggie were busy on their phones, Salty told Lil to get her purse, and to make sure she brought all their credit cards and the checkbook to their American bank account, in case Cal needed bail. Within minutes they were on their way to Lucy's house, where Lil would stay with the twins while Salty helped his daughter do whatever needed to be done to keep her husband out of jail. Pete and Lorraine wanted to come too, but Salty told them it would probably be a long night and Lorraine should get her rest; they both would likely be needed tomorrow.

Flash bounded into Grady's truck beside Aggie, because there was no question of him letting them go alone. Grady got behind the wheel, his jaw tight and his eyes like thunder. He said, "They'll hold Cal in an interview room until we get there, then take him up to booking."

Aggie said, "I told Lucy to have his lawyer meet us there. He probably won't be arraigned until Monday, but most people don't know what to do when something like this happens, and I think it'll make them both feel better to have a lawyer there."

Grady covered her hand with his own. "Thanks, baby."

He said nothing else until they pulled up in front of the Murphy County Detention Center twenty minutes later. Flash had been to the jail before, but usually went no farther than the administrative offices where Aggie sometimes dropped off papers or talked to lawyers. It wasn't his favorite place, and unless it was too hot he generally preferred to wait in the car. Tonight he didn't hesitate about jumping out of the truck and walking inside between Aggie and Grady. It was pretty clear they were going to need him.

Both Aggie and Grady were in jeans and tee shirts and wore only visitor's badges, but they knew everyone on duty and got their share of nods and "Yo, Cap" and "Hey, Chief" on their way to the interview room at the end of a short gray hallway. Because none of those greetings seemed particularly cautious, Aggie assumed word had not yet spread that it was Captain Grady's brother-in-law who had been brought in for the hit and run.

Grady had called Spence Foster, one of the B-shift deputies who had served the warrant and brought

Cal in, to meet them, and he was waiting outside the interview room for them. He handed Grady a copy of the warrant and went over the details again, even though they already knew them.

"Mr. Bertram dropped off his car at the body shop this afternoon, about six. A green Prius with a broken headlight and dented hood on the right side. He said he thought somebody sideswiped him in the parking lot, that he'd come out of his office and found it like that. Said he wasn't going to file an insurance claim, he just wanted it fixed. He left a number to call with the estimate and got in the car with his wife and kids—at least that's who the fellow that wrote up the work order assumed it was—and drove away. When Billings saw the damage, he called the sheriff's office. Deputy Jackson and I responded. Jackson thought he saw blood on the fender, took a sample, and sent it in for a rush match. It came back human, same type as our victim, so we swore out a warrant and picked Mr. Bertram up at his home about ten o'clock this evening." He looked a little awkward. "I'm sorry, sir, we would've called you sooner, but nobody made the connection. It was Judge Wilkins that signed the warrant, and he recognized the name."

Grady said brusquely, "It's not SOP to ask the family's permission before making an arrest, Foster." Then, with a slight apologetic downward turn of his lips, he added, "But I appreciate the heads-up." He nodded toward the closed door of the room. "What did he have to say for himself?"

Foster shrugged. "Says it's a mistake, we've got the wrong guy, the wrong car...he admits the car is his, though."

Aggie asked, "Does he have an alibi for last night?"

"Says he was working late," Foster answered. He added with a regretful lift of his shoulder, "Alone."

Grady muttered, "Crap," under his breath, and then slapped the palm of his hand with the rolled-up tube he had made of the arrest warrant. "Okay, let's see what we've got. Foster, you got coffee? Good, come sit in, just to keep us honest. After all, the guy is family." And he added, again under his breath, "More or less."

Aggie didn't know her brother-in-law very well. He was tall and lean and going bald; he wore long-sleeved plaid cotton shirts and neatly pressed gray or black trousers, even at family picnics. He was quiet, maybe even a little shy, and if she thought about it, Aggie guessed he probably hadn't said a dozen words to her since she'd known him. When she and Grady attended the requisite family dinner once a month at his house, Cal usually politely excused himself after the meal and went into his study to watch television. But he did their taxes for free and made sure Lucy and the kids lacked for nothing, so Aggie had always assumed he was a good man. But she didn't know him.

He was sitting with his hands clasped on the metal table when they came in, looking as disheveled as Aggie had ever seen him and as distressed as she had expected. Flash came over to greet him, but Cal ignored him, lurching to his feet. "Thank God," he exclaimed. "Maybe you can get this straightened out. This is insane! What am I doing here? What's the matter with these people? They just walk into my house at ten o'clock at night and put handcuffs on me—handcuffs! I'm a respected member of this community, for God's sake! I own my own business! What the hell is going on?"

Those were, Aggie decided, the most words she had ever heard him speak at one time, and definitely the most impassioned.

Grady said, without expression, "Sit down, Cal. You're making Deputy Foster here nervous."

Cal shot a quick frightened glance at Spence Foster, who stood by the door. He did not look in the least nervous, but he was wearing a gun. Cal dropped back into his chair, swallowing hard. Grady pulled out a chair across the table and flung himself into it, tossing the rolled-up arrest warrant onto the table in front of him. Aggie seated herself next to him. When he was upset, Grady sometimes forgot his manners.

Flash, finding an empty chair next to Aggie, hopped into it and prepared to listen.

Cal licked his lips and clasped his hands together again on the table. He leaned forward and said anxiously, "There are metal rings screwed into the floor." He shot an uncertain glance toward Deputy Foster and lowered his voice. "And the table!"

"Leg restraints and handcuffs," Grady answered briefly.

"Christ," whispered Cal.

Grady said, "Okay, Cal, let's get down to business. Why don't you tell me what happened?"

Aggie laid a calming hand on her husband's arm but spoke to Cal. "Lucy's probably here already," she said. Her tone was kind but even. "Lil is taking care of the boys. Your lawyer is on his way and you can wait for him if you want to. We might be family, Cal, but we're still cops, and we're investigating this case. You don't have to talk to us if you don't want to. Do you understand?"

Grady shot her a dark look, but Cal swallowed again and nodded. "Yes," he said, with some difficulty. "Yes, I understand. They read me my rights." He ran a hand across the glistening expanse of his forehead and exclaimed again softly. "Christ! They read me my rights." And he simply stared at his in-laws as though expecting them to share his incredulity. But Aggie and Grady had seen too much, and most of it worse than this, to be impressed.

Aggie went on, "The only reason you're here instead of booking right now is because you're family. But when we're done here, you will be fingerprinted, and photographed, and assigned a cell. You'll probably have to spend the night. I'm sorry, that's how it works. We're going to try to help you, Cal, but talking to us could also hurt you. I just want to make sure you know that."

Cal looked at her helplessly.

Grady said, "What were you doing on Dogleg Island last night?"

Cal stared at him and swallowed hard. It took perhaps half a beat before he managed, "What? What are you talking about? What would I be doing there? I don't have any clients there. I don't even know anybody there except you guys, and Pete and Lorraine. Why would you think I was there?"

Aggie said, watching him, "A man by the name of Elijah Wiesel was struck by a car and killed on Island Road last night around 9:30. The blood on your fender matches his."

All the color drained from Cal's face. Flash sat up alertly, and Aggie half-rose from her chair, ready to call for a medic. Grady glanced at Foster and said, "Can you get us some water from the cooler?"

Foster hurried out and returned in a moment with a cone-shaped paper cup filled with water. Cal gulped it down, holding it with shaking hands. Some of the water spilled on his chin, and he did not appear to notice. He said, at length, "Dead? A man is dead?"

Aggie nodded solemnly.

Grady said, completely without expression, "So where were you last night between eight and eleven o'clock? You're going to hear this question a lot, so think before you answer."

He blinked. "I was at work. I told your people—I mean the deputies—before, I was at the office."

"Your office closes at six," Grady said.

"Quarterly taxes are due December thirty-first for most of our corporate clients. It's a busy time for us. I work late almost every night in December. Ask Lucy."

Grady's jaw tightened but he said nothing. It was Aggie who prompted, "You were at the office the whole time? Can anyone vouch for you?"

His Adam's apple bobbed, and he shook his head. "Everyone else went home. I locked up."

"What time did you get home?" Grady wanted to know.

"I don't know. Eleven, eleven thirty."

Grady said, "And you drove your own car home?"

He seemed confused. "Of course."

Aggie said, "When did you notice the damage?"

Cal looked down at his hands, twisted together on the table. Aggie followed his gaze. It was impossible not to notice the white scar on his finger where a wedding band had been removed. He moved his hands to his lap. He said, "It was dark when I got in the car last night. I parked in the garage when I got home and didn't look at the passenger side. This morning, same thing. I got in, drove to work, parked. I had no reason to look at the passenger side until one of my employees noticed it at lunchtime and asked me what happened. It looked like someone had hit me in the parking lot last night, or maybe this morning. I was pretty upset, but the damage didn't look that bad. I made arrangements to drop the car off for repairs. Lucy followed me over, we took the kids out for pizza, and went home. The next thing I know two deputies are banging on my door..."

Aggie said, "Why didn't you file an insurance claim?"

He blinked. "What?"

"The repairs are going to run into the thousands of dollars," Aggie explained patiently. "That's a brand-new Prius, I know you have full coverage on it. So why did you tell the body shop this wasn't going to be an insurance claim?"

"I—I'm not sure I said that, I—"

"Because in order to file an insurance claim, you need a police report," Grady broke in shortly. "And you didn't report the accident to the police. Why not?"

Cal stared at him. "What's this about?" he demanded. "I don't see what this has to do with—"

Grady said, "When you parked your car, did you back into the space, or pull in straight?"

Cal blinked. "I pulled in straight, like I always do. My spot is right beside the front door. That's why I didn't notice—"

"Then how do you suppose the front headlight got damaged in the parking lot?" Grady demanded. "The front of the car was facing the building, right? How did it sustain damage to the front?"

Cal's expression slowly changed from confusion to muted anger. "How am I supposed to know that? I thought you were here to help! Whose side are you on?"

Grady drew in a sharp breath. but Aggie spoke before he could. "We're on the side of truth, Cal," she said. "And so far here is what we know to be true." She ticked off the items on her fingers as she spoke. "A man was killed last night on Dogleg Island at about

9:30 in a hit and run incident. Your car has damage consistent with the accident. Blood on your car matches that of the victim. And no one can vouch for your whereabouts at the time of the incident."

Cal just stared at her. Aggie wasn't sure whether it was because he hadn't understood what she said, or whether he was genuinely just that scared. She suspected it might be a combination of both.

Grady said quietly, "Here's the deal, dude. You asked whose side I was on. I'm on your side, and because you're married to my sister I'm going to give you the best advice you ever got. You need to level with us right now before things get any worse. There's nothing we can't deal with as long as you tell the truth. But this is a homicide case. It may be vehicular homicide, but it's still some serious shit. And the worst thing you can do right now is lie to me."

"I'm not lying!" Cal cried. There was desperation in his eyes and a sheen of sweat on his face. "I didn't have anything to do with that man's death! It wasn't me, I swear! You've got to believe me!"

Neither Aggie nor Grady said anything in reply. Silence was an effective interrogation technique, but in this case the fact was that neither one of them knew what to say.

Cal swiped a hand across his face in a frantic gesture. He said quickly, "Maybe the car was stolen. That must be it." Relief crept across his face. "That's got to be it! Somebody stole my car and used it to commit the crime!"

"And then returned it to its parking space when they were done?" Grady did not do a very good job of keeping the skepticism out of his voice.

Cal looked at him helplessly. "That's got to be it. What other explanation can there be?"

Grady said nothing. He just looked at him with eyes that were hard and unforgiving.

Aggie said, "Your car is push-start ignition, isn't it? You can't start it without the key fob."

Cal looked embarrassed. "I know it's stupid, but I've gotten in the habit of leaving the fob in the console when I'm just driving around town. I kept getting it confused with Lucy's car and walking out of the house with the wrong one, so it's easier not to carry it with me. I know that means anybody can just open the door and push the button to drive off, but this is Murphy County, for crying out loud. You don't think about things like that." He dropped his head to his hands and his voice was muffled as he said, "Maybe I should have."

Aggie and Grady shared a glance.

Aggie said, "I'll go see if your lawyer is here. He'll explain what happens next. They probably won't let Lucy in tonight, but she can see you tomorrow during regular visiting hours. Is there anything you want us to tell her meantime?"

He raised his head, looking stricken. "Tomorrow? Do you mean I have to spend the night? Can't you do something?"

Aggie said patiently, "It isn't up to us. It depends on the judge's schedule. Your lawyer will explain."

She thought he might cry.

Grady said, "Are you sure you don't have anything else to tell us?"

Cal dropped his gaze and shook his head miserably.

Aggie, Grady and Flash got up and left the room.

They were silent as they walked down the short corridor toward the visitor's lobby, but before they got there, Aggie touched Grady's arm and said, "Hold on a minute." She turned and went down the hall that led to the intake desk. Grady and Flash followed.

She asked the clerk for an inventory list of Cal's belongings when he was brought in, and she studied it, frowning. Grady looked over her shoulder. "Key fob?"

She shook her head. "He would've left it at the repair shop."

"Then what are you looking for?"

Aggie pointed at the third item on the list and looked at the clerk. "All of this was the contents of his pockets?"

The clerk replied, "That's right. They keep their own clothing until they go into general population."

"What about the wedding band?" Aggie asked.

"If it's on the list, it was in his pockets."

Aggie thanked her and slid the paper back beneath the slot in the window.

Aggie thrust her hands into her own pockets as they walked back toward the lobby. It was after midnight on a Saturday which, sad to say, was one of the peak traffic times for the Murphy County Detention Center. Lucy and Salty waited among bail bondsmen, angry wives whose husbands had been brought in on a DUI, a man with a black eye talking loudly on the phone about the complaint he was going to file, and a big-boned, heavily made-up woman—or perhaps man—in gold lame bellbottoms whose business there was anyone's guess.

The minute Lucy saw Grady she launched herself from the chair and into his arms. He hugged her hard. Salty got to his feet, smiling wearily at Aggie, just as Lucy pushed away from her brother and hit him on the chest with her closed fist. "Is *this* what you do all day?" she demanded angrily. "Arrest innocent people? What's the matter with you? Where's Cal?"

Lucy had her mother's round face and predisposition toward plumpness; she unfortunately did not have her mother's personality. She wore her brown hair in a ponytail, and was dressed tonight in an unflattering pair of beige cargo shorts and an oversized tee shirt with flip-flops. Her face was blotchy with emotion.

Grady said, "Look, sis, you need to calm down. We'll do what we can but—"

"I have *children*!" she cried. "Your—your *storm troopers* broke into my house in the middle of the night in front of my children and dragged their father away in handcuffs! In *handcuffs*! What are you going to do about it? What's the point of having a cop in the family if this is how you get treated? You need to do something and you need to do it now, do you hear me?"

Her voice was starting to rise to a hysterical note, and Salty put a firm hand on her shoulder. "Lucy," he said, "it's not your brother's fault that you're here, nor that your husband is behind bars instead of at home with his children where he belongs. So what I need you to do right now is be quiet and listen, can you do that?" He looked at Grady. "What can you tell us, son?"

Up until that moment, Aggie would not have left her husband to deal with Lucy, no matter what it cost her. But with the battering wave of overwhelming fatigue came relief when she looked at Salty and she thought, *He's got this.* She touched Grady's shoulder. "I'm going to take Flash to the car," she said.

She didn't wait for him to respond. She was just glad to get out of there.

Aggie got into the truck and cracked the windows just a fraction to keep them from fogging up. She leaned her head back against the headrest and said tiredly, "What about it, Flash? Do you think he was telling the truth?"

Even if Flash had been able to answer, he wasn't sure he would have. Despite Cal's unfortunate relationship with the twins, he was still family, and there was such a thing as loyalty. So Flash just rested his head on Aggie's knee, offering what comfort he could. Aggie sighed and stroked his head.

"Yeah," she said. "Me, neither."

Grady returned to the truck forty-five minutes later. He got behind the wheel and started the engine, but seemed for a moment too weary to speak. "Well, he's in booking," he said eventually. "The lawyer got there. Thinks bail might be set tomorrow."

"That'll be good," Aggie offered.

"Twenty-five-grand bond."

"Not good," she said.

"Yeah."

He put the car into gear and left the parking lot. Before they reached the bridge, he said, "Do you have any aspirin?"

Aggie dug into her purse and found a bottle, but couldn't get the top off. "Sorry," she said.

They drove the rest of the way home in silence.

Hours later, they lay beside each other in bed, listening to the ocean pound the shore two blocks away with such force that it seemed to shake the house. The doors were open to the balcony where Flash slept, and a restless breeze billowed the curtains and rattled a vase of dried flowers on the dresser. Grady lay with one arm across his forehead and the other stretched across Aggie's pillow, fingers resting lightly on her shoulder. Aggie stared at the ceiling, her eyes aching with fatigue, wide awake.

She said softly, "How's your headache?"

"Almost gone," he lied.

They listened to the surf slapping and splashing, groaning and hissing. After a long time, Aggie said, "Ryan...do you ever take off your wedding band?"

He gave a soft grunt of surprise and amusement. "What, are you kidding me? I worked too hard to get this thing. Why would I take it off?"

"Not even to work on the boat or the water heater or—"

"Crap," he muttered. "I forgot the water heater."

"—or, I don't know, to make pastry? Not even then?"

"Not even."

She said, "I love you so much."

"So," she went on hesitantly, "why would a happily married man take off his wedding band and put it in his pocket?"

He was quiet for a time. "I can only think of one reason."

She turned to him, trying to read his expression in the dark. "Because he's not happily married?"

He didn't answer, but he didn't have to. Aggie slid close to him, her head on his shoulder, her arm across his chest. He drew her into his embrace, and eventually they slept.

CHAPTER EIGHTEEN

His name was Samuel Harris Roosevelt, Jr.—
people called him Rosie—and he was, for the
most part, a good man. He'd worked hard and gotten good grades in school, helped his father out on
weekends sweeping up and loading the truck and
making deliveries when he was old enough. He got
a guitar for his ninth birthday and picked it up like
he'd been playing all his life. By the time he was sixteen he'd earned enough working part time to buy
his first used saxophone, and he was good at that,
too. Music was easy for him. He learned the cello
and a little violin, and he could play any tune on the
piano after hearing it once. He played in the school
orchestra and took private lessons on the side, and
even got a partial music scholarship to Florida State.

His Pop had been torn between pride and disappointment. Samuel Harris Roosevelt, Sr. was a
proud black man from rural Murphy County who
had started his own business in 1966 with nothing
but a used Ford pickup truck and a knack for getting things done. He believed in hard work, a winning attitude, and making the customer happy, and

those were exactly the qualities he had passed on to his son. He'd always planned for his boy to go to college—why else would he have worked so hard, building up the business, making it into something his family could be proud of—unless it was for his kids? So Rosie would go to college, get a degree in something important, like business or finance, and when the time came he'd be ready to take over the business, build it into something fine for *his* children. Music was not part of the plan.

But neither was the stroke that brought down Sam Roosevelt, Sr. eighteen months later. Rosie left college in his second year and came home to run the shop, and, except sometimes late at night in the privacy of his dreams, he never looked back. He took care of his mother until she died and sisters until they married, and he built up the business, just like his Pop had raised him to. He married a curvy blond woman who still, after all these years, made him go all quivery inside when he thought about her, and they had two boys who went to a school where they had to wear ties. He had a pretty little Colonial house in a nice part of town, with big pots of geraniums on the porch. These days he didn't do much with the saxophone, but he played a little guitar now and then at church. He was doing okay. Sam Senior would've been proud. Life was good.

Or at least it had been, until 2009. He wasn't sure what had happened. Sure, online shopping was eating away at the small businessman. Sure, everybody had been hit hard during the recession. He'd had to borrow, for the first time in his life, just to stay afloat. But the interest on the note was higher than the principal, so he'd refinanced his house to pay it off. That had seemed liked a good idea at the time, but now the money was gone and the mortgage payments kept coming. And then the hurricane in April ripped half the roof off his house and shut down his business for two weeks. A store full of perishable inventory gone, just like that. Deliveries disrupted. Utilities off. Customers lost. Insurance had paid for about half of it. He was still waiting for the money he had applied for from federal disaster relief, but he didn't think it would be enough to make a difference.

His credit cards were maxed out and sometimes he couldn't even make the monthly minimum. Their retirement fund had gone first, what there was of it, and now he was looking at the kids' college fund. He hadn't told his wife about that. He didn't know how much longer he could keep the boys in that school where they were so proud to wear ties. And then, the last straw. The letter came from the IRS, the one he must have surely known was coming, but had somehow hoped, desperately prayed, would never find him. The one demanding immediate payment of $12,345.17 in back taxes and penalties, or face jail time.

Jail time. Last month, he'd given a speech at the Rotary Club. Now he was facing jail time. What would his Pop say? How could this have happened?

What happened next was an answer to prayer. How could it have been anything else? He was a good man who woke up every day with a dry throat and a weight on his chest, praying to God until sweat ran down his face for some answer, some help, some way out. And at the darkest, most terrifying moment of his life, the answer had come. Manna from heaven. Provisions from the Almighty. He was a good man and God had taken pity on him. He deserved this. Finally, finally, everything was going to be all right.

Except that, in his heart, nothing had ever felt more wrong.

And he didn't know what to do.

Sometimes in his dreams Flash remembered the time when he was new, and the world was covered in blood and thunder. It had been Grady who unlocked the cage and pulled him out, and Flash remembered how safe he'd felt in Grady's arms, even later, when they were alone and the big man's whole body shook with sobs. Sometimes in his dreams the smell of blood and the wail of sirens would make Flash whimper softly in his sleep, but not for long, because then he would remember the nest Grady had made for him on the pillow next to his in the bed where Aggie and Grady—and usually Flash—now slept every night. They'd spent a lot of nights together, Flash and Grady, waiting for Aggie to wake up in the hospital where she slept far away. And every morning, when the first pale light speckled the scarred oak floor, they would get up and go to the beach and run.

Except for in his dreams, Flash didn't think much about the old times, the sad times. He didn't see the point in it, when in the today times they all were sleeping under the same roof and waking up happy to be together every day. Still, he and Grady ran on the beach every morning while they waited for Aggie to wake up, and if he *had* thought about it, Flash would think that, in an odd way, that special time they had together running on the beach was like remembering. And like saying thank you.

Sometimes, when the sun was hot and Grady didn't have to hurry to go to work, they would dive in the waves before coming home to Aggie, but usually they only did that in the summer. Today had been a treat, although Flash thought it might also have something to do with the dark thoughts that had pounded at Grady like the sound of his running shoes on the sand. After their swim, though, Grady seemed to feel better, and was more or less content to find a sunny spot on their deck at home and wait for Aggie to wake up. Grady checked his phone and drank coffee and was silent with his thoughts, which was okay with Flash. The best part about their mornings together was that, most of the time, Flash didn't have to think about anything at all.

The temperature had dropped thirty degrees overnight. Aggie awoke a little past ten to find that Grady had covered her with an extra blanket, which she wrapped around her shoulders when she got out of bed. Shivering, she pulled on a pair of sweats and wooly socks and went out onto the deck, where Grady and Flash sat in the sun, sheltered from the chill sea breeze by the adjacent wall. Flash's fur was damp, and so was Grady's hair. She sat on Grady's knee and kissed him good morning, spreading the blanket over both of them. Grady slipped his arm around her waist, resting his hand on her hip bone. Flash came over for his morning petting. She kissed him too, on the nose.

"Did you guys go for a swim?" she asked. "That water must've been freezing."

"Warmer than the shower."

She brushed her fingers lightly across the abrasion on his cheek, a series of small scabs and a yellow bruise beneath his eye. "How does it feel?"

"Like it never happened."

"You're a rock." She ruffled his hair lightly. "And insurance is not going to pay for this if it turns out you have a concussion later."

"Noted."

He offered her his coffee cup and she took a sip, holding it with both hands. Flash returned to his sunny spot to finish drying his fur. The three of them sat easily for a while, gazing at the brilliant blue strip of ocean in the distance, listening to the sigh of waves.

"You know," Grady observed, retrieving his coffee cup. "There are times when I could just sit here all day, watching the ocean. This is one of them."

"I know what you mean." She caressed the back of his neck, then let her arm drop to his shoulder. "Did you hear from your folks?"

"I had a text from Mom." He sipped his coffee. "They're going to stay with Lucy until Cal gets home. The lawyer thinks he can get him in front of a judge this afternoon, but the problem is going to be raising enough money for bond on a Sunday. We're all pitching in, but I've only got about five hundred left on my credit card."

"I've got almost a thousand," Aggie volunteered. She added, almost apologetically, "I haven't done my Christmas shopping yet."

He smiled his gratitude and handed his cup to her. She took another sip. She said, "You know what we should do? Sail to Bimini."

"Where's that?"

"I'm not sure, but I've always wanted to go there. It could be our honeymoon."

He slanted a grin up at her, caressing the small of her back. "I like the way you think. Can you be packed in an hour?"

"What's to pack? A couple of bikinis and a box of dog biscuits, and we're set."

He laughed softly, and they finished off the coffee, passing the cup back and forth between them while Flash dozed in the sun.

Aggie said after a time, "You know, if somebody did want to steal a car, a Prius would be the one to take. It's silent below twenty-five miles per hour. And it's quieter than other cars on the road, which could explain why a hit and run victim might not have heard it coming, even at normal speed."

He gave a skeptical grunt. "So you're telling me a car thief wandered around town looking for a Prius to steal, happened to find one sitting in an empty parking lot in front of an accounting office with the key fob in the console, went for a joy ride across the bridge, killed somebody, drove it back where he found it, and went home."

"Maybe," she said. "Maybe somebody saw Cal leave the key fob, or knew that he did it, or maybe somebody walked around checking doors until he found one unlocked. Happens all the time. As for returning it...what would you do if you'd just committed a hit and run? Leave the car at the scene and run away on foot? Take a stolen car home with you?"

"Me?" he said. He glanced at the empty coffee cup and leaned forward to set it on the rail. "I'd drive it into a swamp and leave it there. Then I'd get the hell out of Dodge."

"That's because you're smarter than the average crook," she conceded.

"Why, thank you, darlin'." He traced the knobs of her spine with his fingertips. "You're not really buying that 'I was framed' defense, are you?"

"Well, you know what Sherlock Holmes said. 'When you've eliminated the impossible, whatever remains, however improbable, must be the truth.'"

Grady scrunched his eyes closed briefly and rubbed the bridge of his nose. "Damn it," he said. "It was all I could do not to punch the guy out last night."

She caressed his shoulder. "I was proud of you."

"It's just that..." He blew out a breath through his teeth. "She's my sister, you know?"

Aggie dropped her chin to the top of his head. "I know."

They were quiet for a time, listening to the sound of the surf, watching the sun-sparks on the water. Aggie said, "He's got a clean record. It's second-degree homicide. He could plead down to five years, be out in two. But his lawyer has got to convince him to confess."

"Anybody can make a mistake," Grady said, his voice still tight and angry. "But you don't lie about it. You don't get yourself arrested and then *lie* to the law, to your wife, your *family*, for God's sake."

Aggie said carefully, "We don't know the whole story. Innocent until proven guilty."

He gave a grunt of derision. "How much more proof do you need? Jesus, I can't believe we're talking about a member of my family."

Aggie said, frowning a little, "The only thing I can't quite figure out is the money. The counterfeit hundred with blood on it. How did it get way across the field next to Park Street, when the body was over a hundred feet away?"

Grady shrugged. "Wind?"

"It was foggy that night," she reminded him. "Not that much wind."

"Maybe we'll get a fingerprint match tomorrow," Grady said. He added, without much conviction, "Maybe it won't be Cal's."

"Did you listen to the 911 tape?"

Grady said, "Yeah, yesterday afternoon. It was a male, that's all I can say for sure. I'll listen to it again, but the voice didn't sound familiar to me the first time. I don't think it was Cal."

Aggie's tone was thoughtful. "Then it had to be a witness. Somebody saw the accident and for whatever reason didn't want to be identified. That's who we need to find. I mean, there's always traffic on Island Road—maybe not much, but some, and 9:30 isn't that late. You'd have to be the luckiest man in the world to have an accident there with no witnesses."

"Or unluckiest," Grady pointed out, "if you were the victim."

Aggie sighed. "Right." She added, "I've still got some doors to knock on."

Grady said, "I'm going to go down to the impound yard to have a look at the car for myself."

"You shouldn't have to work this case," Aggie said.

"I'm in charge of investigations," he pointed out. "No choice. Even if it was you sitting behind bars, I'd still be on the case."

"If it was me sitting behind bars," she said, "there's no one else I'd want on the case."

He looked at her. "Exactly."

Grady's phone rang. He glanced at the ID, then at Aggie. "It's Lucy," he said.

Aggie said, "She probably wants to know why you're not there."

"Wherever 'there' is," he agreed, staring at the phone.

"You should answer it."

"I'm going to."

Aggie said hesitantly, "You know, it's not that I'm unsympathetic to what she's going through, but I really think I can be more useful right now as an investigator than a sister-in-law."

Grady gave her a sour glance. "I think you're getting off easy."

"Maybe you could explain it to her," Aggie suggested.

"Coward."

Aggie kissed his hair and stood up. "I'll keep you up to date."

He answered the phone with a resigned, "Hey, sis. How're you holding up?"

The day did not go exactly as Flash had expected. For one thing, there were no waffles for breakfast, and he was certain he had heard Grady say something about waffles last night. Grady made eggs with cheese, though, which were fine, then got in the truck and went across the bridge, just as though it was a normal work day. Aggie put on her navy pants and white sweater and her blue wool jacket with the gold badge pinned to it, and they went to the office, which was strange, because it wasn't a normal office day. Sally Ann wasn't at work, and the only cars in town were parked in the lot that surrounded the church. Even the bakery was closed, and the good smells that usually floated from its kitchen and in through the cracks around the doors and windows of the police station were absent. Aggie made coffee and turned on her computer, but didn't turn on the Christmas lights or the music. It was all rather depressing, and Flash lay beneath her desk with his head on his paws and thought about waffles. But his ears pricked up when Aggie spoke.

"I don't know, Flash," she said, her eyes on the computer screen. "People make such a big deal over family, but if you ask me most of the time we're a lot better off with the people we choose than the people we were born with, you know what I mean?"

Flash did not, but he listened anyway.

"The thing is," she went on, clicking the mouse, "when it's family, you're stuck with their mistakes, their problems, and you have to deal with them whether you like it or not. I mean, what's Grady supposed to say to his sister? 'Too bad about your husband and the father of your children, but he's lying to us all and he's probably going to jail and he deserves it'? If he does his job as a cop, she hates him. If he tries to be a good brother, she hates him. Not to mention me," she muttered, clicking the mouse again, "who she's always hated. I'll tell you, Flash..." She stopped, her eyes scanning the screen for a moment in silence. Then she said softly, "Bingo. That's what I thought."

She glanced at the clock on the opposite wall—now wreathed in plastic greenery and shiny red jingle bells—and pushed up from the desk. "Come on, Flash. We've got just enough time to check out the scene before our witness gets out of church."

Beach property was valued differently than in other places. For example, in the average community, a corner lot that overlooked the back parking lot of a bar on one side, a row of rental houses on another, and a dirt road on the third would not have been particularly desirable. But Betsy Everest's three-story Victorian with its tiers of wraparound porches, architectural shingles, and gingerbread trim, had a view of the ocean from the second floor and a view of the lagoon from the third, not to mention—as Sally Ann had pointed out—a perfect sight line to almost everything that happened in any direction from the big bay window in the living room. Its size, location and beautifully landscaped yard made it a landmark on Dogleg Island. Aggie drove past it almost every day, either on patrol or on her way to Pete's. Still, she wanted to check it out one more time, just to make sure.

Aggie parked in front of the Everest house and looked around. Five hundred feet away to the west was the back parking lot of Pete's Place. It was closed on Sundays, and would have been even if Pete and

Lorraine, along with the rest of the family, hadn't been sucked into Lucy's crisis. The parking lot was empty. So were most of the driveways down Old Stillwater Way, the majority of them marked by "seasonal rental" signs. Half a block down Grady Plantation Drive, a bunch of red and white balloons bounced in the wind in front of a house for sale, indicating an afternoon open house. An occasional car cruised down Island Drive, but for the most part all was quiet on this chill, bright Sunday morning.

"No security system," Aggie observed to Flash, who was staring fixedly out the window toward Pete's Place. Following the direction of his gaze, she shook her head. "Pete's cameras are pointed in the wrong direction. They wouldn't reach the street."

Actually, Flash had been wondering whether they might be stopping by Pete's for lunch, since he still had unfinished business there. But when Aggie spoke he decided it might be best to concentrate on one case at a time. He shifted his weight in the seat and looked forward, paying attention.

"Sally Ann was right, though," she murmured. "Mrs. Everest has a perfect view of everything that goes on around here for three blocks."

Eighteen oh eight Stillwater Way, about which Betsy Everest had called in the report Friday night, was two houses down across the street, the driveway completely visible from where Aggie sat, and probably even clearer from Mrs. Everest's second-story bay window. "Of course, it was dark," Aggie admitted. "And she's an old woman." But there were four sets of windows on 1808, Aggie couldn't help noticing, all facing this way.

Her phone buzzed. It was a text from Grady: *Arraignment postponed. Lucy ballistic. Home in a couple.*

She replied: *I'm sorry. Not enough evidence?*

They both knew Judge Wilkins, who covered weekends in December, was a fair man who would not force a first-time offender to spend a weekend in jail if there was sufficient evidence that he was being held on a technicality or could easily bond out. On the other hand, he wasn't likely to give up a family dinner to hold Sunday court for someone who was clearly guilty. It made her heart sink when Grady typed back, *Right.*

She knew she was giving false hope, but false hope was better than none at all, so she replied, *Working on something. I'll let you know if it pans out. See you soon. Xxoo*

He answered, *Love you more,* which made her smile.

She started the engine and drove to St. Michael's Episcopal Church, where she and Flash got out of the car and waited for their witness to come out.

Chapter Nineteen

Rosie had been raised in a Bible-thumping country church where Sunday service lasted most of the day and the judgment of the Almighty was nothing to be trifled with. When he married a white woman, he found that judgment turned on him—not necessarily by God, but by most of his sisters in the Lord, who somehow felt betrayed when one of their own married outside their race. In the end it was easier for him to start going to church with his wife Elise over on the island, and after a while, he found he actually preferred the gentility and ritual of the Episcopal church, and enjoyed the welcoming, accepting nature of the island congregation.

Father Dave wasn't much like the preachers he had grown up with, but he was still a man of God, and he had the added advantage of being easy to talk to. Rosie had known, as he was getting dressed for church that morning and he couldn't even look his wife in the eye—as he was folding down the collar of his gray turtleneck, adjusting the lapel of his sports jacket, and listening to her prattle on in the background about needing to go back to the church after dinner to help the ladies wrap Christmas presents for the church party later that night and organize the children's coat distribution and it was all he could do not to shout at her to shut up, to just *shut up* for one minute and let him *think*—he knew then he had to talk to somebody. Father Dave would know what to do. He might not look or sound like a real preacher, but he knew about things. Rosie could trust him.

So he slipped two folded one-hundred-dollar bills into the collection box with a silent prayer for blessing and took his place at the side of the podium with the other musicians. He accompanied the soloist in a rendition of "Mary Did You Know?" and did an acoustic background piece while Father Dave read the devotional. He was dimly amazed by the way his fingers could remember the chords when his mind was on nothing that resembled the music.

He wouldn't tell the priest what had happened, he decided. He wasn't ready for that, not yet, not until...just not yet. Instead, he'd present a hypothetical: *Father, do you think God sometimes uses the devil to do his work?* Or *Father, suppose you went to the ATM and instead of a hundred dollars it gave you a thousand, and when you tried to fix the mistake the bank added a thousand dollars to your account and nothing you could do would convince them the money wasn't yours. Wouldn't it be okay to keep it?* Or *What if a man had a child who needed an operation and he found a bag full of stolen money that would pay for that operation...wouldn't that be the hand of God? Wouldn't it?*

Once, a long time ago, he'd been wrestling with a decision—he couldn't remember what it was now—and his Pop had told him, "Son, if you have to ask somebody else whether you're doing the right thing, chances are you're not. So what you really need to ask yourself now is can you live with your choice?"

Those were the words he had been trying not to remember for two days. And now, sitting in church while Father Dave talked about wise men from afar and their gifts of faith, he could hear his Pop's voice as clearly as if he were standing right in front of him: *Can you live with your choice?*

The Lord did not reward iniquity. God didn't use the devil to do his work. There was right, and there was wrong. Father Dave ought to try preaching on that some day.

Rosie knew what he had to do. And that was even before he left the church and saw the police in the parking lot, waiting for him.

Betsy Everest was a small, neat woman with silver hair worn in a stylish clip and practical, block-heeled shoes. She distinguished herself as the widow of a prominent citizen by her discreet diamond stud earrings and the snow-white cashmere shawl she wore over the jacket of her lavender silk pantsuit. Aggie watched as she paused in the vestibule to say a few words to the rector, and then she and Flash moved forward. She caught up with the other woman as she was activating the remote to unlock her car.

"Mrs. Everest," Aggie said, holding out her hand. "I'm Aggie Malone, Dogleg Island Police."

The woman looked at her, looked at her extended hand, and replied, "I know who you are, you silly girl. I read the papers, don't I?" She glanced down at Flash. "And this, I presume, is your deputy?"

Aggie let her hand drop. Other parishioners, filing out to their cars, glanced at them and moved on. She said, "I'm following up on a report you filed Friday night. I didn't want to interrupt your Sunday afternoon, so I thought if you could take a minute to answer a quick question or two..."

Betsy Everest lifted a skeptical eyebrow. "And you couldn't do this during normal business hours?"

Aggie smiled apologetically. "Like I said, it will only take a minute."

Betsy Everest put on a tolerant expression and folded her gloved hands at her waist, her classic black purse dangling from her wrist. "Very well. Go on."

Aggie tucked her fingers into her jacket pockets. The sun was bright, but she was freezing. She said, "I noticed you called in the report of a disturbance at around 9:00 on Friday night. Could you tell me what first alerted you?"

She sniffed imperceptibly. "Well, it's an empty house, isn't it? Pure dark outside, car doors slamming, lights on, music...It was a nice night out," she explained before Aggie could ask. "I had my windows open. There's nothing wrong with my hearing."

"Did you happen to notice the make of the cars in the driveway?" Aggie prompted. "The report didn't say."

Again her nose twitched with disdain. "That's because it turned out to be nothing but that real estate agent, gallivanting around at all hours again. But how was I to know that? She got a new car. A red SUV. She used to drive a Lincoln. *That* I could recognize."

Aggie nodded sympathetically. "You did the right thing, Mrs. Everest. It's always better to report suspicions than not to get involved. And I'm sure the homeowner appreciates your vigilance."

The other woman gave a small eye roll, and Aggie tried not to smile.

"So that was all you saw?" Aggie prompted. "The red SUV in the driveway, and the lights on in the house? Were there any other cars?"

"Not unless you mean the one her gentleman friend parked behind my house, on the street across from the bar," replied Mrs. Everest. "One of those electric jobs that don't make any noise. But I saw the headlights. That's the first thing that was suspicious. There's plenty of parking over in that bar's lot, no reason to be leaving your car on the street."

Aggie's heart sank. "Do you know what kind of car it was? Maybe the color?"

She shook her head. "Some kind of sedan, not very big. Light colored, maybe pale green or blue. You know how streetlights wash everything out."

Streetlights. Of course. There were two of them there on the corner, which was how Mrs. Everest had seen so much in the dark. Aggie said, "What about the driver? Did you recognize him?"

She gave a firm shake of her head. "I did not. If I had, I wouldn't have called the police. I'm not a troublemaker. Youngish man, maybe late thirties, but bald on top. Plaid shirt, beige trousers. Nervous way about him. That's the first thing I noticed. He walked right across my yard, almost tripped over my sprinkler, real quick like. Nervous. Then I saw him again through the window across the street, when the music started. That's when I figured I'd better call somebody. I knew the house wasn't rented. He didn't have any luggage. It just looked suspicious to me. I'm not a busybody. I'm just trying to be a good neighbor."

Aggie smiled weakly. "Yes, ma'am. We appreciate it, really. Do you remember what time you noticed the car? The sedan, I mean?"

She thought for a moment. "Maybe eight thirty, eight forty-five? I remember it was before my show started at nine, because when the sheriff's office called back I had to pause it. That was probably around nine thirty."

Aggie said, "Thank you, Mrs. Everest. You've been a big help." She started to turn away.

"Of course," added the older woman, "the car was gone by then."

Aggie looked at her.

"The sedan," she explained, "the one parked on Grady Plantation behind my house. The SUV was still in the driveway, but the car was gone. I know because the phone is by the window, and when I went to answer it I couldn't help looking out and noticing."

Aggie said, "Did you notice what time it left?"

She replied, "Like I said, those electric things don't make any noise. And I was busy with my show." She was thoughtful for a moment. "Here's something odd, though. When I hung up the phone I looked out the window again and that man, the one in the plaid shirt, was closing the blinds in the house across the street. I saw him plain as day. So I guess it wasn't his car that was parked there, after all."

Aggie said, "You're certain? You saw the man in the house across the street, but the car was gone?"

She looked annoyed. "That's what I said, isn't it?"

"And that was while you were on the phone with the sheriff's deputy?"

Her lips pursed in irritation. "Young lady, if you're going to ask questions, you really ought to pay attention to the answers. And I'll tell you something else. When I went to turn off the lights at eleven—it was a two-hour show—the car was right back there under the streetlight. So whoever the driver was must've left and come back. I just don't understand why he had to park in the street and walk across my yard. There ought to be some kind of regulation against that, don't you think? Aren't you in charge of traffic control?"

Aggie said, "I'll look into it, Mrs. Everest. Thanks again for your help. Come on, Flash."

Flash, whose attention was elsewhere, turned to follow her, disappointed and confused that she hadn't once noticed the bourbon-and-roses man who was staring at them from across the way.

Grady had told Aggie once that Wendy Coker used to be a model at boat shows. The photo on her real estate sign must have been from those days: wind-blown blond hair, perky boobs in a V-neck tee, a blinding white smile. Of course, that was fifteen years ago. Today's reality was sun-baked skin, too much makeup, and an over-sprayed platinum bob. But the perky boobs were the same, despite a slightly larger midriff, as was the brilliant smile with which she greeted Aggie and Flash when they walked in.

"Oops!" she said. "No dogs, I'm afraid, the house is staged. But he's a cutie, isn't he?" She thrust out her hand to Aggie, shook it firmly, and pushed a brochure into it before Aggie could take a breath. "Wendy Coker, so glad you could come. I'm afraid we're not quite open yet but, oh, what the heck, let me take you through. Can I get you coffee? A brownie? Oh," she said suddenly, staring. "You're with the police. There's no problem, is there? This is just a regular open house, I don't usually have to get a permit..."

Aggie interrupted firmly, "There's no problem. I'm Aggie Malone, Police Chief here on the island, and we're not staying. I just wanted to ask you some questions about the disturbance on Old Stillwater Way the other night."

She made an impatient face, turning away to put the remaining brochures on the mermaid-shaped credenza by the door. "Oh, please. I already explained that to the sheriff's office. That nosey old woman calls every time somebody burps on that street. I own that house. I shouldn't have to ask permission from the neighbors to use it."

Aggie said, "The report says you told the deputy you were showing the house."

She busied herself with straightening the brochures on the credenza, her back to Aggie. Flash was fascinated by the mermaid, and sniffed the marble legs, tail held down cautiously.

"That's right," said Wendy, without turning around.

"That seems kind of late to be showing a rental house."

She didn't reply.

Aggie said, "Do you mind telling me who your client was?"

Now she turned around, her expression defensive. "I most certainly do. I haven't done anything wrong, Chief. What's this about?"

Aggie said, "Who does your taxes, Ms. Coker?"

The other woman stared at her. "What?"

"Would it happen to be Cal Bertram?" she pressed.

She looked uncomfortable. "Maybe. Yes, but I honestly can't see what business it is of yours. Really, Chief, if there's nothing else, I have a lot to do."

Aggie said, "Was it Cal Bertram you were with here Friday night?"

Wendy widened her eyes, but a stain of color on her well-bronzed cheekbones betrayed her. "Excuse me?"

"It's a simple question, Ms. Coker," Aggie said.

Wendy squared up her shoulders, her lips tightening defiantly. "So what if it was? Any reason why my accountant shouldn't be interested in buying one of my properties? It's a nice place, three bedrooms, two decks, granite countertops, jetted tub, ocean view..."

Aggie nodded, wishing she could believe her. "And it's not for sale," she pointed out.

Wendy faltered. Most people, when challenged with lying to the police, would stumble sooner or later. "Well, that doesn't mean I can't show it to him, does it?" She managed at last. "Anyway, I really don't see why I should explain myself to you. I didn't do anything wrong."

Aggie didn't see any choice. She inquired simply, "How long have the two of you been having an affair?"

Wendy's color flashed hotter. "Well, honestly, I've had about enough of this." She pivoted on the toe of one red high-heeled shoe and started to walk away. "What I do on my own time is none of your business, and unless you're interested in buying this house..."

Aggie was out of patience and in no mood for games. She said, "Cal Bertram is sitting in jail right now charged with a felony hit and run that occurred Friday night around 9:30. He claims he was at his office all night. You claim he was with you. Somebody's lying. If you have any information that relates to this case, you need to come forward now, or you will subject yourself to being charged as an accessory."

It was not, perhaps, Aggie's most subtle or graceful attempt at interrogating a witness, but it worked. Wendy's face sagged as she turned back to Aggie, and she grasped the edge of the credenza behind her for support. She said, "Felony? Cal? What are you talking about?"

Aggie said, "A man was killed on Island Road by a hit and run driver around nine thirty Friday night. The damage to Cal's car is consistent with the crime, and blood on his fender matches that of the victim. Do you have anything to tell me that can shed any light on the situation?"

Her eyes grew bigger with every word that Aggie spoke. There was an awful silence for a moment, and then her words rushed into the void. "Well, I can tell you it wasn't Cal, that's for sure! He got here a little after eight and didn't leave until eleven thirty, not even when the police called. He wanted to, he got anxious about it, but it's my house, for crap's sake! I had dinner all made and everything. But he's so paranoid. Always afraid his wife..." She stopped, and swallowed, and looked at Aggie. "Come on, okay? It's not like I didn't know he was married, but this was just for laughs. And now he's in jail? Are you kidding me? Totally not worth it. I don't know what happened with the dead guy, but Cal was here with me until after eleven. He's a sweet guy, you know? A little geeky but sweet. This is crazy. He was here the whole time. I'll swear in a court of law."

Aggie said, "Did he park his car in the driveway?"

She shook her head. "No, like I said, he was paranoid. He parked around the corner and walked. He was afraid somebody might recognize the car."

Aggie looked at her steadily. "Ms. Coker, this is very important. Did Cal leave here for any reason, maybe to get more wine, to step outside to make a phone call, for any length of time at all, between eight p.m. and eleven thirty?"

Wendy shook her head adamantly. "I told you, no!"

Aggie said, "And you'd swear to this under oath?"

"Of course I would! I said I would! It's the truth, and I've got nothing to hide. I'm not ashamed of what we did." She hesitated. "I know Cal is worried about his wife finding out, but come on. You said jail, right? Why wouldn't he just tell the truth?"

Aggie thought she knew the answer to that, but even if she wanted to, it was too complicated to try to put into words. She said, taking out a business card, "Ms. Coker, I need you to stop by the office tomorrow and give a statement."

She took the card with a muffled groan, wrinkling her forehead as she stared at it. "Jeez, I hadn't planned to be back on the island tomorrow. Maybe Tuesday? I have a showing at 2:00."

Aggie stared Wendy down. "Tomorrow, 8:00 a.m."

Wendy shoved the card into the pocket of her form-fitting slacks, looking unhappy, and Aggie didn't say another word until she got to the car.

She slammed the door, fastened her seat belt, and took out her phone. She stared at it for a long moment, then looked at Flash. "I'll make you a tuna casserole," she told him, "and take you to Pete's for hamburgers every day for a month if you'll make this call for me."

Then, reluctantly, she dialed her husband.

Flash would have done anything for Aggie, even without the tuna casserole. But he was glad that, this time, he didn't have to.

Aggie put the phone on speaker as she drove home. "So I've got two witnesses who can place Cal in Wendy Coker's house at the time of the crime," she summarized. The relating of the details had been much more difficult, and had come first. "It's not enough to get the charges dismissed, but it might be enough to get a bail hearing today. Do you want me to call the DA?"

Grady was silent for a moment. She wished more than anything she could see his eyes. Finally he said, "No. Follow procedure. Get your statements, file your report. One more night in jail won't kill him, and I'm for damn sure not going begging to the DA for that son of a..." He sucked in a sharp breath. "I mean, he's sitting there in a private cell, getting his meals served to him three times a day while he watches the gardening channel and reads Grisham and all this time my sister is at home crying herself sick and my mother is wearing herself out taking care of those damn brats of his..."

"Deep breath," Aggie cautioned him sternly, turning into their driveway.

He was silent for a moment, and when he spoke his voice was more subdued. "Yeah, okay, you're right. I'm leaving the impound yard now. I'll call his lawyer and have him meet me at the jail. My guess is Cal will revise his statement before morning. If you can get what you have to the DA by noon tomorrow, that'll be soon enough. The hearing is set for 2:00, I think."

"No problem." She put the car in Park but didn't turn off the engine. "Did you find anything at the impound yard?"

"That car is like the inside of an operating room. The man is completely anal. Nothing but a piece of gum in the cup holder, probably belongs to one of the kids. Smells like cherry."

Aggie frowned. "I think I heard Lucy say one time that Cal doesn't allow the kids to ride in his car."

"I bagged it," he said. "I'll ask Cal if it's his, but I've never seen him chew gum."

"Yeah," Aggie agreed thoughtfully. "And it doesn't make sense that a man who's that obsessive about keeping his car clean would leave gum in the cup holder. You know Mrs. Everest's testimony will support the claim that the car was stolen. This could be a lead on who stole it."

"I know." But he didn't sound very happy about that, or even interested. He blew out a slow breath. "God. I don't know what I'm going to tell Lucy."

"Nothing," Aggie said firmly. "You're not going to tell her anything. This is a marriage, Ryan. Stay out of it. Do your job, and come home."

He was silent for a long time. Then he sighed again. "Yeah, okay. Give me another hour or so. Love you."

"Me too."

The minute Aggie opened the car door, Flash bounded out and dashed through the pepper tree hedge toward the cottage. Aggie called after him, but it was more of a question than a command, so he kept going. He and Aggie had lived in the cottage for a good, happy time before they moved all their things into the big house with Grady, and Flash always enjoyed coming back. But this time there was another reason: Grady's mother was there, and company, like surprises, almost always meant good things.

Aggie almost turned back when she rounded the corner and saw the white rental car parked in front of the cottage. But Grady's mother had seen her, and waved to her from the porch.

Lil was sitting in the turquoise porch swing, wrapped in a brightly colored heavy cotton shawl and chuckling as she petted Flash, who sat happily beside her. Aggie couldn't help smiling when she came up the steps, remembering all the times she and Flash had sat together in that same spot. "I hope he's not bothering you," she said. "I think he still thinks of this as his house."

Flash leapt down from the swing when he saw Aggie and, nosing open the screen door, went inside to explore his old haunt. Aggie drew a breath to call him back, but Lil just laughed. "Oh, let him go. Everyone needs to go home every now and then." She patted the spot on the swing beside her that Flash had vacated. "Come visit, if you have a minute. I just came back to pack a bag for another night, but couldn't resist this swing." She gestured to the mug of tea on the painted wooden table beside her. "Can I get you some? The water's still hot."

Aggie would have liked a cup of hot tea, but when she took her hands out of her pockets to button the top button of her coat against the chill of the shadowed porch, they were trembling so badly she knew she wouldn't be able to hold the cup. Worse, she knew Lil noticed, and was embarrassed. She tried to be casual about it as she sat beside her mother-in-law. "No thanks."

But Lil nodded kindly toward the hands Aggie once again tucked into her pockets, trying to hide the unsteadiness. "That must be hard to deal with," she said, "in your line of work."

Aggie tried not to be self-conscious. "It can be scary," she admitted. "But it hasn't been happening that long, and it's only when I'm tired." She shrugged. "It's always something. It'll probably go away."

"It might," agreed Lil. "But, honey, you know you're taking an awful lot of different medications. I couldn't help noticing them lined up on the kitchen counter last night. And some of them can cause tremors when taken with anti-seizure meds. You might want to talk to your doctor about cutting back the dose."

She said it so easily, almost offhandedly, as though she had no idea how those words could change Aggie's life. A medication reaction? That was it? It had never occurred to look for an explanation that simple. For a moment the relief of the possibility—the mere possibility—left Aggie weak, and all she could do was stare at the other woman in wonder. "That's right," she managed after a moment, remembering. "You're an RN."

"But not a doctor," Lil reminded her. She gave her a reassuring smile. "I'll be happy to go with you, though. Sometimes all that medical jargon can confuse even someone who's heard as much of it as you have."

"Oh," Aggie said on a breath, and she sank back against the swing. "That'd be nice. Thank you."

Lil kicked her foot gently and set the swing into a soft gliding motion. "That's what family is for."

Aggie sat beside her in contented silence for a time, just glad to be there. Then she said, "That's a gorgeous shawl. Is it handmade?"

"It is." She picked up her mug and sipped the tea. "A mother and daughter weave them, and sell them at the market in town on Saturdays, right between the dead chickens and the fresh oranges. I'm glad you like it." She winked at her. "You're getting one for Christmas."

Aggie smiled. "I'm awfully sorry things turned out the way they did for your visit," she said. "I know it hasn't been exactly what you expected."

Lil looked thoughtful. "Oh, I don't know. I was thinking about that just this morning. If we'd kept our original schedule we wouldn't have been here when Lucy needed us, so everything really worked out for the best. Families should be together at a time like this."

Aggie didn't know what to say to that.

Lil said, "Did you know Salty and I lived in this cottage when we were first married?"

Aggie was surprised. "Ryan never mentioned it."

She smiled reminiscently. "Oh, we couldn't begin to afford a place of our own, and base housing was...well, let's just say, base housing. Salty was overseas most of the first two years we were married, but when he came home...my goodness, it's amazing how a man can make a place seem twice as small! We didn't care, though, we were so much in love. Still are," she added with a tender glance at Aggie. "If you have even half the happy years we've had, Aggie, you'll be a rich woman. Oh, there'll be some hard times—you've seen them already—but believe

me, what you gain in the process will all be worth it."
She squeezed Aggie's hand. "Thank you for letting
us stay here, dear. It brings back so many wonderful
memories. That's why I just wanted to sit here for a
minute, and be with them all."

Aggie said, "Do you ever regret moving away?"

Lil chuckled. "Well, if I did, the past twenty-
four hours with my grandchildren would have
cured that!" Then she added, "We've talked about
coming back, and maybe we will some day. But we
wanted the children to have their inheritance while
they could enjoy it, and, my goodness, we live like
royalty over there for a fraction of what it costs
to live here! There's a nice ex-pat community—
although I suspect they're close to growing tired of
Salty's stories by now—and I have my bridge club
and my volunteer work at the free clinic. But I miss
my family."

She smiled. "I missed getting to know the woman
my youngest son was falling in love with. I missed
your wedding. You know, my Salty always said he'd
die a happy man once he'd sung at all three of his
children's weddings." And she laughed lightly, a
spark of mischief in her eyes. "Not that I wish him
any bad luck, of course!"

The laughter faded, and her eyes gentled with
regret. "I missed being here when you and Ryan
were going through that awful business. We wanted
to come, to be with our boy when he needed us, but
Pete said it wasn't a good idea, that if we came back it
would only make things seem worse than they were.

So we didn't." She looked at Aggie tenderly. "But I want you to know we were here in our thoughts, and you were in our prayers, the whole time. It's so hard for a mother not to be there when one of her children is hurting. That's why I'm glad we're here now for Lucy."

Aggie said uncertainly, "I guess I never thought about how worried you must have been. All of this, the family thing, is new to me. I never had a mother, you know, or a father either."

Lil reached over and covered Aggie's hand with hers. "Well," she said, "you do now."

Aggie looked down at her hand, so confidently covered by the older woman's, and for a moment it was hard for her to speak. "Listen," she said, at length. "I probably shouldn't tell you this, but...we found some evidence that may help Cal's case. It's just that...it's not going to make Lucy happy." She looked up at her mother-in-law and added simply, "I'm sorry for that."

Lil sipped her tea and held Aggie's gaze thoughtfully. "Do you think this will clear Cal of the charges?"

Aggie said, "I can't promise. He'll probably have to go to trial, or at least have a hearing. But I think so, yes."

Lil smiled. "Then thank you, dear, for doing your job. And Lucy will thank you too."

Aggie couldn't prevent a rueful shake of her head. "I don't think so. Lucy's never liked me much, and this is not going to put me at the top of her list of favorite people."

Lil gave a dismissing wave of her hand. "Oh, honey, Lucy doesn't dislike you. She's just jealous of you."

Aggie looked at her, surprised. "Jealous?" she parroted. "Of me?"

"Of course," replied Lil. "You're smart, you're pretty, you're tough, you have an amazing job, and worst of all, you stole her brother. Before you, Lucy was the only girl in Ryan's life. He was always there to fix the broken sprinkler or repair a loose shingle—heaven knows, Cal was never any good around the house—or just to call to make a fourth for cards. She made Sunday dinner for him, told him where to shop and how to dress, got to be the big sister she's always been. Now he has you, and she can't compete." She took another sip of tea. "It's an adjustment."

"Oh," said Aggie, beginning to understand.

"That's why Lucy pushed her way into planning this party," she went on easily, "and believe me, I know how bossy she can be. She just wanted to prove she could do something better than you."

Aggie couldn't prevent a half laugh. "No problem there." And then it occurred to her. "I guess no one will be in the mood for a party, now. And after you spent all that money..." She was already thinking about all the people she'd have to call, the things she'd have to cancel. She didn't even know what half of them were.

But Lil seemed unconcerned. "Let's see what happens, shall we?" She put her tea aside. "This new evidence of yours—is it something we're going to have to deal with tonight?"

Aggie glanced at her watch, noted visiting hours at the jail were over, and said, "Probably not. But tomorrow, for sure."

Lil gave a satisfied nod and set aside her cup. "Good. I could use a break. I noticed the sign outside the church said they were having their Christmas program tonight. Would you like to go with me?"

Flash came out of the house, having found nothing of interest to report, and let the door bounce gently closed behind him. Aggie smiled. "Ryan and I were planning to take Flash. They're having a blessing of the animals."

Lil's face lit with approval, and she clasped her hands together. "Perfect. I could make us an early supper if you like—maybe shepherd's pie out of the leftover roast beef? But," she added quickly, "only if you want me to. I don't want to be pushy. It's your house."

Aggie laughed. "That kind of pushiness I'll take. It sounds wonderful. Should I ask Lorraine and Pete to come too?"

"Of course! And, sweetheart?" she added as Aggie stood. "If you get a chance, will you please tell that darling girl she doesn't have to keep hiding her hands? I know she lost the ring. Pete told me, and Ryan after that, and both of them made me promise not to say anything. But for heaven's sake, I don't care! The only thing I care about is the pain it's causing her, so the sooner we get this out in the open the better."

Aggie smiled. "Yeah," she said. "I'll tell her." And after that, it seemed the only appropriate thing to do was to hug her mother-in-law. So she did.

Chapter Twenty

There was not much in this world Flash enjoyed more than a party, and even though Grady didn't appear to be much in a party mood when he came home, he seemed glad for an excuse to change that when he found Aggie and his mother working and laughing together in the kitchen. It turned out Salty had promised to have dinner with Bishop, but Pete and Lorraine came over and there was a lot of hugging and key lime pie for dessert. Aggie put on a long skirt with the black suede boots that she hardly ever wore, and a red felt hat with a sprig of silk mistletoe on the brim. Grady changed into a shirt with a collar and a pullover sweater, and Lorraine tied a red Christmas bandanna around Flash's neck and told him how handsome he looked. They all went off to church together, with Flash feeling as proud as he could be, all dressed up and sitting in the front seat of the car between Aggie and Grady.

Flash had only been to church once or twice before, and never with so many lights or so many people. It was really quite magnificent. He sniffed the sheep in the nativity display and discovered they were, as he suspected, plastic. He said hello to some of the people he knew: Sally Ann was there, as were some of the waitresses from Pete's Place, and a red-haired boy named Benji who sometimes threw the ball for him. After that he and Aggie stood in line on the lawn with a bunch of other people and some dogs who clearly had not been told it was impolite to bark at church, a few cats, and even a parrot, waiting for their turn to be blessed. All the other people gathered around and smiled a lot while Father Dave gave a speech and put his hands on each animal in turn. Afterwards, Flash did not feel much different than before he had been blessed, but he did appreciate Father Dave's kind words.

Most of the animals had to go home, or wait in the car, when the blessing ceremony was over, but Flash went inside the church with everyone else, and that was when he remembered what he had wanted Aggie to see yesterday.

"Oh, my," said Lil, gazing around in delight. "Look at all the roses. How beautiful!"

The altar was banked with greenery and decked with red roses and white baby's breath. On either side of the podium were rose topiaries, and the whole was lit with tiny white lights. For the Christmas program, a backdrop of midnight blue sky, also studded with tiny white lights and one particularly bright light, had been built. Music played from the organ and tall white candles flickered in a candelabra at each entrance. Flash thought it was all spectacular, and wondered why they didn't come to church more often.

Lorraine said, "A florist from Ocean City donated the arrangements. Actually, they were ordered for a wedding that was canceled—the couple eloped—and they were already paid for. They go to church here—the florist and his wife, I mean—and since his wife is on the Hospitality Committee, she knew exactly what to do with them. The florist was nice enough to deliver all the roses after work Friday night and the ladies worked until all hours to finish up." She tucked her arm through Pete's and smiled. "It reminds me of our wedding, doesn't it you, honey?"

"Oh, yours was gorgeous," Lil agreed. "There's something about a candlelight ceremony. And remember all those camellias at Lucy's wedding? Oh my goodness, what a time we had trying to keep those things alive until the end of the service!"

The two women moved to their seats, laughing softly together, and Flash looked at Aggie, waiting for her to decide what they should do next. But all she did was look at Grady and say, "Are you sorry we didn't have a big wedding?"

"Of course I am," he answered. "I'd want it to look just like this, too. Well," he added, considering, "maybe a few more lights. And maybe not roses."

Aggie half-frowned, half-smiled as she looked around. There was an absent expression in her eyes, as though she was trying to remember something. "Yeah," she agreed. "Maybe not roses."

Grady touched her back lightly and she followed his mother into the pew, wondering why all those roses made her think of the smell of bourbon.

Clearly, Flash concluded, Aggie had decided the time to move had not yet come. That was okay. He knew how to be patient.

Jerome Bishop and Sean Grady had served together for four years aboard the USS *Independence*, where Bishop was Chief Petty Officer and Salty was a signalman. After a particularly memorable leave in Rota, Spain, in which they both barely escaped disciplinary action for being off base, drunk and disorderly and fighting—among other infractions—they became drinking buddies and, eventually, fast friends. In 1973, an A-4 Skyhawk came in low and crashed on deck; four men were killed and twelve injured. Bishop sustained minor burns pulling Salty from the path of danger, and Salty spent three weeks on a hospital ship recovering from his injuries. Salty still limped a little in damp weather, and Lil still sent Bishop a box of homemade key lime cookies every year on his birthday.

Lured by the picture his friend had painted of an idyllic life on the Gulf Coast of Florida, Bishop settled in Murphy County after the war, and for the most part he hadn't been disappointed. He'd met and married the love of his life there, built a house there, raised his kids there. Salty stood up for him when he got married, and Bishop was the unofficial godfather to all three of Salty's children. They'd been through sunshine and storm together over the decades, and even now, after having lived in different countries for years, when they got together it was as though they'd never been apart.

They tackled two of Riverboat Charlie's surf and turf platters with all the sides, brandishing forks to emphasize the point of a story and occasionally bursting into laughter so uproarious that heads turned. After one such episode in which Salty spun an elaborate yarn about a river baptism, an African-American church choir in full regalia, and an alligator, Bishop wiped his streaming eyes and declared, "Lord have mercy, Salty, after all these years you still don't know a damn thing about black culture. That was damn near offensive. But I swear, nobody can tell a tall tale like you."

"And I'd say you don't know a damn thing about Irish culture," retorted Salty, lifting his near-empty beer mug, "to let a man sit before an empty glass with his throat half-parched."

Bishop lifted his hand to the waiter, and when the mug was filled, said, "How did you manage to tear yourself away from your lovely bride tonight?"

"Ah, it was a hardship, all right," admitted Salty, taking a satisfying drought of the beer. "She'll be pestering to have you to the table before we're off again." His expression grew reminiscent as he added, "What times we used to have together, the four of us, eh? How I miss your sweet Esther."

Bishop said, "You can bet she's smiling down on us now. She always did say nobody could put away steak and lobster like you, you old fool."

Salty raised his glass and declared quietly, "To Esther. Always in our hearts."

Bishop saluted somberly with his glass of iced tea, and the two men's gazes met and held for a moment of memorial before they drank.

Bishop finished off the last of his baked potato and then sat back, his expression serious. "So," he said. "We might as well get to it."

By unspoken agreement they had not mentioned Cal or Lucy throughout the meal, nor the fact that Bishop was the sheriff in charge of the jail that held his best friend's son-in-law. They were both old enough to know there would always be time for bad news; enjoying a good laugh and a good steak should take priority whenever possible.

Salty lifted his beer. "Am I going to need a refill for this one?"

"Maybe," allowed Bishop. "Maybe not. It's not my place to tell you the details, you'll have to go to Cal's lawyer for that. But the investigation has uncovered some witnesses who place Cal elsewhere at the time of the crime. This means he'll probably be cleared of the charges. The only problem is that when those witnesses give testimony, you're probably going to want to horsewhip your son-in-law. I have to ask you not to do that. One of you people in my jail is about all this county can handle."

Salty leaned back, pulling at the hairs of his silver beard, regarding his old friend steadily. "If I'm hearing you," he said at length, "my daughter's going to get her husband back, but she might not want him."

Bishop did not answer.

Salty gave a slow, sad shake of his head and lifted his glass. "Children," he said. "They'll rip the soul right out of you if you let them."

"You raised good kids," Bishop said. "They're going to be fine."

Salty sighed. "Aye," he said and drank.

They were quiet while the waitress came and took their plates. Bishop gazed into his iced tea glass, absently swirling the ice around, debating. Then he said, "There's something on my mind. I could use some advice, but I don't know if I should ask." He looked at Salty. "It's about another one of your kids."

Salty smothered a groan. "Lord save us, and to think it wasn't more than three months ago I was sitting by my pool drinking mango juice—mango juice, mind you—and thinking in my head what a good idea it was when Lil said, 'Let's go visit the children for Christmas!' It's Ryan, isn't it? He always was a loose cannon. Well…" He took a long draw on his beer. "Out with it then. Might as well get the worst all in one package, I always say."

Bishop smiled faintly. "Actually, it's Aggie."

Salty put his mug down, surprised. "That sweet girl?"

Bishop said, "I don't know how much you know about her family."

"Doesn't have much of one, I hear tell. Mother dead, no-account deadbeat father never even darkened her door, raised by a sainted grandmother, also passed, God rest her. About right?"

Bishop nodded. "A couple of years ago, they tried to find her father, but ran into a dead end. She pretended it didn't matter, but I think it would have meant a lot to her, just to know whether he was alive or dead. Now I've come across what might be a lead on the man, but I don't know whether to say anything."

Salty looked at him intently. "Is it something bad?"

"Safe to say, it's probably not good. From what I understand, the kid was no Boy Scout even back then, drugs, alcohol, in and out of jail, running out on his pregnant girlfriend...hard to make a decent citizen out of that kind of material." He shrugged. "Then again, the whole thing might be bogus. I'd track it down if I could, but the man with the information won't talk to me. He'll only talk to Grady."

Salty lifted his eyebrows. "I'm waiting for the question."

Bishop regarded his old friend evenly. "You know, there are some things a man never gets over. What happened here three years ago...well, Aggie's scars you can see. In a way, that makes it a little easier for her. But Grady, he keeps his wounds down inside, pretending they're not there, hoping they'll go away on their own, I guess. These things never do. They just keep growing and festering until they either eat you alive or blow you apart." He frowned. "I'm just not sure he's ready to do what it's going to take to see this thing through, and I'm not sure I want to ask him to go down that road if it turns out to be a hoax."

With every word that Bishop spoke, the lines in Salty's face grew deeper, his eyes grew older. He said, in a voice that was raw with dread, "God's beard, Chief, don't tell me this has something to do with the shooting."

It took Bishop a moment to reply, "It does."

Salty's gaze did not waver. "Then, sir," he said, "you don't need me to tell you what to do. You know." He gazed mournfully into his glass. "And I'll be needing another one of these before the night is done, that's for true."

"No, you don't." Bishop raised his hand for the check. "Let's head back to my place, where I can share a drink with an old friend without half the county counting my sips. I'm a pillar of the community, you know, have to set an example. And I've got a bottle of Jamieson's waiting for someone who knows how to appreciate it."

Salty lifted his eyebrows. "Jamieson's, eh?"

"It's your Christmas present."

Salty grinned. "Lord bless you, but I can't take that on the plane."

Bishop placed his credit card in the black folder that was placed before him. "I know," he replied and smiled back.

Salty said, nodding toward the bill, "I'll get the next one."

"Damn right," said Bishop. "You owe me."

"That I do," said Salty somberly, and raised his glass to him. "That I surely do."

Rosie remained endlessly amazed at the healing power of music. Even after all these years, even in circumstances as dark as these, he could feel each chord sweeping through his soul, cleansing the stain, making him whole. Whether in the midst of an orchestral swell or strumming the quiet chords of "Hallelujah" while Father Dave read the Christmas Story, Rosie was at peace, at home, completely right in the world. Forgiven.

He'd been sick with worry the whole day, swimming in sweat, too nauseous even to eat. That worried his wife, of course, so he choked down some casserole and greens and suffered the consequences of heartburn the rest of the day, miserable and anxious, until he'd finally gotten back to church, and done the only thing he knew how to do to make things right. Now, except for some minor lingering heartburn, he was at peace.

He'd been lucky so far, but this morning God had sent him a sign. He had made a mistake, but he'd been given a second chance. This was the season of renewal, of good and powerful things, and he had to believe that by the grace of God somehow all would be well with him again. Things would turn around. He was a good man. He'd done the best he knew to do.

Fear not, said the angel, *for behold I bring you good tidings of great joy…*

Great joy. It was coming his way. There in the sweet shadows of the musician's corner, surrounded by music and the twinkling stars overhead and the wonderful pageantry of the greatest story ever told, he believed it. But that was before the lights went up, and he looked out over the congregation and saw the black and white dog sitting in the pew. And he remembered where he had seen that dog before. A wave of cold sweat washed over him, and he thought perhaps everything was not going to be all right, after all.

Father Dave said, "Friends and neighbors, thank you for joining us tonight in this commemoration of the most sacred event in Christendom, the birth of our Blessed Savior. I hope you'll be with us again on Christmas Eve to celebrate the Eucharist, and remember our doors are always open to the members of the community we serve. Just before I pronounce the final benediction tonight, I'd like to remind you that the more secular portion of our program will begin in a few minutes in the Parish Hall, where there just might be a tree filled with presents, one for every little boy and girl here tonight, so be sure not to miss it. And if you're like me, you won't want to miss the refreshments our Hospitality Committee has prepared, either. I understand they've outdone themselves this year."

Smiles went around the congregation, young-sters shifted in their seats with excitement, and Flash looked up hopefully at Aggie at the mention of refreshments. Her attention, however, was directed at the speaker.

Father Dave went on, "Just one more thing before we move on, if I may. We're all so appreciative of our performers and all the other volunteers who made this night possible..." A murmur of agreement went through the crowd. "But there's one man in particular I'd like to acknowledge, not only for the gift of music he brings to us tonight and almost every Sunday morning, but for the beautiful floral decorations he donated out of the goodness of his heart. All of this splendor you see around you tonight, friends, is due to his generosity, as well as the fresh wreaths and the Christmas tree you'll enjoy in the Parish Hall. And if that weren't enough, he spent every minute he wasn't rehearsing this afternoon helping to organize and wrap gifts for our party tonight." He lifted his arm toward the musician's corner, smiling warmly. "Mr. Samuel Roosevelt, Jr. Rosie, would you stand?"

The congregation broke into a spontaneous round of appreciative applause, and Aggie clapped her hands with the rest, all the while staring at the uncomfortable-looking bearded black man who half-stood, half-bowed while awkwardly looking for a place to put his guitar. She tried to remember where she had seen him before. Aggie recognized almost all the residents of Dogleg Island, even the part-time ones, but Lorraine had said he was from Ocean City. Maybe he had delivered flowers to her?

No, it was more recent than that. There had been a florist's van in the church parking lot yesterday, but she was sure she hadn't seen the driver then. She glanced at Flash, who was looking up at her inquisitively. Lorraine said he had delivered the roses to the church late Friday afternoon...

Friday. Roses and the smell of bourbon. "That's it," she whispered, and Flash grinned at her. Grady gave her an odd look and she returned a quick apologetic shake of her head as Father Dave called them all to rise and began the benediction.

The organ played "Joy to the World" while the congregation, smiling and shaking hands and hugging each other, made its way toward the vestibule doors. Aggie did not see the guitarist. She said as they all moved toward the lobby, "Hey, Pete, do you know that man, the guitarist?"

He set his hands on Lorraine's waist, guiding her in front of him. "Rosie? Sure, I see him around. He comes in the bar sometimes."

"He was there Friday night, wasn't he?"

He chuckled. 'Honey, half the people in here were there Friday night." He added, "But yeah, I think I remember him. He was drinking—"

"Bourbon," supplied Aggie.

He lifted an eyebrow. "Excellent powers of observation, Grasshopper," he replied in a phony Asian accent. Then, "As a matter of fact, he had a couple. Stayed a little longer than usual, but seemed okay to drive. Why?"

"Do you remember what time he left?"

"Sorry."

Lorraine said, "Let's go get some hot chocolate and watch the children get their presents. Lil, you don't have to get back across the bridge right now, do you?"

Lil replied, "Well, I don't suppose one cup of chocolate would hurt. Salty won't be back from dinner until ten or eleven, at least."

Flash, who never missed an opportunity to check out a party, thought that sounded like a fine idea, but Aggie touched Grady's arm. "I'll meet you there," she said. "If I can catch Mr. Roosevelt before he leaves, it'll save me a trip to Ocean City tomorrow."

Grady said, "I thought Jason was handling the flowers for the party."

Aggie, craning her neck, caught a glimpse of Rosie leaving with his guitar through the side exit. "I have a hunch about something," she said. "I'll explain later."

By the time she edged her way through the crowd and out into the parking lot, there was no longer any sign of Rosie. The grounds were lit by the glow of the nativity scene, the cross atop the sanctuary, and the gentle light that flowed from the stained glass windows of the church. Aggie stood at the edge of the parking lot, looking around for a moment. A few people were headed for their cars, but most were streaming down the steps to the Parish Hall. Flash, who was much faster and more agile than she was, had already made his way halfway down the first row of cars, and she called out, "Flash! Wait for me."

He barked in return. Aggie started toward him, and he barked again. She quickened her step, and that was when she saw a dark shape on the ground near where Flash was standing, and beside it the crumpled figure of a man. She started to run.

She found Samuel Roosevelt, Jr. collapsed on the ground beside his guitar case, his face ashen and wet with sweat, his breathing labored. He was clutching his chest, and as she dropped to the asphalt beside him, a look of what was very close to relief settled over his face. "I should have known," he gasped, "you'd catch up to me. The ways of the Lord...aren't always that mysterious."

Aggie snatched up her phone and dialed 911. "Flash," she cried, "go get Grady!"

But Flash was already on his way. After all, he knew how to do his job.

CHAPTER TWENTY-ONE

Aggie was at her desk at 7:00 the next morning, by which time Sally Ann had already called the hospital to check on Mr. Roosevelt's condition. He had suffered a mild heart attack but was recovering well and, barring further complications, expected to be released in three to five days.

"Wow, what excitement, huh?" Sally Ann said, big-eyed. "I mean, if you and Captain Grady hadn't been there—someone who knows CPR, I mean—he could have died! Right there in the church parking lot!"

"Everyone should know CPR, Sally Ann," Aggie said, booting up her computer.

Flash trotted over to Sally Ann's desk and checked out the candy bowl, but it was filled with peppermints, which were not his favorite. He went to examine the stockings over the window. Nothing yet. Flash joined Aggie at her desk.

"Yes, ma'am," agreed Sally Ann with an enthusiastic nod of her head that sent the jingle-bell on her elf cap to tinkling. "The Red Cross is having a CPR certification course at the community college next month. I'm making everyone in my business class sign up."

"Good for you. That reminds me, we need to get on their schedule for a CPR course at the community center in April, when we start certifying lifeguards."

"Yes, ma'am," she made a note. "I'll do it right after Christmas."

Mo came in, jangling the sleigh bells over the door, and poured herself a cup of coffee. "Five more shopping days till Christmas," she reminded everyone. "And I sure hope you're not planning to do it at the outlet mall, because I'm here to tell you there ain't a thing left that doesn't look like it's been picked over by buzzards."

Aggie stifled a groan. Christmas shopping. As if she didn't have enough to worry about. But right now she could only deal with one thing at a time. "Okay," she said, sitting on the edge of her desk and picking up her coffee cup. "I need to catch you up on some stuff."

As concisely as possible, she filled in her team on the events of the weekend: the discovery of the car filled with cash, the Secret Service investigation into the counterfeit, the shooting death of one of the principles in that investigation. She went on to describe, however reluctantly, the arrest of Cal Bertram for the hit and run, and her subsequent discovery of two witnesses who could alibi him.

"One of them is due here to give her statement in less than an hour," she said, glancing at her watch. "I've alerted the DA's office, but Sally Ann, I need you to make sure the signed copy gets across the bridge before noon. So..." She glanced at Mo. "We've got the car, but we still don't have a driver in the hit and run. I had an idea that Mr. Roosevelt, the florist, might have seen something. He was leaving Pete's Place at about the right time to put him at the corner of Island and Park when the incident happened, and someone said they saw a white van with a logo on it parked there around nine thirty. He may even have been the one who made the 911 call. Unfortunately, he's in the hospital recovering from a heart attack, so I might have to wait a day or two before interviewing him. Also, there was close to a million dollars in counterfeit in the trunk of Wiesel's car. We don't know how much more might have made it into circulation. The investigating agent thinks Murphy County could be one of the drop points for this whole operation, so even if we manage to control it this time, we can't let our guard down. Keep your eyes open, and make sure the merchants do, too."

Mo said, "Yes, sir, Chief." She gave a disgusted shake of her head as she straightened her Santa hat and started toward the door. "Lord knows I never thought I'd live to see the day when Murphy County was a drop point for anything."

"Times are changing," agreed Aggie. "And Mo." Mo looked back and Aggie busied herself sorting through the papers on her desk, trying to sound casual as she added, "Just so you know, I won't be carrying a sidearm for a while."

Mo replied simply, "Yes, sir." And left on patrol.

And that was exactly why Aggie had hired her.

Wendy Coker came in as scheduled, dressed to the nines in crop jeans and high heels, push-up bra and a form-fitting shirt with the top three buttons undone. Aggie wasn't sure who she was trying to impress, but she supposed some habits were hard to break. In a way, she felt a little sorry for Cal.

She e-mailed the District Attorney's office a copy of Wendy's statement, along with her report of her interview with Betsy Everest, and left the office a little after 10:00. The morning had started out with a cold drizzle, but all that was left of the rain was a gunmetal gray sky and a sheen of wetness on the sidewalks that reflected the Christmas lights from the storefronts and utility poles. The sea breeze was biting and the sound of the ocean was loud. Aggie turned up the collar of her coat as she took out her phone to dial Grady, but Flash loved the breeze and the play of red, blue and green holiday lights in the puddles on the street. He walked beside Aggie with tail swishing gladly.

"Hey, babe," Grady answered. "I just got the autopsy report on Wiesel. Your copy should be in your in-box."

"That was fast," she said. "I thought they didn't work on weekends."

"I think they're trying to clear their decks before Christmas."

She made a face. "That's ghoulish. Can you imagine if your to-do list included cutting up five or six bodies before you could go home for Christmas?"

"Now I can," he responded glumly. "Thanks for that." There were very few things in the world that made Grady squeamish; dead bodies were among them. "Anyway, nothing surprising. His last meal was Chik 'N' Waffles. Cause of death, ruptured aortic artery secondary to crushing injuries consistent with automobile tires. Some other things—portion of a tread mark on his upper arm, sand and debris consistent with the place we found him."

"Can we get anything from the tread mark?"

"Maybe." He sounded doubtful. "I'll send the pictures on to CID, but the best we can hope for is that the forensics will support whatever other evidence we find…if we find any."

"What about the fingerprint on the hundred-dollar bill?"

"Nothing yet. Maybe this afternoon. Since we don't exactly have a suspect, I'm having them run it through military and civil servant databases as well as criminal. It might take longer."

"Maybe the lab is trying to clear its schedule before Christmas too," suggested Aggie hopefully. Then, "I just e-mailed Wendy Coker's statement to the DA. He doesn't need me in court today but maybe for the hearing, if it gets that far. What about you?"

"I guess I'll go, just for moral support." He didn't sound happy about it. "The SOB is still claiming all he and Wendy did that night was work on her taxes."

"Wendy's statement contradicts that," Aggie cautioned.

"Yeah, whatever. I'm out of it. But if I weren't, I'd say he was just trying to buy time until he can talk to Lucy."

"I hope he tells her the truth," Aggie said.

"Well, if he doesn't—"

"You're out of it," Aggie reminded him.

"Right," he replied.

"Listen," she said, "I called the hospital about Mr. Roosevelt. It looks like he's going to be okay. Mild heart attack, no surgery."

"Well, that's good news, anyway. I still don't understand what gave you the idea he might be a witness to the hit and run."

"It's a small island," she tried to justify, looking at Flash. "Not that many vans with writing on them would be parked on Park at the time of the accident, and we know he was in the vicinity. I still think it's worth checking out."

"Let me know what you find out."

"Will do," she said. "And, Ryan?"

"Yeah, baby."

"If you ever cheat on me, I'll castrate you with a rusty knife."

"Good to know," he replied. "I'll be home around five. Love you."

"Me too."

Aggie disconnected and dropped the phone into her pocket, looking up to find herself in front of Saylor's Sea and Surf Shop. "Okay," she said to Flash, squaring her shoulders. "Christmas shopping."

She pushed the door open and went inside.

The first Christmas they were together, Grady gave her a portrait of Flash hand-painted by a local artist. It was the best gift she had ever gotten, and she had hugged him so hard that her arms, still sensitive from anticoagulants, had turned black and blue. The next Christmas he sent her on a scavenger hunt that led to the top of the lighthouse where, on the sand below, he had spelled out I LOVE YOU in seashells. He was waiting for her there with a silver seashell necklace which she still wore every day under her uniform shirt. *That* was the best gift she had ever gotten. The third year he had taken her on a sunset cruise with champagne and chilled lobster, and she thought that was the best gift she'd ever gotten until he took her home to a hundred candles lighting the house and a live band performing the playlist of their favorite songs while a slide show of the highlights of the past three years of their life together played across the high walls of the house. It was magical, it was unforgettable, it was the best Christmas ever.

Meanwhile, Aggie gave him sweaters and running shoes and action movie DVDs. This was their first Christmas as a married couple. She wanted it to be special.

Saylor's was one of the biggest shops on Main Street, and one of the few that could survive year round with its vast selection of boating and fishing gear; surfboards, paddle boards and boogie boards, not to mention an entire clothing section. It was doing a brisk business this close to Christmas, and

Aggie and Flash had to edge their way to the display counter. She waited a full five minutes before Sam Saylor noticed her.

"Good morning, Chief," he said cheerfully. "Help you with something?"

Aggie was out of her depth and she knew it. She said, pointing aimlessly at one of the diver's watches under the glass display, "I'm looking for something for Grady. Maybe this one?"

"Oh, sure, great choice." He unlocked the case and removed the watch. "LED display shows time, depth, and pressure, accurate to 300 PSI, even has an emergency flashlight. Nine hundred dollars, professional courtesy discount, eight-fifty."

Aggie maintained her composure with great difficulty. "It's nice," she agreed, pretending to examine it. "But maybe..." she glanced around a little desperately, and waved her hand toward one of the boards on the wall. "Something more like that?"

Sam looked over his shoulder, his expression doubtful. "Sure, Chief, we could custom make a boogie board for you, but it'll take about six weeks and, you know—if you don't mind me saying—I'm not sure that's something your husband would really get that much use out of. Now if you want to talk surfboards," he went on, gaining enthusiasm as he directed her attention to the opposite wall, "we could really knock out a killer board for a dude like Grady, hand planed, custom paint, sized to spec, I'm talking one of a kind. You down with that?"

Aggie blinked. "Price?"

He replied easily, "We go anywhere from eight to fifteen K on our custom work. Happy to finance. What do you say? What we're doing for Christmas orders is printing up the design and gift-wrapping it, really cool presentation, delivery of the finished product in eight weeks, which is really the beginning of the season anyway, so perfect timing. Do you want me to get your order started?"

Aggie murmured, "Let me think about it."

Flash spotted someone he knew as they turned away from the display, and he trotted over to the checkout line to greet her. Jenny always remembered to put ice in his water bowl when they ate at Pete's, and she gave great ear rubs.

"Hi, Jenny," Aggie said, joining Flash. "Christmas shopping, huh?"

There were bags from other shops piled at her feet, and she juggled several potential purchases in one arm as she bent to scratch Flash's ears. "Hi, Chief," she greeted Aggie cheerfully. "Merry Christmas. They have some really nice stuff here, don't they?"

"They sure do. Expensive, though. Wow, that's a nice fishing reel. For your dad?"

She nodded. "He's wanted this one forever, and he's been so down after his accident that I thought this might cheer him up for Christmas."

She held it out for Aggie to examine and she did, particularly the price tag. "I'd love to get Grady something like this," she said, returning it regretfully, "but I can't afford it."

Jenny laughed easily and agreed, "Yeah, it's a lot, but it's Christmas. And my dad's worth it. He's always worked so hard, and I just really wanted to do something nice for him, you know?"

Aggie tried to find a way to ask the obvious question—how a waitress whose family was struggling to pay their bills could afford such an extravagant Christmas gift—and she had a really, really bad feeling about the answer. How much was Lorraine's sapphire and diamond ring worth, anyway? Not to mention a designer watch and a cell phone and the other things that had gone missing from Pete's, one by one, over the past few weeks. Jenny's name had been on the schedule after each one of those incidents; she'd checked with Mo. Jenny always worked the patio, and the items had all gone missing from diners on the patio.

The line moved forward and Jenny flashed Aggie a parting smile as she placed her purchases on the counter. Aggie stepped out of the way, but not so far that she couldn't see the total: $389.43. And her heart sank when Jenny pulled out a roll of cash to pay.

"Do you know, Flash," she muttered, "sometimes this job sucks."

Aggie fell into step beside Jenny as she started toward the door. "You must've been saving your tips for a long time, huh?"

Jenny cast her a slightly uneasy look, obviously catching on to the fact that the police chief's interest in her financial situation wasn't idle curiosity.

She slowed her pace, glanced around as if concerned about being overheard, and lowered her voice. "Actually, Chief," she said, her eyes growing big with the import of what she was about to say, "it was more like a Christmas miracle. But please don't tell my folks. They don't like to take charity, and I wanted it to be a surprise."

They had reached the door and Jenny stepped to the side, out of the flow of traffic. Aggie and Flash stood slightly in front of her, blocking her access to the door, just in case. Aggie really didn't feel like chasing anybody today.

Jenny glanced around again, and then said, "You know the church Christmas party last night? Well, I took my little sister, Sarah—they always have a nice Christmas tree with lots of candy and dolls for the little girls and trucks and stuff for the boys, and Mama said it might be the only Christmas Sarah gets this year…" She looked momentarily embarrassed to have to confess such a thing, then rushed on, "And, you know, some of the kids, their teacher at school signs them up to get a new coat this time of year, and the church always wraps them up real pretty, and if you come to the Christmas party you can take home your new coat, otherwise they deliver them, I think. So anyway, Sarah left with an armful of presents, and she kept pestering me to open them, so when we got to the car I said she could open just one, and I let her have the one with the coat, because I knew Mama and Daddy wanted her to put the rest of them under the tree..." As she spoke her voice grew breathless with excitement. "And Sarah, she's just the sweetest thing, she likes any present no matter what it is, so she wanted to wear the coat home, and when she put her hands in the pockets..." Jenny dug into her purse, bringing up a crumpled white envelope. "She found this! Chief..." Jenny's voice dropped to a whisper. "It had over twelve hundred dollars in it! Enough to catch us up on our mortgage and pay the electric, and get some nice toys for Sarah and a new outfit for Mama and a ham for Christmas dinner!"

Aggie took the envelope, examining it in puzzlement. On the outside was scrawled, "God Bless You and Merry Christmas!" Nothing else was written on either side, and it was, of course, empty.

"I wanted to go back in and hug Father Dave's neck," she added, "but I couldn't leave Sarah, and then I thought maybe he wanted to keep it a secret. I don't know, Chief, what do you think? Should I go back and thank him?"

Aggie was about to reply when she heard her name called loudly from the front of the store. She turned to see Sam Saylor pushing his way toward her, his face red with anger, waving a bill at her. "Chief! Hold up a minute! Look at this!"

He thrust the hundred-dollar bill at her and declared, "I'm right, aren't I? It's counterfeit!"

Aggie took the bill and ran it through her fingertips, turned it over, held it up to the light of the window. She turned back to Sam. "I'm afraid so," she said.

Sam glared at Jenny. "And I've got three more just like it under my cash drawer. Thank God my clerk called me over before you left the store."

Jenny looked confused and alarmed. "Why are you looking at me?"

Aggie said to Jenny, "Was all the money in that envelope one hundreds?"

"Most of it," she admitted. "Some twenties, I think. But…"

Slowly, it all began to come together. A white van parked at the corner of Island and Park. A bloody counterfeit one-hundred-dollar bill at the scene of a hit and run. A church filled with roses.

"Chief," demanded Saylor, "what are you going to do about this?"

Aggie took out her phone and dialed. "Mo," she spoke into it, "I need you to get down to St. Michael's church and find out how many coats from the children's coat drive have gone out, and where they went. Don't let any more leave until I get there. I'll explain when I see you."

Aggie disconnected and turned to Jenny. "So," she said unhappily, "where did you spend the rest of the money?"

CHAPTER TWENTY-TWO

It was almost 1:00 before Aggie made it across the bridge to the hospital. Flash waited in the car, but he didn't mind. He'd spent a lot of time in that particular hospital, most of it visiting Aggie or Lorraine, and he'd noticed people tended to cry a lot there. He was fine in the car.

Aggie was no fonder of hospitals than Flash was, but she had come to understand over the past few years that those corridors, those smells, those tired, smiling faces in pastel scrubs, were destined to be a part of her life for an indeterminate period of time. In a sense, she had gotten used to it. In another sense, she never would.

Rosie's wife was there to greet her when Aggie knocked tentatively on the door of room 102.

"Chief Malone!" she exclaimed softly, clasping Aggie's hand. "I can't believe you came! I was hoping to get a chance to thank you—you saved my husband's life!"

Aggie glanced past the woman to her husband, who was sitting in a half-incline position in bed and who, despite the sunken features and the oxygen

271

tubes, looked much better than he had last night. And when she met his eyes, she could tell he knew she wasn't here on a social call. She said, "I'm glad it all turned out well."

Rosie said, "Honey, would it be too much trouble to ask you to go downstairs and get me an orange drink from the cafeteria? You know the kind I like, the ones with plenty of fizz. And maybe some ice."

She turned to him with a tender smile. "Oh, look at you, milking this thing for all it's worth. Well, enjoy it, because the doctor says you'll be back at work right after Christmas." She turned to Aggie. "Chief? Can I bring you anything?"

"Thank you, I'm good."

When she was gone, Aggie made sure the door was closed behind her, then came over to the bed. "I'm glad you're feeling better, Mr. Roosevelt," she said. "I guess you've been under a lot of stress the last few days."

His tired brown eyes did not waver. "You've got something to say, Chief, now's the time."

She nodded. "There was a hit and run on Island Road Friday night around 9:30 p.m. The victim didn't survive. We found a bloody one-hundred-dollar bill near the scene, and we're running a fingerprint ID now. I wonder if we compared that fingerprint to yours, would they match?"

He looked at her wearily for a long moment. Then he said, "Things haven't been going so great for me lately. My wife doesn't know. Nobody knows." He was silent for a time, thoughts turned inward.

Oxygen hissed. Somewhere down the hall a chime sounded. He went on, "You know, you try to do the right thing, live a good life, give back even when you don't have much to give...but sometimes it just seems like what's the point, you know? So Friday I was on the island, delivering flowers for the church, and I stopped by the bar afterwards, thinking I'd have just one...but it turned into more than one. I was coming down Park Street, driving really slow because I was..." he looked embarrassed. "I knew I was impaired. I was coming up on the intersection when this car—this little Prius—came out of nowhere, all hell to the floor, and swerved off the road on my side. I thought he was going to hit me and I stopped dead. That's when I saw something go flying out into the middle of the road, something he'd hit, but I didn't get what it was until he stopped a few dozen feet ahead, and backed up and ran over it again. Sweet Lord Jesus, it was a body. It was a man. I don't know, it all happened so fast, but when I think back over it, it was like it took an hour. Everything is so clear."

A fine sheen of perspiration had broken out on his forehead. Aggie glanced at the monitors and saw some of the numbers rising. She said, "It's okay, Mr. Roosevelt. Take your time. You're not in any trouble here. I'm just trying to find out what happened."

He closed his eyes slowly. "I am in trouble," he whispered. "What I did...I deserve it. It wasn't right."

"Just tell me what happened," Aggie encouraged gently.

"The driver." He swallowed hard. "He swerved off the road to hit that man, then he backed up to run over him, and then he got out of the car and he dragged him out of the road and into the grass. Then he kind of squatted down, like he was going through his pockets or something, and that was when I guess my brain kicked into gear and I opened my door and I yelled something—I don't know what—and the guy looked up and noticed me, and then he got back in his car and took off. It was that fast.

"I pulled off the road and got out and ran across the grass to check on the guy, the one who'd been hit. He was a mess. He…" Again he swallowed. Aggie glanced at the monitors. "I couldn't find a pulse. I should have called. My phone was in the car. And then…then I noticed his jacket was open, and there was a twenty-dollar bill sticking out of the neck of his tee shirt. Chief, his shirt was stuffed with money. Hundreds, fifties, twenties…So much money. I didn't count it. I didn't even think about it. I just… God forgive me, I just took it."

He was silent for a long moment. The beeping of the monitors resumed their normal steady rhythm. Aggie waited.

He said heavily, "It was almost a hundred thousand dollars. That money could have saved my family, maybe my business. It was like it was sent by God. But it wasn't, was it?" He didn't look at her when he said it. "I think I knew that when I got home and saw the bills were all bloody. I had to wash them in the kitchen sink. Blood money. Clear as day. Blood money."

The silence lingered. Then he went on, "My wife called a little after eleven to say she was on her way home from decorating the church. That's when I knew I had to try to do something to make this right. So I called 911 to report the hit and run. I couldn't leave my name. I'd been drinking, I knew there'd be questions, and...we needed the money. But it wasn't right."

He drew in a long breath, and let it out. "And in the end, it wasn't worth it. Stealing from a dead man is still stealing, and I knew I'd never have a moment's peace from that money. So I decided the best thing to do was give it back to the Lord."

Aggie nodded. "So you distributed it among the coats in the children's coat drive."

He turned his head on the pillow, seeming exhausted. "I figured those families were the most deserving, and I wanted to see something good come from all this wrongness. Will I go to jail?"

Aggie said, "You'll be charged with theft. But it'll be up to the DA whether to prosecute. You see, Mr. Roosevelt, the money you stole was counterfeit. From what I can tell, you spent a few hundred at Wal-Mart, the pharmacy, some fast food places, but without foreknowledge or criminal intent. For the most part you didn't personally benefit, and I'm sure that will be taken into consideration."

He looked at her with eyes that were numb with confusion, trying to take it all in.

Aggie said, "Anything you can do to help us with our investigation is going to work in your favor, Mr.

Roosevelt, and believe me, things aren't nearly as bad as they probably seem right now." She gave him a reassuring smile, and he latched on to it like a lifeline. She said, "I know it was dark, and you were, as you said, impaired, but is there anything you can tell us about the driver of the Prius? Did you get a look at him at all?"

Rosie replied without hesitation, "Yes, ma'am, I did, and I'll be honest with you, that's the thing that's been weighing on my conscience all this time. I needed to tell somebody, but I didn't know how, not without getting myself in worse hot water."

"You can tell me now," Aggie assured him gently.

He said, "It's not that I know him or anything, and wouldn't even have recognized him if I hadn't been sitting beside him at the bar for half an hour. He'll be easy enough to identify, if you can find him. He's got a tattoo of a scorpion on his neck."

CHAPTER TWENTY-THREE

Bishop looked into Grady's office. "I thought you were going to go to Cal's arraignment."

Grady's tone was absent, his attention on his computer screen. "Yeah, I thought about it."

Bishop came in and looked over Grady's shoulder at the screen. "Do your Facebooking on your own time, Captain. Good-looking couple, though," he added as he straightened up.

Grady glanced up then from the picture he had been studying, one that had apparently been taken of him and Aggie Saturday while they had lunch at Beachside Park. "That's just it," he said. "I didn't post that picture. And this isn't my personal page, it's work." At Bishop's blank look, he explained, "A lot of the guys have them, all linked to the main Sheriff's Office page. One of the suggestions to improve community relations you asked for, remember? It makes it easier for the public to connect with us, makes us more relatable, that kind of thing."

"Oh, yeah." The lack of enthusiasm in Bishop's voice revealed just how much interest he had in the project. "How's that working out?"

"Okay, I guess. We've gotten a few tips, and it makes it faster to reach the public with bulletins, Amber Alerts, pictures of suspects. Not that crazy about people posting pictures of me I didn't know about, though."

"Who put it up?"

Grady pointed to the author, listed simply as John Q. Public. "A fan?"

Bishop shrugged. "Seems harmless enough."

"I guess." He didn't sound particularly convinced. "Maybe it's some reporter working on an exposé of deputies who have lunch on taxpayers' time." He closed the page and leaned back in his chair. "We got the lab report back on the fingerprint we took from the counterfeit bill at the hit and run scene. No match to anything in the system."

Bishop said, "It was a long shot." He pulled up a chair and sat down, a frown settling into his features that made Grady lean forward a little, his attention sharpening. "I just got off the phone with the FBI. John Keenan, bureau chief up in Tallahassee, is an old friend of mine. All I wanted was an update on the investigation into that snitch that was shot on the road Saturday, Lindon…what did they call him?"

"Sting," supplied Grady.

"Right." Bishop looked troubled. "So I tried to talk to the investigating agent. I got a lot of questions, no answers. Next thing I know the bureau chief himself is on the phone. And I gotta tell you, son, I didn't like what he had to tell me." He regarded Grady gravely. "And you're not going to, either."

Even though it was a cool day, Aggie had left the windows of their patrol vehicle cracked, just a little, for air circulation, and that's how Flash caught his first whiff of cigarette smoke. He guessed he'd never smell smoke again without remembering the bad man that he and Aggie had taken down, so the growl was already forming in his throat before he even raised his head to the window. He sniffed the air and swiveled his head around until he located the direction of the smell: a black SUV that wasn't that different from the one Flash was sitting in— except that it didn't have the Dogleg Island Police Department logo stenciled on the door, of course— parked around the corner of the building in the middle of a row of cars. The window of the black SUV was rolled down, and the arm of the smoking man was visible outside of it, the cigarette dangling between his fingers.

Aggie had parked in a "reserved for emergency vehicles" spot near the emergency room entrance, which was partially blocked by the ambulance bay. Flash could not be sure whether the smoking man had seen him, but he knew for certain the man saw Aggie as she came through the automatic doors, paused for just an instant, and looked around. Flash wasn't sure how he knew, but he did.

Aggie proceeded to her vehicle with what she hoped was a casual gait, got inside, and pulled on her seat belt. All the while her eyes were scanning the parking lot. "Did you smell that, Flash?" she said. "Cigarette smoke."

Flash shifted restlessly in his seat, his gaze fixed on the black SUV.

"Remember the way that Agent Carson kept patting his pockets the whole time we were in Bishop's office? And I didn't think much of it until now, but his clothes reeked of smoke."

Flash remembered the cigarette butt in the puddle, on the night of the dead man.

Aggie whispered, "But what would he be doing here?"

And then she knew.

Her focus sharpened on the direction of Flash's gaze just in time to catch the arc of a cigarette ember, red against the gray day, as it was tossed from the window of an SUV with a rental agency sticker on the bumper. She started her engine and radioed the office, watching as the SUV backed out of its parking space. "Sally Ann," she said. "I need you to call Sun Coast Car Rental and find out who rented a black SUV over the weekend with the license plate Sunday Charlie One Zero Eight Niner. Call me back."

"Yes, ma'am, on it."

Aggie disconnected and followed the SUV out of the parking lot. "We could be wrong," she murmured. "Lots of people smoke."

But not many of them had reason to be staking out the parking lot of a hospital where the only witness to a homicide had been admitted.

She followed the SUV on to Hospital Way, and when he turned right on Veteran's Parkway she let a couple of cars get in between them. He drove the speed limit, maintained his lane, stopped at every stop sign. On Highway 44 he turned again, heading out of town. Aggie radioed the office again.

"Anything?" she demanded of Sally Ann.

"I'm on hold," Sally Ann replied. "And if you don't mind my saying, these people are *not* very cooperative. I practically had to threaten them with a subpoena."

"Okay. Let me know the minute you have something." She started to click off, but hesitated, pressing her lips together in frustration. He had turned onto County Road 83, past the power plant, past the elementary school. Mailboxes were fewer and farther between. He was leading her on a wild goose chase, and without a vehicle ID she had absolutely no reason to pull over a law-abiding citizen who had given her no cause whatsoever for suspicion. And then she saw the Santa hat on the seat beside her.

She switched bands. "This is Chief Malone in Dogleg Island-One about to make a Santa Cop stop at mile marker 13 on CR 83. Sorry to step on your toes, boys. Any unit in the vicinity is welcome to attend. Dogleg Island Out."

She switched on her lights and sirens and, after a moment of held breath, saw the vehicle in front of her signal and slow. He pulled over on to a wide sandy spot in the road. Aggie let out her breath and pulled in behind him.

"Okay, Flash," she said. "We're on."

"In the first place," Bishop said, "our friend Agent Carson did *not* return to Miami on Saturday like he was supposed to."

Grady muttered, "I knew that son of a bitch was no good."

Bishop held up a staying hand. "Maybe, maybe not. If he's gone rogue, he might have good reason, or at least in his mind he does. Carson's part of a task force that's investigating what looks like a new crime syndicate forming in the deep South, started to attract some attention four or five years ago. This counterfeit operation we got caught up in is just one part of the business, and it looks like it's being used to finance some pretty major arms deals, both foreign and domestic."

Grady said softly, "Jesus."

"That's just the tip of the iceberg. It appears this operation is a key player in the drug traffic that's coming out of Mexico, and all the fentanyl we're seeing on the streets now? It might've started with them. So this is where Carson comes in. Maybe you remember a couple of years back six DEA agents were injured in a warehouse explosion during a raid in Atlanta, two of them died. One of the ones that didn't make it was Carson's fiancée."

Grady tried, and didn't quite manage, to hide a flinch. He hadn't wanted to sympathize with Carson at all, but that story hit a little too close to home.

Bishop went on, "The guy that set them up turned out to be a dirty cop, working for the syndicate. So for Agent Carson this is personal. He fought to be assigned to the task force and he spent too much time setting up this operation to walk away from it now."

"Great," said Grady, sinking back into his chair. "Now we've got the Mob *and* a cowboy federal agent running loose in our county. What's the procedure for that, Sheriff?"

"Just wait," said Bishop, unsmiling. "It gets better."

Aggie reached for the Santa hat and then hesitated. Instead, she turned, got up onto her knees and felt around in the narrow area between the front seat and the prisoner cage for Flash's Kevlar vest. Her own vest, like her weapon, was back at the office. "It's probably not even him," she muttered, strapping Flash into his vest. "But in case it is, you wait for my signal, understand?"

Flash absolutely understood. He remembered all about the element of surprise, and even though the vest wasn't his favorite—it was hot and heavy and slowed him down—he knew that when he put it on, he and Aggie were about to do some serious work. So he waited while Aggie put on her Santa hat, grabbed a coupon book, and got out of the car, leaving the door open. He waited and he watched and he listened, every sense attuned to her. Waiting for the signal.

Aggie looked around. She couldn't have picked a more isolated area to make a stop. Except for a tumbling-down old shack a few hundred yards down the road, there was nothing but field grass and scrub trees. A faded billboard advertising Danny's Country Restaurant had to be thirty years old; Danny's had burned down long before Aggie arrived in Murphy County. A blue sedan passed, slowing sensibly when it saw the blue lights, then continued down the highway. Other than that, the road was deserted; not even the sound of distant traffic reached her. She swallowed hard and touched the baton on her belt lightly for reassurance, then moved forward.

The tinted window rolled down as Aggie approached the vehicle. Agent Mike Carson looked up at her, unsmiling. "Chief Malone, isn't it?" he greeted her. "Aren't you off your beat?"

Aggie replied, "I could say the same about you. Last I heard, you were being recalled to Miami."

"Change of plans," he replied briefly. "You had no lawful reason to pull me over. You're out of your jurisdiction. I'm within my rights to drive away right now."

"Actually," Aggie replied pleasantly, "in addition to being police chief of Dogleg Island, I'm a duly sworn deputy of Murphy County, which means I can arrest anyone in the state of Florida given just cause. But this is your lucky day. I didn't stop you for a traffic violation. I stopped you as part of our community relations Santa Cop program, designed to reward deserving citizens for obeying the law." She tore off a coupon from her book and thrust it through the window to him. "Congratulations. Have a good day. Also," she added as he scowled over the coupon in his hand, bemused, "as long as I have you here, I'd like to ask you a few questions. For example, if I call your supervisor, will he verify your whereabouts?"

He said nothing.

She decided to risk it. "Because the rental car agency says this vehicle was paid for with your personal credit card. That's not standard procedure for an agent on assignment, is it?"

The very faintest flicker of annoyance in his eyes told her she had guessed right. Aggie said, "Do you mind stepping out of the vehicle?"

Flash watched intently from the patrol car, waiting for her signal. Nothing yet. He licked his lips.

Carson looked at her. "Yes, I do mind. You're interfering with a federal investigation and you have no reason to detain me, Chief, or Deputy, or whoever the hell you are. So if there's nothing further, I'll just be on my way." He reached for the key in the ignition.

"Keep your hands on the wheel, sir," Aggie said firmly. Her heart was pounding. "Please step out of the vehicle."

His eyes flickered over her, although his hand left the key. She correctly interpreted his faint smile to indicate he had noticed she wasn't wearing a weapon. She was intensely aware of her surroundings: the leaden sky, the empty road, the cold damp mist that clung to her skin. The only sound was the distant crackle of the radio from her car.

Flash watched, muscles tensing.

Aggie slowly reached inside Carson's open window, holding his gaze, and clicked the lock on the door. She opened the car door and stood behind it. "Get out of the car," she repeated, very deliberately, "and keep your hands where I can see them, if you will, please."

He said, "Chief, that's not going to happen."

Aggie tightened her muscles, knowing even as she did so her posturing was futile. She could not physically overpower this man, and there was no way he was going to let her take his gun. The only way she had been able to disarm him the first time was with the help of Grady and Flash. The emptiness of the road stretched out on either side of her, and a trickle of damp air crept inside her collar.

She said, "That was not a request, Agent Carson."

He said lowly, "Chief, you need to back off. You're in over your head."

Flash, watching from the car, waited, waited.

And Aggie gave the signal.

Bishop said somberly, "Listen, Grady, for the time being this stays between you and me. The FBI doesn't even have enough information to brief the other sheriffs and police departments in the area yet, and since they've already determined that one of the ways this particular bad guy stays ahead of the law is by using our own cops against us, well, you can see how discretion would be the better part of valor."

Grady's expression had gone still and hard, almost as though he knew what Bishop was leading up to.

"They're calling it the Ghost Syndicate," Bishop went on, "because every time they get close to busting it, or even identifying it, the damn thing disappears. They think it's run by one guy; pretty efficient, if you think about it. People call him Angelo, but not even his top lieutenants know who he is. It seems to have started in south Georgia, but migrated down the Gulf Coast over the past five years or so, probably because of the Mexican connection and, like Carson said, the casinos. The thing that concerns us is that it looks like Murphy County might have, for whatever reason, come to the particular attention of these folks."

Grady said quietly, "Yeah, well, Murphy County came to the attention of a lot of people three years ago."

Bishop nodded gravely. "There's no proof of any connection, of course. But it's possible Briggs might have been one of the first cops recruited by the syndicate here on the Gulf, most likely without ever knowing who he worked for. Everything about the MO matches, and..." His lips tightened briefly in self-recrimination, "I never did think he was smart enough to have pulled it off as long as he did without help." He looked at Grady. "So that brings me to what I came in here to talk to you about. You work in law enforcement as long as I have, and you learn that only a fool ignores coincidence. Four days ago

Briggs was transferred over to Jackson County. And he sent me a message for you."

Flash sprang from the vehicle in a low crouch and closed the distance at lightning speed, the low rumbling in his throat a warning, his bared teeth a reminder. He stopped beside Aggie, head down, teeth up, prepared to lunge. The man in the car looked down at him, hard, and Flash suspected he was remembering what had happened the last time they'd met.

Aggie said, "Just in case you were thinking about doing something stupid, there's a reason I call him Flash. He can tear out your throat before you even get your hand on your gun."

Flash was alarmed. He had never imagined himself doing such a thing. But then he remembered the game Aggie and he played with the rope tug toy, where she sometimes let him win and he shook it until he broke its imaginary neck, and she laughed and clapped her hands and told him how terrific he was. He understood games. He hoped this was a game. But he didn't dare take his eyes off the bad guy to look at Aggie and make sure.

Once Flash had killed a squirrel. He remembered the crunch of bones and the taste of blood. What if he actually had to tear out the throat of a bad guy?

Carson met her eyes with quiet, unmitigated fury. "Call him off," he said.

Aggie gave a small flick of her fingers and Flash, with great relief, whipped around to sit beside her, poised and ready, his piercing blue eyes fixed on Carson.

Carson got slowly out of the car, hands held palm out, his expression tumultuous. "Lady, you don't know what you've stepped into. You're going down for this if it's the last thing I do."

Aggie tried to keep her breathing even. She was not entirely successful. She said, "What are you doing here?"

His eyes flickered from her to Flash and back again. It was a moment before he replied, "Right now I'm going to have a cigarette. I'd appreciate it if you'd control your animal while I reach for my smokes."

He opened his jacket, showing her his shoulder holster and the cigarettes in his shirt pocket. He reached for the cigarettes and lighter.

Aggie thought about the cigarette butt in the puddle at the corner of Island and Park on the night of the hit and run. So did Flash.

She said, "You went back to the scene of the hit and run Friday night. Sting was alone when he killed Wiesel, but when he reported back to you, you came back to the scene of the crime..." She frowned, thinking out loud, trying to piece it together. And then she did. "The money," she said. "Sting tried to get the money off of Wiesel but Mr. Roosevelt stopped him. You couldn't let that money get into circulation; it would have blown your operation. So you went back for it. Or sent Sting for it, while you waited in the car, smoking. Only by the time you got back there the money was gone."

Carson inhaled smoke, regarding her with absolutely no expression. "You're pretty smart, aren't you?"

"Is that why you were at the hospital? Waiting for a chance to get to Mr. Roosevelt?"

He flicked an ash on the ground. "Why would I do that?"

"I don't know. Maybe because he could put you in jail?"

He gave a brief impatient shake of his head and drew in more smoke. "I wanted to talk to him, that's all, see how much he knew. When I saw you go in, I figured it wasn't a good time. I was going to wait until you left, but then I got a call." He glanced impatiently at his watch. "Are we about done here?"

Aggie said sharply, "A call about what? From whom?"

He drew slowly on his cigarette, blew out the smoke. "This is still an active operation. I'm still undercover. and you're interfering with a federal agent."

Aggie said steadily, "And I'm going to go on interfering until I get some answers."

He took a final harsh drag on the cigarette and tossed it away. A sharp arrow appeared between his brows as he squinted against the fine drizzle of rain that had begun to fall. "Look, Chief, I told you before you don't know what you're getting into. This is bigger than one counterfeit operation, one dead hillbilly. The man we're after is a seriously bad dude and the less you know about him the better."

Aggie said incredulously, "Worse than you covering up the murder of that poor Mr. Wiesel? Do you think you're somehow above the law just because you're chasing the bad guys? Are you honestly going to try to make *that* your defense?"

His eyes blazed. Flash tightened his legs, ready to leap, and fixed him with a stare.

Carson said, "I had nothing to do with that! Do you think I would've let it go down if I had?"

Aggie replied coolly, "I don't know. Would you?"

He jerked out another cigarette from the pack, lit it, and took a short drag. His eyes restlessly scanned the horizon behind her. He said, "I told you, Sting was my man on the inside. The way he stayed alive was by *staying* on the inside, do you understand what I'm saying? He had to take orders. When that driver, the guy they called Weasel, walked away from the exchange with the keys still in his pocket, Sting's orders were to track him down and kill him."

Aggie stared at him. "And that was okay with you?"

Another impatient shake of his head. "I didn't know what he'd done until he came back with blood on his clothes. He got a phone call. The guy on the other end had a car waiting for him, an unlocked Prius with the key fob in the console. He told Sting to run the driver over, make sure he was dead, and return the car where he'd found it."

Aggie worked hard to keep her tone flat. "So that's what he did. And you just stood by and let it happen."

He scowled and flicked ash on the ground. "I told you, I didn't know about it until it was over. I thought he'd just gone to try to track Weasel down. When I got the real story, of course I was pissed. More than pissed. It'd taken months to set up that operation, and now my CI had gone rogue, I was going to have to take him in. My cover would be blown, other agents put in jeopardy, the entire mission falling apart. I felt like killing the stupid son of a bitch myself, with my bare hands."

He took another harsh draw on the cigarette. "Sting told me there was a witness to the hit and run, and he was scared—not of the law, but of his boss. He wanted to cut and run, and I was half-inclined to let him. I figured what his boss would do to him for running out on orders was worse than anything the justice system could manage, and as it turns out, I was right. But I wanted to see the scene of the crime for myself, so I made him take me by there. I expected emergency vehicles, police tape, bystanders...but all we found was a quiet corner and a body in the weeds. Nobody had called it in. I started to think there might be a chance to save the operation after all. And that's when I started to put it together. The guy we were after—the man called Angelo, the head of the entire operation—was right there on the island. He had given the order to kill. He told Sting where to find the car to steal. There was a good chance he'd been watching us the whole time, and he might even be planning to pick up the counterfeit himself. This was the closest we'd ever gotten to him. There was no way I was going to let him slip through my fingers."

Aggie said, "So instead of following procedure, calling in the hit and run and arresting the man who confessed to it, you decided—on your own—to continue your operation."

He replied, "On my own is how I work. I was within hours of bringing down a major league player. Maybe minutes. And then you showed up."

"And another man got killed."

He replied shortly, "I already told you, you have no idea what was at stake. I used my judgment."

"You broke the law!" Aggie could not keep the outrage, the simple incredulity, out of her voice. "Do you really think you can fight crime by turning into a criminal yourself? You covered up a murder because it was convenient. Is that what we do now? Is that who we are?"

His look was laced with contempt. "Spare me your self-righteous sermons, lady. Why don't you just go back to your winter carnivals and your Christmas coupons and let me get back to taking care of the kind of criminals who give the order to kill an innocent man for a few grand in counterfeit, and then shoot the killer with a high-powered rifle to get him out of the way. You don't get to talk to me about who I am until you've had to do the things I've done. In the meantime, I don't have to stand here in the rain trying to make you understand something that's none of your business." He tossed the stump of the cigarette to the ground and glanced again at his watch. "I've got someplace to be."

Aggie said, "Was it Angelo who called while you were waiting at the hospital?"

He said, "As far as he knows, I'm still working for him. He set up a meeting ten minutes from now, and I'm sure as hell not going to blow it for the sake of some small-town cop with nothing better to do than get in my way. So if your curiosity is satisfied, I'll be on my way, and I expect you to be on yours. I don't have to waste any more time with you."

Aggie swallowed and nodded. "No, sir, you don't," she admitted quietly. "What you have to do now is surrender your weapon, and come with me. I'm placing you under arrest for accessory after the fact to a felony homicide, withholding evidence, and interfering with a police investigation."

He gave one short grunt of laughter and a shake of his head. "I'm not playing this stupid game again. You don't even have a gun."

He turned toward his car and Flash prepared to spring, wondering if this was the time, this was the moment when he would be called upon to do the unthinkable, if Aggie would ask him to, and if she did, would he? Could he?

And then Carson, with his hand on the door handle, stopped, having seen what Aggie had noticed moments before: A Dogleg Island Police cruiser pulling in behind them, and two Murphy County Deputy Sheriff vehicles approaching with lights flashing, one from the north and one from the south.

"I don't need a gun," Aggie replied simply, dropping her hand to Flash's head. "I've got backup."

Mo got cautiously out of her vehicle, her hand on the butt of her service revolver, watching the suspect with a fierce scowl.

Aggie said, "Kindly surrender your weapon to Officer Wilson here, and accept a ride to Booking with one of these nice deputies. I believe you know the routine."

Bishop watched Grady's face grow tighter, his eyes harder, as he finished his story. Grady said, "Briggs is just messing with you. Trying to mess with me and Aggie. He remembers when we were trying to find Aggie's father four years ago. He helped me do an inmate search. Sick bastard."

Bishop nodded. "That's why I wanted to check out a few things before I talked to you. It turns out there was a guy named Jimmy Joe Jackson who transferred into Briggs's cell block right before Briggs was moved up here. He was from Macon, Georgia, about the right age to have known Aggie's mother, and he was in juvenile detention when Aggie was born, just like Aggie always said her father was."

Grady's eyes narrowed. "You're sure?"

"All public record. It's entirely possible Briggs talked to him, put some facts together, and decided he had some currency with you."

"For what?" Grady demanded.

Bishop shook his head. "I don't know. But remember what I said about ignoring coincidences? Jackson was released last week, due to what prison officials are calling a 'clerical error.' He was found shot to death that same night, execution style, in a hotel room in St. Pete."

Grady brought his fist to his mouth, tapping his knuckles against his lips thoughtfully. "Do you think Jackson—or whoever he was—was a plant?"

"Could be. The Feds aren't ruling it out, anyway. They're putting Briggs in high-security lockup until they can question him."

Grady blew out a breath. "This sure as hell isn't what I thought I'd be worrying about when I got up this morning."

"Never a dull moment," agreed Bishop.

They were silent for a time, then Bishop said, "This Jackson character was part of the system. His DNA is on file. If you wanted to do a paternity match, all Aggie would have to do is submit a sample."

Grady looked at him. "Or we don't have to say anything to Aggie about this at all. Maybe she's better off not knowing. After all, she's lived without him all these years, and now he's dead. What good can come of it?"

Bishop was thoughtful for a moment. "You might be right," he said. "She might be better off not knowing. Then again, maybe this isn't about Aggie."

Grady frowned. "I don't follow."

"There are two kinds of marriages," Bishop said. "The kind with secrets, and the kind without. So I guess the real question is, what kind do you want to have?"

Grady's frown deepened. He drew in a breath for a reply, but before he could answer, the phone rang. It was Aggie, with the news that she was bringing in a prisoner.

As they watched the sheriff's department cruiser depart the scene with Carson inside, Mo demanded of Aggie, "Lord, child, what were you thinking, making a traffic stop without your gun? You trying to get yourself killed? Don't you watch the news?"

Aggie smiled. She still felt shaky inside, but also triumphant. She had done it; she and Flash. She had done her job even though she couldn't handle a weapon. She hoped she never had to do it again, but this time...this time she'd done it.

She knelt to unstrap Flash's vest, ruffling his fur. "Thanks, Flash," she said fervently, pressing her forehead briefly to his. "Great job. You're the best partner I ever had."

Flash shook himself off and grinned his own congratulations to her. Aggie stood up.

"Thanks for getting here so fast, Mo," Aggie said. "What were you doing on this side of the bridge, anyway?"

"I get a dinner break, don't I?" she replied, mildly defensive. "I was just finishing up my chicken and fries when your call came in. Then when you didn't answer your radio I figured it wouldn't hurt to have a couple of county units on the way, just in case. People are crazy these days, honey," she added, and her dark eyes clouded with worry. "You got to be careful."

"I will," Aggie promised her. "But right now I need you back on the island, keeping our people safe. Flash and I have got some explaining to do to the sheriff."

"Yes, sir, Chief." And as she sauntered back to her car, she called over her shoulder, "Sally Ann said for you not to forget the Christmas Open House tomorrow!"

Aggie got into her SUV, stifling a groan. "Flash," she said when he jumped in beside her. "We have *got* to do some Christmas shopping."

From the loft window of the shack across the road, Angel watched the sheriff's department cruiser with Mike Carson inside round the bend and disappear down the long flat stretch of road. He lowered the scope of his long-range rifle and smiled faintly as he began to disassemble the weapon, packing it into its case. "And so Agent Carson," he murmured, "you live to fight another day, courtesy of Police Chief Aggie Malone. Merry Christmas."

He waited until Aggie and Flash were on the road to leave the building, cross the grassy field and get into the blue sedan that was parked at the end of the sandy trail where he'd left it. He turned the car around, got back on the deserted highway and drove off into the cold, gray day.

CHAPTER TWENTY-FOUR

Aggie and Flash sat on the floor in front of the fire, watching the twinkling Christmas tree lights. She smiled her thanks when Grady carefully handed her a mug of hot chocolate, and then sat down beside her, his own mug in hand. Flash looked at him hopefully, and he dug a couple of dog biscuits out of the pocket of his jeans. Flash set to crunching them up happily. As far as he was concerned, the day couldn't get any better.

Aggie had given her report and managed to make it out of the building before the barrage of men in suits swarmed in to take custody of her prisoner. While Grady and Bishop dealt with the aftermath, she had time to finish her Christmas shopping: a cute purse for Sally Ann, an embroidered Bible cover for Mo—because Aggie had heard her talk about how she admired the one her sister had— and from a thrift shop in town, a Hermes scarf for Lorraine. It was probably a knock-off, but it was gorgeous nonetheless. She stopped by the pet shop and got a chew bone and a flying disc for Flash, and in the bookstore found a beautiful photo scrapbook that reminded her of Lil. She still didn't have anything for Grady, but all in all, the day had turned out better than she expected...in some ways. In others, not so much.

They got home in time to make spaghetti for dinner, and while Grady called his mother, Aggie took a bath and put on her flannel pajamas. The night outside was cold and damp; it was good to sit by the fire and be with those she loved.

Grady dropped a kiss on her head. "You doing okay, baby?"

She managed another quick, vague smile. "Just thinking about things." She tasted the hot chocolate. "You make the best hot chocolate," she said, trying to keep the topic neutral for another moment. "What did your mom say?"

"They're letting the twins stay with them in the cottage tonight," Grady said, and Flash rolled one eye toward him warily, "to give Lucy and Cal a chance to talk."

"Oh dear," murmured Aggie, taking another sip of the chocolate. "I hope the perimeter holds."

"Yeah," agreed Grady. "I wouldn't want to be a fly on the wall of either one of those houses tonight."

Cautiously, Flash went back to munching his dog biscuits.

Outside, the wind rattled beneath the tin roof and sent dead palm fronds scuttling across the yard, spattering fine droplets of rain against the windows. Inside the fire crackled and golden red shadows danced across the wood floor.

Aggie said, "It's weird. I was just sitting here thinking how much fun I had the other night with your folks around the fire pit, laughing and listening to the stories and feeling like part of such an amazing family…"

He put his hand on her knee, caressing it gently. "You are part of the family."

"And even when all of this happened with Cal, everybody held together, supported each other…I never knew people did that," she said simply. "You and Pete and Lucy are so lucky."

She leaned forward and set her mug carefully on the hearth with both hands, then scooted in close to him, resting her head on his shoulder. He encircled her with his free arm, caressing her ribs.

"And just when I was starting to get a taste of what a real family was like," Aggie said, "I find out my birth father is a convicted felon who was killed in a street crime a matter of days before I found him. It's just…weird."

"We don't know it was your father," Grady reminded her. There was an edge to his voice. "It could all be a mistake. Or, more likely, a sick joke."

Nonetheless, Aggie had not hesitated about taking a DNA kit from the equipment room and supplying a cheek swab. Bishop insisted they submit it through the county lab because "anything that threatens one of my deputies is county business," so Grady had hastily filled out the paperwork and finished just before the lab made its final pickup for the day. The driver said they were trying to get routine matters such as that cleared before Christmas, but there was no guarantee.

Grady said, "I almost didn't tell you."

"I know," replied Aggie, with such casual certainty that he bent his head toward her suspiciously. "You're always doing dumb things like that, trying to protect me."

"Not dumb," he corrected. "Selfish. I don't like to see the people I love hurt. Speaking of which…"

"Yeah, I know," Aggie reached for her mug again and took a sip. "No more traffic stops without a weapon. I'm going ask the town council to authorize tazers for Mo and me, too. They're lighter weight and easier to handle. We should've had them before now."

"No argument there. Although," Grady added, ruffling Flash's ears, "you and your team did okay for yourselves today with limited armament, I've got to admit."

Flash gave him an appreciative glance for the well-deserved compliment, then turned back to his dog biscuit.

"Anyway, look." Aggie cautiously held up her mug with both hands. "No trembling tonight. Your mom thinks it might just be a medication reaction. I've got a doctor's appointment next week."

"Good deal." He kissed the top of her bristly hair again. "Need some company?"

"I've got it covered."

Aggie held the mug close to her chest, listening to the rain, watching the firelight flicker on her husband's face. "So," she said, "what changed your mind?"

"About what?"

"Telling me."

His face fell into somber lines. "I don't know." He sipped his chocolate. "It was like…I didn't want to give Briggs any more power over us. He had taken so much from us already, I couldn't let him wreck what we've built together. I couldn't let him be the reason I lied to you."

She pressed her head against his shoulder again. "I know how hard it is for you, thinking about him, dealing with him…or with anything from that time, really. I mean, I was unconscious. Most of it I don't remember. You had to go through it all, the pain, the fear, the worry—not just for you, but for me, too. I understand. It's just that…hating him like you do gives him a kind of power, too. You know what they say. You don't forgive for the other person, you forgive for yourself."

Grady was silent for a moment. "When you first came to work for Murphy County, back when your hair was long and you wore it in the regulation bun, you know, pinned back, there were always a few pieces that wouldn't stay put, and you had this thing you'd do, a habit really, where you'd reach up and push your hair back behind your ears all the time. I used to watch you sitting at your desk, pushing your hair back while you worked on reports, and every time you did that my gut would clench, I wanted you so bad. Sometimes I'd dream about you doing that, just pushing your hair back."

She smiled up at him, but his eyes were dark and far away. He went on, "After you were shot, and in the hospital, you know, when you were conscious and moving again, I remember one day you reached up like you were smoothing your hair back, a habit, you know, just something you always did. And when your fingers touched the bandage on your head, I remember this look of horror, and confusion, and—I don't know, disorientation—in your eyes, like, just for a minute, you couldn't remember who you were anymore. It was a little thing, maybe, but he'd taken that away from you, a part of who you were. I don't forgive him," Grady said flatly. "I never will."

Aggie searched his eyes. "It's Christmas," she said softly. "Isn't that what you do?"

He didn't answer, and she didn't press.

"Why do you suppose he reached out to you?" Aggie said. "What do you think he wanted for the information?"

Grady shrugged. "To make some kind of deal, I guess. Who knows?"

"Or maybe," suggested Aggie, "he just used Jimmy Joe Jackson's name to get your attention. Maybe he really wanted to see you about something else."

Grady considered that. "Could be. But unless it comes out in the federal investigation, we'll never know. He's way out of our jurisdiction now, thank God."

"Maybe not," Aggie said somberly. "With what Bishop said about Briggs possibly being involved in some kind of crime syndicate, we might be right in the middle of it."

"I don't think it matters," Grady said. "Crime is crime, whether it's organized or not. Sucks either way."

Aggie frowned into her mug. "I just don't get it. People like Carson, Secret Service, for God's sake. Do you know how squeaky clean you've got to be to get that job? And he still managed to convince himself that it was okay to try to trap a criminal by breaking the law."

Grady lifted one shoulder, perhaps a little uncomfortably. "These guys, they go undercover, start talking the talk, living the life...it's a whole different world out there than you and I are used to, baby. It's easy to lose your way."

"Not if you have a moral compass," she countered. "He wasn't even sorry. He was just annoyed that he got caught."

"I don't know." Grady was frowning too. "Sometimes I think that line between right and wrong that we've all got inside us is a little easier to slip over than most people like to admit. And once you step over it, it can be hard to find your way back."

When she looked up at him, a question in her eyes, he reminded her, "I almost didn't tell you about Briggs."

"But you did," she said. "You have a moral compass. Besides, it's not the same thing. Not by a long shot."

He didn't answer for a moment. Then he said, "What if it turns out to be true? What if this Jackson dude really is your father?"

"I don't know," Aggie admitted. She dropped her gaze to her cup again. "I mean, we always knew there was a chance he'd be in prison, and now he's dead and I never got to ask him why...I don't know. I'll have the truth, I guess. That's something. I just wish I'd had it sooner."

He caressed the back of her neck lightly. "You know, honey," he said in a moment, "I was going to wait until Christmas morning, but these last few days, all this talk about family...is it okay if I give you your Christmas present now?"

Aggie watched quizzically as he got up and went to the Christmas tree, then returned with a small wrapped box. He sat beside her again, and offered the gift in his open palm. "When I asked you to marry me," he said, "I really botched it up. I wanted it to be this big production, with music and lights and some kind of grand romantic gesture—I never did decide exactly what—and a ring that would blow your mind. But I think I kind of knew you'd say no."

And she had. The first time.

"Later," he went on, "well, I was just so happy you finally said yes nothing else mattered. Wal-Mart wedding bands are still wedding bands, right? Things have never been traditional for us. But I always felt bad you didn't have a real ring."

"Ryan," she protested, both delighted and mildly dismayed. "Is this a ring? We can't afford..."

But at his meaningful look, she trailed off, and set her mug aside to accept the package.

"This is what Lorraine and I have been working on," he explained as she tore off the wrapping. "She helped me design it and coordinate with Mom on getting it made. I knew you'd see the e-mails if I tried to do it by myself."

Aggie paused with her hand on the lid of the small velvet box. "Your mother?"

"She had a jeweler put it together down there for practically nothing, and got it here in time for Christmas. Open it."

Aggie did, and for a moment she couldn't speak. It was a rich blue diamond-cut sapphire in a filigree silver setting, surrounded by small diamond chips. "Oh," she managed at last. "Ryan."

"I'm not saying that story about Peg O'Brien is true," Grady said, "but there's this necklace that's pretty old, made up of sapphires and diamonds. Over the years, the Gradys have more or less taken it apart piece by piece to use the stones for engagement rings. All the women of the family have one, either passed down from an ancestor or custom made for her. And since you're Peg O'Brien's living counterpart," he added casually, removing the ring from the box, "it only seems right that you should have one custom made."

He lifted her hand and slipped the ring on her finger, right above her wedding band. Perfect fit. "Welcome to the family, baby."

Aggie threw her arms around him, her breath caught in her throat. "Oh," she said. And again, "Oh!" That was really all she could manage for the longest time.

He wiped away the tears from her cheeks with both thumbs when she finally pulled apart from him. "Yeah," he said wryly, smiling, "this really would've been better in front of the whole family."

"Ryan." She impatiently swiped the remaining moisture from her eyes so that she could better see the sparkle and glitter on the hand she held out in front of her. "I don't know what to say."

"Yes," he replied simply. "Let's pretend I did it right the first time and you said yes."

She choked on a laugh, swiping at her eyes again. "Of course I'd say yes, dummy! Who wouldn't? But now you get to brag you got me even without the ring."

He grinned. "There's that."

She held her hand out to the glow of the firelight again, the twinkle of the Christmas lights reflecting in its facets. She couldn't help smiling from pure joy. Centuries of heritage, of family legend, of tradition smiled back at her. She understood now, in a way she hadn't before, how devastated Lorraine must have been when she lost her own ring.

She lowered her hand to her lap. "It's like Lorraine's," she said quietly.

"Honey, she knew I was giving it to you. She helped plan the whole thing."

Aggie threaded her fingers through her husband's. "I know. It's just…"

"You don't feel right wearing it around her." He tried not to sound disappointed, but he was. Aggie could tell.

"Just for now," she said quickly. "Just until, I don't know, until she feels better." She searched his face anxiously. "Does that hurt your feelings? Because I love it more than anything, and I don't want you to think…"

He drew her close, laughing softly. "No, it doesn't hurt my feelings. It only makes me love you more. But…" He looked down at her, her face held in his hands. "Will you at least wear it the rest of the night?"

"Yes," she whispered, sinking into him again. "Yes, yes, yes…"

And it turned out to be a perfect day after all.

CHAPTER TWENTY-FIVE

The day finally came when Flash arrived at the office, sniffed his stocking, and found it filled with treats. There were platters of cookies everywhere, and paper cups filled with warm apple cider, and people wandered in and out of the open door all morning. Aggie and Mo and Sally Ann laughed and hugged each other when they opened their presents, and Flash and Aggie wore their Santa hats on patrol. The Christmas lights were on in all the shops, and there were cookies and cheese trays and candy and dog treats everywhere they went. Flash decided, as he did every year, that the world would be a better place if Christmas never stopped happening.

At the end of the day they met Grady and Lil and Salty and Pete and Lorraine on the patio at Pete's Place. Flash had not expected the twins to be there, and when he saw them he started to turn and go back to the car. The reproving look Aggie gave him made him ashamed of himself, though, so he put on his most watchful air and approached the table with caution.

Aggie was not surprised to find the twins at the table, but she was surprised to see them sitting quietly between their grandparents, faces scrubbed and neatly dressed, each absorbed in a coloring book. She distrusted the moment almost as much as Flash, and approached the table with equal caution. When she had greeted all the adults, she said uncertainly, "Hello, boys."

They ignored her, and Lil raised her eyebrows at them. "Your Aunt Aggie spoke to you, boys."

The boys looked up and replied as one, "Hello, Aunt Aggie."

Aggie sat down next to Grady, speechless. Flash eased his way under her chair.

Salty said indulgently, "All our two young gents here needed was an idea of where their boundaries lay, just like any other wild thing exploring its turf. That, and a little something to occupy their time."

"They washed the windows on the cottage this morning," Lil said.

"And scrubbed our pool patio this afternoon," Lorraine added.

"And now," concluded Salty with a benevolent smile, "we're having a wee competition to see who can put the most colors on the page, all while remaining seated and not speaking until spoken to."

"The winner gets to make his own ice cream sundae in the kitchen," Pete added.

"Wow," said Aggie, noticing that the images on each boy's book were exceptionally colorful, if not entirely recognizable. "I should have gotten here earlier. Maybe I could've gotten in on that deal."

"You wouldn't have a chance, baby," Grady assured her. "When is the last time you went more than two minutes without speaking unless you were spoken to?"

Aggie kicked his ankle lightly, and he winked at her, enclosing her hand in his under the table. She wasn't wearing her ring, but his smile told her it was okay.

It was a slow night, and they had the patio to themselves. The Christmas tree twinkled in the corner and carols played in the background. There was a big platter of fried shrimp, clams, flounder and hushpuppies on the table, along with a family-sized bowl of salad and baskets of fresh bread. The others had already started, so Aggie helped herself while Lil explained, "Lucy's on her way to pick up the boys. I told her we'd be glad to bring them home, but she insisted."

Aggie was as curious as anyone would have been to know how matters had been resolved between Cal and Lucy—if in fact they had been—but she knew it wouldn't be appropriate to ask in front of the children. She did know, however, that one of the reasons they were all having dinner together tonight was to decide what to do about the party. She and Grady had been up late talking about it.

"Good for her to get out of the house," Salty observed. "And isn't that drive across the bridge at night just the most magnificent thing? The whole project turned out right nice, if I do say so myself." He gave a satisfied nod. "Money well spent, no arguing that."

Aggie was confused. "You knew about the bridge decorating project?"

He gave a snort of amusement. "Knew about it? The Grady Foundation has been trying to get that thing off the ground, so to speak, for eight years or more. So much bloody red tape. But worth it now, don't you think?"

Aggie paused in the middle of spooning a pool of cocktail sauce onto her plate. "The Grady Foundation?" she parroted. "*That*'s the anonymous donor?" She turned to her husband, accusing. "You have a foundation?"

Grady tilted his beer toward his father. "*He* has a foundation," he corrected. "I have a busted water heater."

"Do you need help with your water heater, son?" Salty said, concerned.

A younger, less confident man might have disdained an offer of help from his father, but Grady said, "Thanks, Dad. I've got the parts in the truck, just haven't had a chance to get to it."

"Right after supper," his father assured him.

Aggie was still dumbfounded. She repeated, "You have a foundation?"

"It's just a small one," Lil assured her, "restricted to the 'betterment, protection and beautification' of Dogleg Island. Some of the items in the museum were paid for with foundation money, and we helped replant the trees along Island Road after the hurricane. But Salty has been obsessed with those blessed bridge lights since before we left here." She smiled at her husband affectionately. "They do look nice," she admitted.

Aggie said simply, "Wow. I married a trust fund kid. Who knew?" And that made everyone laugh.

Lil turned back to Aggie. "We walked around town a little this afternoon, after the boys finished their chores," she said. "Everything was so pretty! And it was so good catching up with old friends. Did you ever get that awful business with the children's coat drive straightened out?" There were very few secrets in the small island town, and word of the counterfeit Christmas bounty had spread like wildfire.

Aggie cut up some flounder and put it on a paper napkin for Flash. He was very good about not eating the napkin, having learned early on that just because something smelled good didn't mean the taste was up to par.

"Only a couple of them went out before we could stop them," Aggie said, placing the flounder on the floor for Flash. "The church Benevolent Fund stepped in to make up the loss to people who thought they'd gotten a Christmas miracle. After all, no one wants to see kids disappointed. Some of the money had already been spent, here and out of town, though. There's no real way to make that up to the merchants."

"Tell me about it," grumbled Pete, and Lorraine elbowed him in the ribs.

"Twenty dollars," she scoffed. "You give away more than that every night in free beers."

Grady lifted his eyebrows. "Free beers? I didn't know there was such a thing."

"Giving away," Pete pointed out, still disgruntled, "is a lot different than being stolen from. So what's the deal with how that phony cash got here, anyway?"

Aggie and Grady shared a glance. "Sorry," Aggie said, "ongoing investigation. I think most of it's under control, but you're going to have to keep your eyes open for a while."

"Mercy," murmured Lil. "The world we live in."

Again, Aggie and Grady shared a glance, this one more somber.

To change the subject, Aggie said, "Just so you know, I talked to Jason and he said that Brett hasn't started on the dessert table yet, but if we're going to cancel, the absolute last possible day to do it is tomorrow. He doesn't think we can get the deposit back on the flowers, though."

"Cancel?" demanded an indignant voice behind her. "After all this work, you're going to cancel the party? Why on earth would you do that?"

Aggie turned to see Lucy striding across the patio floor to them, ponytail swinging. The boys cried, "Mommy!" and scrambled off the bench to run to her. She knelt and opened her arms to them.

"There are my babies! There you are! Did you have a good time with Grandma and Grandpa? Were you the best babies ever? Of course you were! Give me kisses!"

All this was peppered in between screeches of, "Mommy, see what I did! Mommy, look at me! Mine is better! No, mine is! Come look, Mommy, come look!"—which was the kind of cacophony that usually accompanied any interaction with the twins, and in a way was rather reassuring. Those at the table shared a wry smile, and then Pete got up.

"Okay, you little hooligans," he declared, "as the duly appointed judge of The Great Coloring Book Contest, I officially declare the winner is..."

The boys were abruptly silent, jiggling on their tiptoes, watching him expectantly.

"It's a tie," said Pete, and placed a hand on each of their shoulders as they broke into squeals of delight. "Let's go in the kitchen and claim your prize."

Lucy hugged her parents and thanked them for watching the boys. Lorraine half-rose and offered Lucy a drink, but she refused. Flash, having determined that the twins were well and truly gone, gave his napkin a final lick and jumped up into the seat Pete had vacated. Lucy glared at him in disapproval, but he didn't care. He was part of the family too and he needed to know what was going on. As long as the twins weren't involved, of course.

Lucy sat next to her father and folded her hands on the table. Aggie noticed she had taken trouble with her appearance, wearing makeup and earrings and a white sweater with push-up sleeves. Her eyes were still puffy and bloodshot, and her face showed lines of stress, but there was a resolute set to her mouth, and her shoulders were squared. She said, "So, no point in beating around the bush. Here's what's happening. Cal will be moving out after Christmas. I don't know for how long. He'll see the boys every day. We'll start marriage counseling after the first of the year. We're not canceling the party. That's stupid. We've been planning it for three months, half the island is planning to come, you'll never get all your deposits back, and we're not ruining everyone's Christmas at this late date." She turned a hard look on Aggie. "Okay?"

Aggie swallowed the piece of bread she'd been chewing and said, a little meekly, "I just thought..."

"And another thing," Lucy interrupted. "Mom and Dad told me how hard you worked to get the evidence that cleared Cal of the charges. Thank you. His lawyer says the DA has already started the paperwork to formally drop the charges so he probably won't even have to go to court. I appreciate everything you did."

Aggie could tell by the stiffness of her manner how difficult that was for her to say and she wished she had some gracious reply at hand. But all she could think of was, "Sure."

Lucy braced her hands on the table in preparation for rising. "Well then. I'd better get the boys home to bed. I hope Pete's not feeding them ice cream. All that sugar will keep them awake all night. By the way, Cal won't be coming to the party, in case you were wondering, but I will. And I'll see everybody at my house for Christmas dinner just like we planned. One o'clock. I'll make the turkey, Pete's making the dressing, and don't forget the wine. Good night, everyone."

It was at that point that something caught Flash's attention, which was perfect timing because a quick glance around told him no one was eating, so it would be perfectly acceptable for him to sniff around. He sprang off the bench and hurried to the Christmas tree while people at the table were hugging and saying good-bye. Flash caught the scent of his prey and he only had time for one quick bark to alert Aggie before he dived under the Christmas tree after it.

Behind him, the Christmas tree rattled and swayed and toppled, crashing against the empty table and chairs beside it. People screamed. Aggie cried, "Flash!" Flash scrambled through the hole in the plastic behind the fallen tree, barking.

Grady pushed through an opening in the plastic wall; Aggie climbed over the fallen tree and lifted the torn bottom seam of the plastic and crawled through it after Flash. They each arrived on the scene at about the same time. Flash stood with his legs braced and his head down, barking a warning at a hole in the lattice that covered the crawl space beneath the restaurant. Aggie unclipped her flashlight from her belt and switched it on just in time to catch a blur of movement streaking past Flash. Grady cried, "What the hell!" and grabbed for his gun. Aggie shouted too, but with laughter.

"Easy, cowboy!" She swept the wide beam across the alleyway, where a furry ringed tail could be seen disappearing over the top of the stockade fence that separated the back of the restaurant from the dumpsters. "It's a raccoon."

Flash, having chased the animal as far as he could, trotted back to Aggie, tongue lolling and tail waving. Grady, looking annoyed, holstered his weapon and came over to her. Aggie grinned at him, already enjoying teasing him about the time he'd drawn a gun on an unarmed raccoon.

Lorraine called over the fallen Christmas tree, "Is everything okay? What happened?"

Aggie knelt and swung the flashlight beam inside the hole beneath the building. She smiled and sat back on her heels, reaching out a hand to ruffle Flash's fur. "Everything is fine," she called back. "I think we found our thief."

All in all, Aggie and Flash recovered one bejeweled cell phone case with cell phone still intact, one gold-foil wrapped watch, one brightly beaded wallet with $57.00 inside, two dominoes, origin unknown, a couple of Christmas tree ornaments, $4.50 in quarters and one sapphire and diamond ring. "I always heard about raccoons collecting shiny things," Aggie admitted with a shrug, "but I've never actually seen it before. That's why Flash was so interested in the Christmas tree every time we came in here. The raccoon must've chewed a hole in the plastic there, and whenever a customer put something shiny on the floor that attracted his attention, he came in and stole it. All the things that went missing were from these tables along the plastic wall here, by the Christmas tree. And that's where you must've dropped your ring, Lorraine."

"Damnedest thing I ever saw," admitted Salty with a shake of his head. "A raccoon, do you say?"

"Dad," said Grady, struggling to right the tree. "A little help?"

Salty hurried to help set the Christmas tree upright in its stand again, and Aggie added, "I'm really sorry about the Christmas tree."

Lorraine couldn't seem to stop crying—or laughing—and she knelt to hug Flash. "You're the best dog who ever lived!" she exclaimed. "And you're getting the biggest steak we have in the cooler tonight!"

Flash thought that sounded just fine, but he was even prouder when Aggie smiled down at him and said, "Flash is definitely the brightest star in the crime-solving business this week." Because everyone knew Aggie was brilliant, and if *she* thought he was a star…well, that must mean he was brilliant too.

That was something to think about.

Lorraine stood up and hugged Aggie again, hard. "You don't know what this means to me," she said, for perhaps the fifth time. "You just don't know."

Aggie, hugging her back, smiled. "Yeah," she said, "I think I do."

And when she saw the look on Pete's face as he slipped the ring, freshly washed and shined with dish soap, on his wife's finger, Aggie suddenly knew exactly what she was giving her husband for Christmas.

She turned to her other sister-in-law and said, "Lucy, can I talk to you for a minute?"

CHAPTER TWENTY-SIX

ACW Analysis and Lab Services was scheduled to close for the holidays at noon on December 24, and Bill Channing, genetics lab supervisor, was trying to sign off on as many reports as he could before he left. He had a houseful of grandkids and a big bowl of eggnog waiting for him at home, and he wanted to enjoy the holiday without worrying about what was waiting for him in his in-box when he got back. So far, that in-box was not diminishing quite as rapidly as he had hoped.

Scowling with annoyance, he pushed the PA button on his telephone and said, "Fielding, my office."

Thirty seconds later a bespectacled young lab technician appeared at his door. Channing waved a report at him without glancing up. "Where's the S-10 form on this?"

The technician stepped in and took the paper, examining it. "Yes, sir, this was the gum sample that was submitted for a general fingerprint and DNA match by Captain Grady in the Murphy County Sheriff's Office a couple of days ago. The next morning a Deputy Parker called and requested we add a paternity test."

Channing flipped back through the paper work on his desk. "Didn't we just do a paternity test for them? An inmate match?"

"Yes, sir," agreed Fielding. "It came back negative, but the gum came back positive for paternity within a 12 percent degree of error."

Channing grunted. "They're going to have a hard time in court with nothing but a piece of gum to test. They need to get a cheek swab. And submit an S-10." He took the report back from the technician and slapped it impatiently back into his in-box. "We've got an audit coming up the first of the year and I'm not taking any chances with paperwork. Go ahead and send out the reports on the DNA and fingerprint search, and the first paternity test. I'll call them about this one when I get back."

But by the time the lab reopened after Christmas, both the report on the paternity test and the gum on which it had been run were gone. Channing, with an in-box that was overflowing by then, didn't even notice, and forgot all about calling the Murphy County Sheriff's Office. If he had, he would have learned, among other things, that there was no Deputy Parker working there.

But Angel, whose network was infallible, had learned all he needed to know.

The party was scheduled to start at 4:00 p.m. on Christmas Eve. Aggie darted around like a bee without a hive all day while Grady, bemused, kept to his

routine: running on the beach, doing laundry, checking e-mail. At 3:00 Aggie told him Lorraine had some
kind of crisis, kissed him briefly, and said she would
see him at the party. At 3:30, when he had showered
and changed into fresh jeans and a shirt and was
thinking about going to the pavilion to help set up,
his phone chimed with a new e-mail. It was from ACW
Lab Services, and he scanned through it immediately.

He skimmed through the graphs and statistics
and scientific jargon to the bottom line:

> *Probability of a match between inmate specimen*
> *FL978452 and submitted specimen 387861:*
> *0.021 Negative for paternity as required by Florida*
> *law.*

Grady stared at it for moment, feeling the bitter-
ness of disappointment on Aggie's behalf, but also a
certain relief. This was what they had wanted. Now
they knew. Briggs had lied. This Jimmy Joe Jackson
was not Aggie's father. The whole damn thing had
been a hoax.

There was another attachment, and he opened
it. It was the DNA analysis and fingerprint report
on the piece of gum he'd found in Cal's car, which
he expected to turn up a positive match with Sting,
who, according to both the eyewitness, Roosevelt,
and Agent Mike Carson, had stolen the car and committed the hit and run. They didn't need a positive
match to convict, but it would've been solid backup
evidence. Once again he scanned to the bottom line.

The first thing that jumped out at him were the words: *No fingerprints found.* That was bizarre, because unless the guy had spit the gum directly into the cup holder, he had to have taken it out of his mouth with his fingers. The next report was even more puzzling.

Genetic comparison of specimen 674509 (chewing gum, partially chewed, artificial cherry flavoring) and specimen 41675 (epithelial cells taken from Stanley Robert Lindon, deceased) show no significant similarities. Conclusion: genetic material taken from specimen 674509 (chewing gum) was not deposited by deceased victim Stanley Robert Lindon.

Grady gave a grunt of surprise. They had already ruled out everyone else who had contact with the car—Cal, Lucy, the kids, even the guys at the body shop and the impound yard. Had the evidence been crucial to the case, he would probably have asked the lab to run a series of elimination tests, but they already had enough to convict Sting—and by association, Carson—without it. Still, he would have liked to know how the gum got there, just for curiosity's sake.

The back door opened and Pete called, "Yo, bro, you here?"

Grady sent the report on the gum to the DA's office, knowing they wouldn't get it until after the holiday, but not wanting to have another chore waiting for him when he went back to work. When he looked up, Pete was standing there with a dry-cleaning bag in his hand.

"Mom wants us in jackets for the family photo," he said, thrusting the bag into Grady's hands. "And khakis and white shirts. Come on, get a move on. I've got twelve pounds of barbecue chicken going bad in the car." He glanced down at Grady's sneakers and added with a downward twist of his lips. "And put on some socks, will you? Jeez, were you raised in a barn?"

Grady, who was busy forwarding the paternity report to Aggie's phone, barely glanced up. "Yeah, whatever."

He should have known something was up when Pete insisted on waiting for him to change, and then driving him the couple of blocks to the party. Cars already lined the street in front of Beachside Park, the bluegrass band was going full volume, and the minute he got out of the car Grady forgot all about lab reports and paperwork and why his mother had suddenly decided she wanted Pete and him to wear matching jackets for a photograph.

The day had turned balmy and bright, and as the sun grew low in the sky, a few distant clouds shimmered with gold. The big Christmas tree in the pavilion sparkled against the deep blue background of the sky, and the long tables were covered with white tablecloths and lined with evergreens and red carnations. Dozens of white candles in hurricane shades marched down the center of each table, flickering in the ocean breeze. Even the picnic tables outside were decorated with tablecloths and candles, and several couples were already trying out the dance floor that was set up near the band. The air was filled with the aroma of Sterno and salt air and good things cooking. Grady grinned and slapped his brother on the back, then helped him carry a couple of bags of ice and some coolers from the car before moving off to mingle with the crowd.

He might have guessed something was up when he saw Father Dave in full vestments, but he assumed the cleric was on his way to officiate at a Christmas Eve service, and before he could greet him, someone pulled him away. He started to wonder where Aggie was, and thought about texting her, then was vaguely aware that he hadn't seen any member of his family except Pete, but he really didn't suspect anything until he felt his brother's hand on his shoulder. "Come here for a minute," Pete said, and nodded toward the Christmas tree.

"Where are the girls?" Grady asked.

"On their way," Pete replied rather enigmatically.

Grady thought a couple of people gave him funny grins as he passed, but he really didn't get it until he saw his father talking to the priest and, as Pete and Grady reached the Christmas tree, the band stopped playing. Father Dave smiled at him, and Salty beamed. The chatter in the crowd faded to murmurs and Pete said, winking at him, "Sorry, dude. She wanted it to be a surprise."

The band started playing a funky country version of Pacabel's Canon, and Father Dave raised his arms. The crowd moved to either side of the pavilion, forming an aisle.

Lucy and Lorraine wore red dresses and carried nosegays of red and white flowers with streaming velvet ribbons. Flash wore his red Christmas bandanna and carried a blue velvet ring box down the aisle and presented it to Pete, the best man. Everyone laughed at that, which gave Grady a chance to surreptitiously wipe his eyes, laughing too. Then the band changed to "The Wedding March" and Jerome Bishop, wearing a white tuxedo and practically bursting with pride, escorted Aggie down the aisle. She wore a long white dress and a big picture hat wrapped in netting with pearl earrings that Grady thought belonged to his mother. She carried a bouquet of red and white flowers. Grady repeatedly fought the misting in his eyes because he didn't want to miss a minute of it, he wanted to memorize every detail. But when Bishop took Aggie's hand and placed it in Grady's, and when she looked up at him and whispered, "Merry Christmas," he lost the battle.

Father Dave stepped forward, smiled at them, and spoke to the crowd. "Dearly beloved," he said, "inasmuch as Agatha and Ryan Grady, having committed themselves to each other in the lawful ceremony of marriage, have expressed a desire to share the nature of that commitment and the tradition of the sacrament of holy matrimony with this community of family and friends, we are gathered here today to bear witness to a public renewal of the vows of marriage..."

There was the sharing of the candle flames, and the way his mother's eyes glistened with tears as she kissed her son's cheek and embraced her new daughter. There was Salty, stepping forward to sing "O Holy Night" in his rich, operatic baritone that left Aggie wide-eyed with wonder and the crowd breathless. There were the vows, which had been spoken and meant with equal fervor before, but which this time caused Aggie's voice to tremble and Grady to wipe his eyes more than once before they were done. And when Pete passed the ring to him, it was Grady's hand that shook as he slipped the sapphire on her finger.

"This time," she whispered to him, "it stays on."

He kissed her fiercely on the mouth and then lifted her off her feet with his embrace, swinging her around until she squealed with laughter and grabbed at her hat. The crowd cheered and the band played and Grady said, "I can't believe you did this!"

"I can't believe you didn't figure it out," she replied. "Some detective you are!" But her eyes were glowing and her cheeks were flushed with happiness and she wrapped her arms around his neck and kissed him one more time before demanding, "Now put me down before you ruin Lorraine's dress."

Pete broke out a case of champagne from his New Year's Eve supply, and there were toasts, and cake-cutting, and enough photographs to satisfy even Lil. When Aggie, who was terrified of spilling something on Lorraine's wedding gown, went to change, Grady sat on a bench next to Bishop and demanded, "How long have you known about this?"

Bishop grinned. "About four hours. I've got to admit, though, it's long been a dream of mine to walk that girl down the aisle." He lifted his champagne glass to Grady in a salute. "Hell of a shindig, son, and thanks for the chance to see if I could still fit into this tux. Haven't worn it since my little girl's wedding, but not bad, huh?"

He puffed out his chest, and Grady grinned. "You look good enough to take to the prom, Chief."

Bishop chuckled good-naturedly and sipped his champagne. "This is the way it should have been the first time, your folks here, the whole town turned out...it's not often you get a do-over. You're a lucky man."

"You don't have to tell me." Grady was thoughtful for a moment. "Listen, I haven't talked to Aggie about it, but we got the paternity test back on Jimmy Joe Jackson. It was negative."

Bishop nodded somberly. "Well, I can't say that's bad news. Maybe in this case it's better not to know anything at all than to live with a truth like that one." He sipped his champagne. "I had a feeling all along Briggs was playing us."

Grady frowned. "That's just the thing," he said. "What if he wasn't? What if—"

Lorraine swooped in and planted a big kiss on his cheek, leaving a smear of lipstick behind. "Merry Christmas, darling! I feel like everybody's fairy godmother tonight! Aggie was wild about her ring and the look on your face when she walked down the aisle was worth every sleepless minute we spent trying to pull this thing off! A wedding in less than forty-eight hours, can you believe it?" She kissed Bishop's cheek too and wiggled her way in between them on the bench. "Now tell me the truth, boys," she demanded, draping an arm around each of their shoulders. "Have you ever seen a more beautiful bride?"

Aggie changed into the floral print dress she had bought for the party, but she kept the hat. The band stayed late, and Aggie slow danced with her husband in her bare feet while candles sputtered and the moon backlit a scattering of clouds high in the sky.

"Where'd you get the hat?" Grady asked, mostly because it was hard to kiss her while navigating the thing. "Lorraine?"

"Lucy," she said, leaning back with her arms around his neck. "Christmas present."

"No lie," he observed, surprised.

"No lie," she assured him.

"Did you ever think about keeping your hair short?" he said. "You look good in hats."

She chuckled deep in her throat. "No way, José. I'm growing it down to my butt."

He let his hands slide down to that region.

"You know, Ryan, I was thinking...it wouldn't hurt you, now and then, to stop by Lucy's house, make sure the sprinklers are working, clean the gutters, that sort of thing."

He knew better than to question. "You got it."

She rested her head on his shoulder. He turned his head to avoid the brim of the hat. "Hey, good news," she murmured. "Your mom said they might stay a few weeks, maybe into February. Just until they see Lucy on her feet."

"Cool," he agreed. "I like having the old man around. We're going fishing next week. And Mom's something else, isn't she?"

"Yeah," Aggie agreed with a contented sigh. "She really is."

Grady said, "Sweetheart, I sent you an email earlier…"

She replied, "Yeah, I know, I always read your emails when they come in."

"So you know the lab results…"

"Right. No match." She tilted her head back to look at him. She said, "I'm okay with that. Ryan…" She lifted her hand from his shoulder to gesture to the dance floor around them. Among the dancers were his parents, their faces tilted toward each other, their eyes soft with adoration. "Look what you've given me. Look what we have. I'm good. I'm more than good. Someday you're going to sit around the fire pit and tell your grandchildren about this night, about who we are, about what we've done. Baby, this is enough."

Grady pushed back her hat, rested his forehead against hers. He said, "I was thinking about what you said. About Briggs, and forgiveness, and what Bishop said about do-overs, and I was wondering, what if we could make it like it never happened? What if we could skip the crap and just make this our happy ending?"

She smiled, a little sadly. "Doesn't work that way."

He said, "I think I need to talk to Briggs."

She said, "I love you."

He raised his face to look at her; she stretched to kiss him. She said, "We are going to have such amazing babies."

He said, "Damn right." He kissed her again.

She said, "I'm going to make love to you until sunrise."

He smiled. "Baby, you'll be asleep in half an hour."

She cupped his face with her hands, and she looked into his eyes. She said, "Watch me."

For Flash's part, there couldn't have been a more perfect holiday. Pete's barbecue chicken, lights that twinkled in the sky, music thrumming and booming everywhere. He was front and center in every single photograph, wearing his Christmas bandanna. The cake—minus its raspberry filling, which wasn't his favorite—was amazing. Aggie laughed all the time, and so did Grady. The bad guys were behind bars, and even the raccoon who had caused Aggie so much aggravation had been chased away. All the stolen property had been returned, and Flash had enjoyed the best steak he'd ever eaten. Aggie thought he was brilliant. Best of all, he hadn't had to tear anyone's throat out. Who could ask for more?

The only thing that bothered him—and this was just a little thing, nothing he'd ever worry Aggie about—was that every now and then, from out of nowhere, he caught a scent that made the fur on the back of his neck prickle. It reminded him of the day at the beach, when they were having lunch in the sun, and someone was watching. It smelled like cherry chewing gum.

But by the time Flash figured that out, the guy with the cherry chewing gum was gone. And really, Aggie was so happy, there was no reason to bother her with it at all.

CHAPTER TWENTY-SEVEN

Sheriff Derrels had complained for years about
security in the holding room of the courthouse,
where prisoners were brought from the jail to await
their time in front of the judge. It wasn't any worse
than any other small southern courthouse, and
except for the one time a meth-head had taken a
swing at a guard and almost made it to the door
before he was tazed, there had never been any incidents. Still, it bothered him.

Prisoners were taken from a van or a patrol car up
a small ramp that led from the parking lot to the back
door, a walk of about fifteen feet. The glass on that door
was wire-reinforced, but not bulletproof. There were
two windows inside the holding room, and another
door that led directly into the courtroom. What worried Sheriff Derrels was how easy it would be for a prisoner to break away and attack a judge or a lawyer, or
even a witness. He didn't think about the windows, or
the glass door, or the fifteen-foot walk from the parking lot. It was always the things you didn't think about.

Due to some maneuvering by the defense attorney, the trial had been held over past the holiday,

and Briggs was scheduled to give testimony on December 27. No one was happy about that except Briggs, who had enjoyed the county jail's Christmas dinner of catered baked ham and all the trimmings, as opposed to the tasteless institution food served at state prison. Court resumed at 10:00 a.m. Briggs was brought up at 9:55.

Grady had cleared his presence at the court-house with the sheriff and both the defense counsel and prosecutor. It was unorthodox, but since Briggs would be returned to Wakulla directly after taking the witness stand, this would be Grady's last chance to talk to him. He was granted access to the hold-ing room for the few minutes it would take before Briggs was called to the stand. Briggs would be the only prisoner in the room that morning.

Grady was in uniform, but he surrendered his weapon at the security checkpoint. The bailiff took him through the door that led from the courtroom to the holding room. He was nervous. He thought this might be a mistake. He'd told Bishop that he wanted to follow up on that whole Jimmy Joe Jackson busi-ness, since so far it had led them nowhere, and that was part of it. But the bigger part was what Aggie had said, about forgiveness buying freedom. He wasn't sure it worked that way, and he was even less sure of his ability to forgive, but he knew he'd never be free of the man who haunted his nightmares until he looked the monster in the eyes.

He hadn't been in the featureless little room more than a few seconds—long enough to note the windows, the wood paneled walls, the tile floor, the long bench with shackle rings on the east wall—when the metal exterior door clanged open. A deputy held the door open while another one escorted Briggs, shackled and cuffed, up the ramp. Grady moved forward.

Briggs noticed him, and smiled. "Well, if it isn't Deputy Sheriff Ryan Grady. What do you know about that?"

Briggs had always been a rotund man; prison food and lack of exercise had turned fat into flab. His face was puffy and his eyes sunken and he had lost even more of his hair in the months since Grady last had seen him. This man in whom he had invested so much power, who had tried to take from him everything he had ever valued and who had almost succeeded, this old, fat, shuffling shadow of a human was not a monster. He was just pathetic. Grady looked at Briggs, and he felt mildly nauseous.

Grady said softly, "This is bullshit." He turned to go.

Briggs said urgently, "Grady, wait—"

Grady was vaguely aware of a muted thump, or cracking sound, and something sprayed his cheek. He reached up in annoyance to wipe it away, and his fingers came away red. Droplets of blood darkened his uniform. In slow motion he turned back to the door, saw the deputy who was standing there frozen in place, saw the other deputy, his face and his shirt bright with blood, his expression utterly astonished. Roy Briggs slumped to the ground, one side of his face completely blown off.

He never got a chance to say another word.

Security footage would show the sun glinting on the barrel of a rifle from the barely cracked, deeply tinted window of a black Mercedes parked among the rows of other cars twenty feet away. It would show that car pulling away at a normal rate of speed less than a minute later, but it would not reveal a license plate or any other identifying information. By the time Ryan Grady wiped the blood from his face, Angel had already rolled up the window and begun packing away his weapon.

He had known there would be some things to clean up when he arrived here. He hated to go this far, but it was important that his people understand he could get to them anytime, anywhere. He'd have thought a man like Briggs would have figured that out by now. After all, this was personal.

It was family. And you didn't mess with a man's family.

wed 10:00

leg compress

Alex

619-
797-
4519

ABOUT THE AUTHOR

Donna Ball is the author of over a hundred novels under several different pseudonyms in a variety of genres that include romance, mystery, suspense, paranormal, western adventure, historical and women's fiction. Recent popular series include the Ladybug Farm series and the Raine Stockton Dog Mystery series. Donna is an avid dog lover and her dogs have won numerous titles for agility, obedience and canine musical freestyle. She divides her time between the Blue Ridge mountains and the east coast of Florida. You can contact her at www.donnaball.net.

50549392R00214

Made in the USA
San Bernardino, CA
27 June 2017